Preacherman

Preacherman

Trina F. Winde

PALMETTO

PUBLISHING

Charleston, SC

www.PalmettoPublishing.com

Hardcover ISBN: 979-8-8229-2706-3
Paperback ISBN: 979-8-8229-2707-0
eBook ISBN: 979-8-8229-2708-7

To my husband Robb, my home, thank you for always supporting and loving me as only you can. To Laken and Luke, God blessed me so well when he made you mine. Ryan and Jake, you enrich my life more than you'll ever know. Israel, Jonah and Levi, you have my heart. And to Denna, you've been my North Star and encouraging light from the beginning.

In loving memory of my mama, Rosie Ellen and my dear friend Gammie.

Part One

Chapter One

Praise music vibrated from the giant speakers around the stage, and Charlie's temples were soaked with the excitement of his message. He was on fire. His left arm lifted into a soulful sway as he mouthed the words to "How Great Is Our God" while Marianna sat in the front row immersed in the music with her hands folded across her heart. Her long, dark, curly hair flowed along her shoulders as she caught Charlie's gaze. Charlie smiled at her as the music faded into the background. The love he felt onstage, bringing people to God, could only compare to the love he had for his wife and son. Her presence set him at ease.

It was time for the invitation. The moment of truth. How effective was his message? By the end of the day, all the salvations from all five campuses would be totaled, and the results would dictate Charlie's approach for future messages. Saving souls was in his DNA. Creating beauty from ashes, as his daddy would say.

"I know that many of you are dealing with loss, heartache, situations that make you feel out of control. But never forget that there is hope; there is *always* hope. All you have to do is surrender." Charlie stood at the front of the stage between the two teleprompters, feeling the energy in the room shift when he shared his own testimony of losing his mother at such a young age.

His heart raised its tempo with his words. "Surrender the pain of the past; surrender the hurt of divorce, of loss, of abuse; surrender all at the feet of Jesus. You don't have to do this alone. Lay your worries at the feet of The One that gave it all for you. All you have to do is step out of the aisle and leave through the back door. Someone from our response team will be waiting for you." Charlie strode across the stage as people filtered out. He lost count at 15 when he noticed Marianna moving to the end of the aisle and exiting out the back. *Where is she going? Must be going to get Chan.* "I see people moving. If you feel moved, but you haven't made your way, this is your time. It appears there are still some of you that feel anchored to the floor right now but get whoever brought you today to walk with you. You don't have to do this alone." The music grew louder as Charlie swayed into the satisfaction of more people stepping out of the aisles and into the light. *God is good.*

After ending the service with a prayer and funny anecdote, he pulled his earpiece out, removed his audio pack from the back of his pants, and handed it to a volunteer at the edge of the stage.

"Great message, Pastor Charlie," the volunteer said, collecting his equipment.

"Thanks. I appreciate that," he replied, striding from backstage to the hallway leading to the offices. He felt good—until the impact of the busy weeks ahead weighed him down like a sinker on a fishing line. He was scheduled to leave for Jerusalem, followed by a long trip to a sister church in California. Anxiety leached into the pool of joy that had collected in his chest during the service. *When did my life become all business and less ministering to people?* he asked himself.

He was exhausted.

For months he'd shelved the feeling resting deep in his soul that something big was on the horizon for him. Little did he know that the road ahead was going to lead him back to where it all started.

—◦◦◦—

Charlie Nettles had been born into an era of change and the passion that Mary Francis and Elroy Nettles shared for making a difference. Ministering to those in need filled their spiritual cups, and Charlie's formative years consisted of traveling around the country every summer in a battered pickup truck, firmly planted in the front seat between his parents' sweaty shoulders and strong values. As a child, Charlie watched in amazement as Elroy transformed hearts and changed lives through his ministry. But Charlie showed no interest himself in following the path of the Nettles men who had come before him, much to Elroy's dismay.

Elroy was a slight man with a crooked smile and partial limp caused by a fall in his youth that, without proper medical attention, had, over the years, grown into an aggravating disability. While he offered Charlie guidance when time permitted, his priority was always answering the call of the ministry, whether from the pulpit of his tiny church or a revival tent. While the echoes of his voice resonated like a bomb on a battlefield to those who gathered to hear the word, he often missed the immediate needs of his son.

Charlie entered the world within ten months of his parents pledging their hearts to each other in a grassy field just north of nowhere with only their parents in attendance. It was the summer of 1988, and Mary Francis had not been much more than a child herself. But even as the heat rose and her belly expanded, she watched Elroy preach with a peaceful smile covering her face. She understood the importance of her role in Elroy's journey and embraced it with a grace beyond her years. Even more important was the feeling in the depths of her soul that she was carrying a child who would one day set the world on fire with a ministry of his own, one unlike anything the world had known.

Mary Francis's water broke two days shy of her eighteenth birthday just as the final amen echoed throughout an old tent. Elroy's face contorted with a silly grin as he noticed the puddle around her dusty Mary Janes.

"It's time, Elroy," Mary Francis said, waving her hands with controlled panic.

Hopping off his makeshift podium after an abbreviated prayer, Elroy announced, "Kind folk, we are blessed this beautiful day of our Lord." Tucking her arm into his, he led her carefully to their truck parked just outside. Within minutes of reaching the county hospital, Matthew Charles Nettles was born in the back seat, weighing in at eight pounds twelve ounces. Mary Francis and Elroy cried as Charlie took his first breath.

"He's the most beautiful thing I ever seen," Elroy said, holding her hand.

"Oh, Elroy, it's like God laid a sweet angel in my arms."

"I know, Mama. I know."

"Hear me when I say this, Elroy. This child is special."

"I hear ya, Mama. And he's going to make his daddy proud. We gonna raise him up strong, yes, we are."

Charlie became the center of their small universe. For Mary Francis's lack of parenting experience, she made up with unconditional love. Her love was like a warm blanket that wrapped around his tiny shoulders.

So, it was a good, consistent childhood full of grace, until the summer after middle school, when Charlie's world shifted on its axis. Resting his elbows on his knees in a hot, dusty tent, Charlie watched Elroy's greased hair shine against the light. His daddy's words made little sense to him but seemed to be honey to the drones of little prayer bees buzzing around him. They raised their hands shouting "amen" as Elroy made an impacting remark, pounding the top of the pulpit, and clenching his other fist in the air.

"Praise Jesus," Mary Francis said, shaking her head in agreement while she stifled a cough.

"Mama, can I go grab something out of the truck?" Charlie whispered loudly.

Resting her hand on Charlie's faded overalls and patting his leg with light taps, she leaned into his tufts of dark curls and touched her lips to his ears. Her whisper was strained but kind. "Baby, you gonna sit here by me today. No more lollygagging outside the tent while your daddy is preachin'. It's important that you watch and take note of what he's sayin'. One day that's gonna be you up there."

"When I grow up, I ain't preachin' like Daddy. As soon as I am old enough, I'm gonna get a real job and leave these tents for sure," he said with assurance.

Mary Francis stared ahead, raising her hands in praise without acknowledging Charlie's declaration. Charlie slumped into his seat with boredom as the eyes of the hopeful sinners around him felt like irons searing holes into his flesh. Most times he felt like coming out of his skin when the volume rose, and his daddy's sweat-basted face contorted with conviction.

"Can we go through the Burger King drive-through when we leave here?"

"Lord, have mercy on my soul, son. You are testin' my patience. Now listen and be quiet."

Charlie shifted in his seat. He could feel her aggravation covering him like a white sheet on Halloween night. He sighed, straightening his back and crossing his arms over his chest.

Mary Francis retrieved a piece of Wrigley's Juicy Fruit gum from her dress pocket and placed it flatly onto his thigh. Her shoulders convulsed as she stifled another cough. "Amen, good Reverend. Amen."

Before Charlie could unwrap the stick of gum, he heard the words that he dreaded more than having his face wiped with one of his mama's handkerchiefs as a little boy. "Before we end this evening of praise and worship I wanna introduce you good folk to my wife, Mary Francis, and my boy, Charlie. Come on up here, family, and meet the Lord's people," Elroy said, waving them forward.

Charlie pulled his shoulders back and marched to the podium beside his mama, leaving a wake of dust as they joined Elroy front and center. He felt like a trophy. Plain and simple. The sea of faces with knotted brows and hopeful smiles raised their hands in praise and cheered as Elroy paraded them down the center aisle and exited the tent. His daddy glowed from the mix of admiration and sweat.

Finally, Charlie thought. *My favorite part—leaving.*

Charlie stood close to his mama as she shook hands and praised Jesus with everyone who approached. Pulling at the side of his mama's pale-blue dress, he scanned the crowd for his daddy, who was sure to be bent out of shape with him for talking somewhere between the fire and the brimstone.

"Excuse me one second," Mary Francis said to a rotund woman who was flailing her fleshy arms in the air and praising Elroy's sermon. "Son, why in heaven's name do you keep yankin' at my dress? Mercy on my soul, child." Even the aggravation in her voice could not outweigh the love in her eyes.

"I'm seriously about to starve." Charlie looked at Francis with pleading eyes.

"Why don't you just step outside and catch a quick breath of fresh air, and before long we'll be leavin'. But don't dillydally too long. Your daddy will have a fit if you are off wonderin' around when he finishes."

"Thanks, Mama," Charlie said and eased out the back. The night air was cool, providing him with a needed reprieve from the thick heat of the tent. He shoved the stick of gum in his mouth and stood off to the side. Hunger pains gnawed at his stomach, and the urge to pee added to his misery. Charlie peeked his head inside the tent as his daddy raised his hands in praise, engrossed in one of his stories, while his mother and an older couple listened. Neither seemed concerned with his whereabouts. A port-a-john in the distance looked and probably smelled less appealing than he liked, and he knew that once they got into the truck, his daddy wouldn't stop. Charlie scurried into a patch of brush, settling behind a tree some distance from the leftover praising and clapping. He watched his daddy slowly folding through the crowd with the broken gait of a politician on election day, shaking hands and embracing small children. His window of opportunity was closing, so he hurriedly unzipped his overalls. Charlie turned to the dark sky, closing his eyes with relief. The voices in the distance faded into the melody of the cicadas around him. Just as he finished and zipped his pants, a hand took a firm grip on his shoulder.

"What in tarnation has gotten into you, boy? I been hollering your name. Your mama is already in the truck, and I am worn to a frazz." The perspiration on Elroy's cheeks shone like a glass bowl, flush with anger.

"Sorry, Daddy, but nature was calling."

Elroy's grip tightened on the scruff of Charlie's neck as they trudged through the brush. Charlie picked up the pace, fearing Elroy might grab a switch if the opportunity presented itself. As they reached the clearing by the tent, Elroy stopped and stared Charlie squarely in the eyes. With a tart smile, Elroy canvassed the crowd before speaking. Charlie took a breath, preparing for the promise of a whoopin' when they got back to the motel. "Now you listen and listen good, boy. You pull another disappearin' act like that, and you gonna be pickin' a switch, you hear me?"

"Yes, sir."

"I done told you how important it is for you to watch your mama when I'm done. She ain't well and has no business making her way to the truck on her own. You hear me, boy?"

"Yes, sir."

"Now git to the car and settle in with your mama. I will be there shortly."

As Charlie turned to leave, the sea of people parted, presenting the most beautiful girl he'd ever seen. Her hair was like spun waves of sunlight, creating a halo around her rosy cheeks and flowing to the bottoms of her shoulders. A very tall gentleman with a straightforward stride led her carefully through the crowd and extended a large hand to Charlie's daddy. Elroy's dark, weathered hand provided the grip of a toddler compared to his counterpart's.

"Reverend Turner, it is good to finally make your acquaintance—in person, that is."

Elroy shifted nervously onto his good hip. "I hope you enjoyed tonight's sermon."

"I have to say, Reverend Nettles, you are every bit as charismatic as I'd heard you'd be."

The leathery lines around Elroy's eyes creased as he lifted his shoulders back a full inch. "Well, it is an honor to have you here tonight. I've watched your preachin' on the cable channel many a night."

"I appreciate that, Reverend."

Charlie swallowed hard. His earlobes were on fire.

As the good ole boy flattery continued, Charlie found it increasingly difficult to breathe. A genuine angel come to life was standing in front of him. He was no longer concerned with the pasty heat around him or the swarm of gnats taking refuge in his hairline. His fingers were numb, and he couldn't tell if he was breathing. *And why in the world is someone famous like Reverend Turner talking to my daddy?* The voices became a low rumble as everyone and everything around them faded to black. Sliding his hands into the front of his overalls, Charlie pinched his thigh to make sure this wasn't a dream. He could have sworn a choir of angels was filling his head with song as the thud of Elroy's palm smacked him squarely in the back.

"Boy, what in tarnation has gotten into you? Say hello to Reverend Turner and his daughter, Abigail."

Embarrassed heat blanketed Charlie's face as he wiped his hand on his trousers before extending it to Reverend Turner.

Then suddenly Abigail reached out. "Hi, Charlie. It's nice to meet you." The silky warmth of her hand lingered as she pulled away and braided her fingers together in front of her white eyelet sundress. If Charlie's heart didn't slow down, he was sure it was going to jump clear out of his chest.

"Hi." That was all he had.

The men's voices became a low hum as he stood with his hands tucked tightly into the front pockets of his overalls and he and Abigail stood quietly for what seemed like three days. Her gaze was steady and certain while Charlie's eyes danced between the ground and her forehead. Every time their eyes locked, he felt light headed.

"So, do you go to school around here?" she asked.

"Uhhhh…"

"Son, Abigail is askin' you a simple question. Cat got your tongue?" Elroy said, leaning into Charlie with a strained smile and robustly squeezing his shoulder.

"Uhhhh, no. I'm not in school."

"I think my boy is a bit confused. I think the heat done got hold of him."

"I mean, I am in school, just not now with it being summer and all." A dry wad of embarrassment rested in his throat. *Please, God, let there be a shovel around here so I can dig a hole and crawl in it. Please don't let my knees buckle.*

As the reverends shook hands and said their goodbyes, Charlie stared at Abigail, wishing away the dark, circular pattern of perspiration displayed around the top edge of his T-shirt. He would have sniffed his armpits if it could have gone unnoticed. He was sure to be ripe from the heat and humidity of the evening.

"I will be in touch, Reverend Nettles. We could use your brand of excitement at our church, though I'd hate to ask you to leave the congregation you've cultivated for so many years."

"Well, I will be talkin' to my missus about this. You don't git opportunities like this but once in a lifetime. I know my people would be in good hands with my associate pastor. He handles things real well on his own in the summers when I take leave to preach."

"I will be looking forward to hearing back from you then. It was a pleasure meeting you all this evening," Reverend Turner said with a smile as he turned and led Abigail across the hard, dry dirt, waving over his shoulder at Elroy. Charlie's breath hitched as Abigail stopped, turned, and waved with a smile of sheer purity. Charlie was certain there was a pair of angel wings tucked beneath her sundress.

The crowd had thinned down to barely a handful as they made their way to his daddy's old pickup truck. Charlie kept pace with Elroy as he scuffed along unusually fast. No words were exchanged, and that suited him just fine. He fully expected a lecture, but his daddy exuded an excitement that was reserved for his sermons, rarely making an appearance outside a clapboard building or tent.

His mama was perched in the front seat with the window down, fanning herself with an old church program. "I sure am glad to see you boys. It is hotter than blue blazes in here."

Elroy's expression softened as he opened the driver's side door, allowing Charlie to climb in the middle. "Are you okay, Mama? If I'd known we was gonna be a minute, I'd a told ya to sit in one of them chairs back in the tent, but boy, have I got some news," Elroy said.

Charlie slid onto the dark-red vinyl seats, exhaling into her shoulder. He was tired and sweaty but buzzing from the inside.

"You comfy?"

"Yes, Mama," Charlie said, edging into her shoulder.

Suddenly Mary Francis retched into a blood-spattered handkerchief.

Charlie's chest felt heavy and numb as he watched his mama's rigid fingers clutch her chest and mouth. The shift dress that once hugged her curves now draped over her jagged edges, reminding him of the tent disappearing in the rearview mirror. The only bright spot with her new edges was Elroy's softer ones. His daddy no longer raised his voice at his mama when his temper got the best of him. He treated her like a paper doll.

"Family, I got some good news. Yes, I do." Elroy eased on the gas as the muffler popped and rumbled. His body swayed between the seat and the steering wheel, working his fingers around the wheel.

"You sho' are filled up with the Spirit tonight. What has got you so fired up, Elroy?"

"Well, Mama, I'm gone tell you."

Charlie closed his eyes, inhaling his mama's lavender perfume and memorizing every line of Abigail Turner's face. Maybe he'd get lucky and dream about her. Now that would make sleeping in the tiny confines of the Motel 6 doable.

"Mama, we gonna make a new start. This is the opportunity we been waitin' for our whole life."

Charlie's limbs were almost limp as he focused on the rumble of the muffler and the sound of Abigail's voice.

"That Reverend Turner wants me to come work as an associate pastor at his church."

Charlie's heart skipped a beat as he jolted upright. "What, Daddy? What did you say?"

"Oh, Elroy, that is such blessed news. It's time for your light to shine," Mary Francis said, hunched over with a staccato of coughs. "That could present some real opportunities for you, hun."

"Boy, your daddy is gone be the associate pastor of the Church of the Golden Light in Sinclair, South Carolina." Elroy needled his thumbs along the worn leather steering wheel with a grin unlike any Charlie had ever seen on his daddy's face.

And as the wheels passed over the miles of road, Charlie felt as though he was melting into the night sky, imagining what he'd say the next time he encountered an angel.

Chapter Two

Within a few weeks, they'd packed up their lives and moved to a new town for a fresh start.

On a Monday morning, the truck sputtered to a stop in front of a low brick building that seemed to stretch on and on. "Now you go on in that new school of yours and make some friends." Mary Francis held the handkerchief to her lips. "And you remember how special you are, you hear me?"

Charlie stared at the building in front of him and wondered what was ahead. His daddy had told him that the reverend's kids attended this school and he needed to make friends with them. That was the only part of the day that he was excited about. His throat tightened as he worked through the dialogue that would likely take place between him and Abigail. He would be witty and charming, unlike their last encounter. After all, she deserved to meet the real Charlie Nettles, not the sweaty, nervous version she had encountered at the tent revival. He'd even run his finger along the top of his daddy's bottle of Old Spice, just enough to dab behind his ears.

"Son, it's time to pee or git off da pot. Now tell your mama bye, and let's git you enrolled. Summer's over, boy, it's time to git your head on straight."

Charlie took another breath, much deeper than the last, and leaned into his mama, wrapping his arm around her waist. He didn't want to leave her. "Bye, Mama. Maybe you should go back to the doctor today about that cough?"

"Oh now, you don't need to worry another minute about your mama." Deep cough. "Go in there and make friends. You got your new shirt on, and you gone be the most handsome boy in school. You just wait."

Charlie smoothed down his fresh, out-of-the-bag, white Hanes T-shirt. "Thanks, Mama. But you sure you're okay?" Her brown eyes sparkled from their concave sockets. "I mean you didn't sleep none and…"

"Boy, tell your mama bye, and let's git a move on."

Mary Francis smiled and nodded for him to listen to his daddy. Charlie pulled himself into her one last time and then slid across the seat onto the gravel parking lot.

In what seemed like minutes, he was on his way to his first class, American history. The halls were silent except for the occasional echoes of his tennis shoes squeaking along the smooth concrete surface. Charlie scanned the doors until he reached room 240. It was like being on one of those game shows. Is Abigail Turner behind door number one or door number two? Surely, he couldn't be that lucky. *I got this.*

"Well now, you must be Charlie Nettles." Mrs. Hampton was a rotund African American woman with a close-cut afro. Her smile immediately put Charlie at ease as she guided him to the front of the class among periodic snickers. "Now, everyone, I would like to introduce you to a new student. I will expect each of you to take a moment to introduce yourself when class is over."

Charlie was somewhat immune to the stares of strangers. His daddy's ministry had vaccinated him against them a long time ago. But it was the possibility of seeing Abigail Turner behind one of those metal desks that took his breath away—he spotted her. *No freakin' way. Feet don't fail me now.* There she was, sitting one row over directly beside him. Charlie bumped into the desk, causing it to screech across the floor. "Uhh, sorry about that." All eyes were on him as he awkwardly slid onto the hard, shiny chair. Heat rose in his neck as he looked ahead.

"Sphhhh. Hey, Charlie, glad to see you."

Charlie turned to Abigail, who was leaning on one elbow smiling at him. "Yeah, me too," he said. *Me too—what a bonehead thing to say. Me too. I am glad to see myself.*

Abigail chuckled and looked ahead, whittling her number-two pencil between her fingers.

For the remainder of the class, Mrs. Hampton could have been talking about the rise and fall of Tony the Tiger, and he would have been none the wiser. Abigail's presence made it hard to breathe, much less focus.

As class came to a close and the bell rang, Charlie stood gripping his schedule in his hand. He could hear a boy two seats up mutter, "What's up with that hair? Is he Samson or something?" to another boy as they laughed and walked out.

"So, Charlie, what do you think of our school so far?" Abigail slid from behind the desk unfazed by the comment and retrieved a stack of books from her backpack on the floor by her feet. Her hair was longer than he remembered, and her turquoise-blue eyes stared at him from beneath lashes that reminded him of Bambi. He wondered how she blinked with lashes that long.

"It's alright, I guess."

"Yeah, you have to ignore some of these jerks around here. Not much of a Welcome Wagon."

"Uhhh, yeah, all right." Once again, Charlie was at a loss. Any bravado that he'd conjured walking into class dissipated when he spotted Abigail.

"So where to next?" she asked, reaching out for his class schedule. Charlie handed it over, and she scanned it quickly. "Okay, let's go. My next class isn't far from there, and you *do not* want to be late for Mr. Rodriguez. He gets mad and starts yelling random things that you cannot *even* understand." She had the ease of a tour guide and the grace of a gazelle.

"Spanish. I don't know how to speak Spanish."

"You don't have to, silly. It says 101 Beginner. Aside from his short fuse when you're late, he's pretty cool."

The breezeway between the buildings was bustling with chatter. Abigail made small talk, asking him questions about what it was like where he came from and what he liked to do. Charlie listened and nodded his head a lot. Just as they reached his next class, two arms slung around them, pulling them shoulder to shoulder.

"And what do we have here? Could this be the new preacher man's kid? Is he already your boyfriend, Princess?"

"Wes, you are such a complete dork, I swear."

Charlie pulled away, crossing his arms.

"Come on now, just making a joke. My name is Wesley, but my friends call me Wes," he said, extending his hand. "Assuming you will be a friend but not so sure by the look on your face."

Charlie paused and then took it. He was accustomed to smart remarks. He had been the recipient of lots of them at his last school. Same old nonsense based on his thick, wavy, shoulder-length hair, the color of coal, or the fact his daddy was a preacher. He wished they'd come up with some new material.

"No problem," Charlie said.

"Look, Dummy, we were having a perfectly good conversation before you butted your way in. By the way, Charlie, Wes is my twin brother."

Charlie could see the resemblance only in that Wes's eyes were so blue they looked transparent, and Abby's hair was straight with very little wave. "So, I hear your Daddy is gonna be working with my daddy over at the church. I hope your daddy knows more about cutting grass than the last guy my daddy hired. Boy, he got an earful when he mowed straight over the petunias my mama had just planted."

What is he talkin' about? "Grass? My daddy's gonna be the associate pastor."

"So *that's* what he told him. Well, if he likes preachin' to the possum family that's takin' refuge under the church, then he'll be just fine." Wes waved over his head as he disappeared into the sea of students just as the tardy bell rang.

"Oh boy. I gotta go, Charlie. Here's your schedule. You better hurry up."

As Wesley's words washed over him, he was filled with unease and stood outside the classroom door clutching the paper, the bustle quieting. He'd have to find out more when he got home, but for now, he just needed to make it until he saw Abigail again. Maybe they would have another class together if he was lucky.

A gust of cool air met Charlie with a very abrasive "Hola, Senor." The rest sounded like gibberish.

Within a few short months, Charlie had settled into his new life. He, Abby, and Wes were inseparable. Which was some solace in the face of his mama's worsening condition, but not enough. She now rarely left the house except for doctor's visits. Even then Elroy had to practically carry her to the car. Neither of his parents talked about her condition and when asked, replied with a vague "You don't need ta worry, Charlie. Your job is to go to school. Leave the rest to us." That response sufficed until his mama could barely choke out a full sentence. Finally, his daddy blurted out over a bucket of Kentucky Fried Chicken that she had cancer and didn't have much time left, which was followed by a request for the mashed potatoes by Charlie's hand.

"Dyin'?" Charlie whispered so that his mama wouldn't hear him upstairs. "What do you mean, dyin'?"

"I mean she is dyin', boy," he said, tearing a chunk of meat from the bone and staring at Charlie deadpan.

"Don't you think you shoulda told me this by now?"

"Well, she's my wife, and it ain't none of your concern."

"What do you mean none of my concern? I have a right to know."

Elroy leaned in and swallowed hard. The anger flickered in his eyes like a candle with a damp wick. "I suggest you watch that tone, boy, cause you gittin' ready to go pick a switch."

Charlie stood up and slammed his fist down onto the small table, catapulting the container of mashed potatoes. "First off, I ain't pickin' a switch. I ain't a baby. And second, she's my mama, and she *is* my business."

Elroy jumped up and leaned onto the table, white knuckled, staring Charlie down for a full minute. Charlie watched the red work its way up his daddy's neck and into his cheeks like when he was reaching a heated high note in one of his sermons. Small pieces of chicken catapulted from Elroy's half-full mouth and onto the table in front of him as he spoke. "Imma gonna give you that, boy. You ain't a baby no more, but let's be clear on one thing. I can still take you any day of the week, you hear me? I got enough on my plate with your mama bein' sick and all. I don't need your back talk and sass." He slammed his fist loudly on the table. "If you want to talk to me like a man, then you better be ready to stand up like one too."

Charlie swallowed hard without breaking his daddy's gaze. Just as Elroy opened his mouth to speak again, the faint sounds of Mary Francis's bell came from upstairs.

"Now I suggest you git out of my sight for the rest of the day, or you and me's gonna tangle."

Charlie watched in silence as Elroy smoothed down his hair and wiped his chin with the paper napkin. It wasn't until Elroy was upstairs that the hot tears pooled over his eyes, landing in the puddle of thick brown gravy on his paper plate. His body shook as he held his face in his hands crying, feeling emptiness in his heart unlike anything he'd ever experienced. He'd committed no crime, yet he was sentenced to living with Elroy. Charlie blew his nose with a crumpled-up napkin and tossed it onto his plate. *Well, if I gotta live without my mama, to heck with everybody's stupid rules.* He rested in his new resolve, staring at the cold bucket of chicken in front of him as the puddle of gravy filled with more tears.

Chapter Three

A few months passed as Charlie wrestled with his grief. *My mama is a fighter for sure*, he thought as he lay on his bed staring at the ceiling. But he'd just checked in on her, and she wasn't doing well. She was having more trouble than usual breathing, and Elroy was waiting for her doctor to arrive. Charlie couldn't stand to be inside any longer. He threw on an old gray sweatshirt and walked into the kitchen. "Daddy, I'm gonna go outside for a while."

"You just hold it right there, boy. I just got off the phone with Lenora down at the Feed and Seed. Seems she had some interestin' things to say." Lenora Smith, owner of Lenora's Feed and Seed and local gossip, seemed to take a certain degree of pleasure in reporting back to Elroy after Sunday services. Her thick, rosaceous-colored cheeks glowed as she pressed her pink cotton handkerchief to her lips, speaking softly, "Good Reverend Nettles, you know I absolutely hate to be the bearer of bad news, but…."

"Charlie, you gonna be the death of me, boy," Elroy said, unevenly pacing along the perimeter of the worn, plaid couch. Charlie stared blankly ahead. "You are supposed to set an example, not run Bill Jenkins and the boys over there at the sheriff's department in circles! How am I 'sposed to talk to folks about redemption and the like when you are running round making a mockery of me? She done told me 'bout you trespassing on the judge's land again. You can't find no other swimmin' hole in this town? You gotta go to his?" Elroy stood in front of Charlie with his arms crossed, waiting for an answer. "Whatcha got to say for yo self?"

"I'm sorry?" He couldn't think of anything except for his mama.

"Is that all you got, boy, sittin' there lookin' at me like you ain't even sure if you should be sorry?"

Charlie kept his head down to avoid eye contact with his daddy. He was too tired to fight. The front door was only a few feet away. He could make it if he timed it right, but that would make his daddy mad as a hornet. It would be twice as bad when he got home, and he didn't want his mama to get upset if she heard him downstairs going at it with Elroy.

Elroy's hand shook as his spindly finger pointed toward the door, and he barked, "Now you git up and go git a switch, and you better make it a good one, you hear me? You ain't gittin' away this time."

Charlie sat with his arms crossed over his chest, clenching his jaw.

"Whatchu waitin' on, boy?"

Charlie stared at the tattered area rug beneath his feet hoping his daddy wouldn't notice the chunks of saltine crackers that had spattered everywhere when he and Wesley had filled their cheeks to capacity with crackers and proceeded to have a whistling contest. That would just add fuel to the fire. Picturing the crackers streaming from Wesley's mouth as he whistled with no sound, Charlie chuckled.

"Oh, you think this is funny?" Elroy said, pulling Charlie off the sofa by the scruff of his neck. "Well, we'll just see about that," he growled, removing his belt from his pants in a single swipe. As Charlie danced in circles, making Elroy madder by the minute, the worn leather caught the bare flesh of his legs with a pop. Determined not to cry,

Charlie bit his lower lip until it was numb with pain as he continued moving to avoid the stinging pops to his legs.

Elroy's arm flailed with fatigue as he delivered a final blow to Charlie's calf. Charlie winced, holding in the urge to cry. Breathing heavily, Elroy worked his belt back through the loops. "Now you git on up to your room, and don't come down till supper. You hear me?" he said, wiping his mouth with the backside of his hand.

Charlie took the old hardwood stairs in twos and landed on his twin bed with a thud. "I wish you were the one in there dying and not mama," he said, slamming both fists on his twin bed.

Hot tears stung Charlie's eyes as he pounded his head into the mushy down pillow behind him. *One day I am gonna up and leave.*

Charlie could only imagine what life would be like when his mama wasn't around to buffer their differences. She knew how to turn his daddy into butter with a few simple words. "Elroy, honey, would you mind…that handsome face needs a smile," she would say, looking over her naturally long eyelashes. She had a handful of phrases that snuffed out his anger, turning him into a kitten in her lap.

Charlie eased himself into the hallway. He could hear his daddy on the phone downstairs with Reverend Turner. This was a good time to slip in to see his mama.

The door creaked open, releasing Mentholatum and sickness into the air around him, and the floor moaned softly beneath his feet as he approached her bed. He eased onto the coverlet beside the green oxygen tank that had become a fixture wherever she was. She opened her eyes, which rested in a cave of darkness, and he touched her cheekbone with the side of his hand. "Hey, Mama."

Her voice was hoarse as she coughed, signaling for Charlie to give her a sip of water from the mason jar beside the bed. He secured the white straw against the jar with one hand and eased her head off the pillow with the other. It was bordered with pink needlepoint flowers. She had loved to needlepoint in the truck when they were on the road.

"Hey, baby boy." Her tired eyes smiled.

"Hey, Mama," he said, choking back a sob.

"I done heard you and your daddy going at it," she said in a low whisper.

Charlie only shook his head, placed her hand in his, and lay his other over her cool, brittle fingers. He knew that look. It was the same look of patience that she displayed when he and Elroy butted heads. "He's just mean, Mama. Plain and simple. He don't love me."

A smile worked to the corners of her mouth. "Now, now. He does love you, no mistakin' that. His way is just different," she said with a deep cough.

"I need you here, Mama. I can't do this without you. I mean I believe you could still be healed and all," he said, feeling the need to press into her faith for her sake, not his. He paused and hung his head as tears landed on her crinkled skin. "I just..."

"Shhh. Now you don't go worryin', baby boy. Our Lord and..." she sputtered out the word "savior" before placing the mask over her mouth and closing her eyes. Then she placed the mask on her abdomen. "He's got this, I tell ya. Not you, not me, but Him," she said, fading into a bliss that he didn't understand. "Never forget that baby boy."

He placed her hand against his cheek.

"I believe in you, Charlie."

"I know you do, Mama."

"You already have everything you need," she choked into her shoulder. "Never forget that you have the gift."

"Boy, you need to give your mama some time to rest," Elroy hissed, easing in the door.

"Now, now, Elroy. He just needs his mama," she said, squeezing his hand.

"I just got in here, Daddy. Can't I stay?"

Elroy's arms uncrossed, relaxing to his sides as he spoke, "Mama, you okay? Can I get you somethin'?" His voice no longer rumbled, but Charlie could sense his daddy's reluctance.

Mary Francis shook her head and smiled at Elroy. "I am perfect. But you know, baby boy, your mama could use a nap. I'm just so tired." Her eyes were the kind that could make miracles happen, they were so pure. *How come she didn't get one?* he wondered, placing her hand on the bed but not before kissing the top.

She mouthed *I love you* as he stood up.

"I will be back. You get some rest."

Chapter Four

Charlie rolled into a patch of sunlight peeking through his blinds and onto his bedspread, creating a warm spot on his newly shaved head. His heart was heavy with grief. His mama had been gone for two months, and getting out of bed was still like dripping molasses from the end of a spoon. He ran his hands along the unfamiliar stubble, scrubbing just above his ears. The thick dark curls that his mama had loved were in the bottom of his bathroom trash can.

"You up, boy?" Elroy called from the bottom of the stairs.

Charlie flopped onto his back and fought the urge to cry. He still missed the smell of fresh-cooked bacon on a Saturday morning and the sound of his mother's feet padding to his window to open his blinds. He missed the way she kissed his forehead to wake him up. He missed how she had run interference between him and his daddy. He missed everything about her. But most of all, he just wanted to hear her say those five simple words: *I'm still here, baby boy*.

"You don't want me to come up them steps, boy. You best have your feet on the floor."

Good morning to you, too, Daddy. Charlie pushed the covers back and stretched away the desire to curl into a ball. He slipped on his favorite Mötley Crüe T-shirt and started down the stairs. Elroy was sitting at the kitchen table hovering over a cup of coffee, wrenching his hands together.

"My hands in knots," Elroy said without looking up. He was wearing the plaid green bathrobe that had become his wardrobe staple from the moment he came home from Mama's funeral. If he could have worn it to preach, he probably would have.

"Mornin', Daddy."

"I thought I told you to cut the grass yesterday."

"I had to take the mower over to old man Eddie's shop to get the blade sharpened, remember?"

Elroy didn't look up as he continued massaging his knuckles. "Gaul dang pain in my hands. So, when did he say you could pick it up?"

"Anytime today," Charlie said, opening the refrigerator for a carton of milk. He pulled out the spout, placed it under his nose, made a grunt, and tossed it into an overflowing trash can. He peered into the refrigerator and narrowed down his prospects to a slice of three-day-old pizza or a serving of leftover pork chop casserole. Their only means of survival had been from the folks in the church bringing by meals. As the months passed, the meals were dwindling.

"You gonna stand there all day holdin' that door open? You tryin' to cool the whole house?"

Charlie grabbed the last can of Coca-Cola and popped the tab. The burn felt good going down. *Breakfast is served.*

"I suppose you think you gonna take off today and leave me to do all the chores around this place."

Charlie looked around and pushed down the desire to laugh in his daddy's face. The floors had not seen the underside of a mop since before his mama died unless the church ladies showed up with cleaning supplies to help, but that was rare. Old newspapers and magazines littered every surface. The only time any cleaning got done was when

Charlie did it, and he preferred hanging out with Wes and Abby to picking up after his daddy. Elroy was just looking for an argument.

"I got to git my sermon notes ready for tomorrow. Reverend Turner is leavin' in the mornin' for a convention. I need you to carry your weight, boy."

"Yes, sir," he answered. Out of respect for his mama, he was trying to keep his mouth shut, but there was always the looming threat of a whipping.

His daddy stood up and tucked his Bible under his arm. "I'm goin' upstairs, and when I come down, you best have this place shinin' like a brand-new penny, boy. Last time you did one shoddy job. Why don't you put your best foot forward and git it right this time?"

Charlie looked at the clock with a sigh. He was supposed to meet Abby and Wes down at Jeremiah's Place. It rested in the center of town and served the best fries within a fifty-mile radius. Charlie knew this with certainty because his mama always treated him to fries when they were on the road. That was their thing. Who cooked the best fries? She always said Jeremiah's were hands down the best, and Charlie agreed.

"I don't hear no water in that sink, boy," Elroy said as he slowly worked his way up the stairs.

Charlie stared at the stack of dishes in the sink and poured the last drop of Dawn dishwashing liquid across the entire pile. He was determined to finish and finish fast.

Within ten minutes he was wiping down the counter tops with a sour-smelling dishrag and putting the last of the papers in a stack on the coffee table.

Elroy shuffled into the kitchen scanning the landscape, lips pursed. "Hmmph...I guess you done poured the last of my coffee out." His daddy was wearing a freshly pressed light-blue oxford shirt and navy pleated pants and smelled like he'd fallen into a vat of Old Spice.

Charlie folded the dish rag and placed it on the side of the sink, "Sorry, Daddy. I thought you were done."

"Well, I guess that's what you git for thinkin'. I 'spose I can go by Jeremiah's on the way in. He always has a pot brewin'."

"You think you could take me with you and drop me off? I can walk back. I'm supposed to meet Abby and Wes."

Elroy scowled, transferring his weight onto the good hip while peering into the living room.

Please let me go. Say I did good, and you will take me. Please, Daddy.

"I 'spose, but before sundown you gonna hit these here floors with a good sweepin'. You shoulda done that anyways without me askin'. I swear, boy." The disappointment in his daddy's voice was as present as the fragrance of his mama in the clothes still hanging in their closet. Some days when his daddy was outside tinkerin' around in the garage or in town, he'd wrap his arms around her old dresses and bury his face in the fabric. He hoped her smell would never fade. It was all he had left.

"Go in there and shut off the lights. I'll be in the truck. And put a move on it."

———◦◦◦———

The diner was packed, as it was on most Saturdays. Charlie could see Jeremiah's wife, Miss Sally, behind the counter through the window that spanned the length of the building. She was always generous with her smiles and the occasional burger or order of fries she'd slide in front of him without a word when Charlie didn't have two nickels to rub together. Miss Sally put every ounce of her heart into simply wiping down counters and serving food. She and Jeremiah treated serving others like a religion in itself. He'd often wished Jeremiah had been his daddy and not Elroy.

Charlie skipped ahead of Elroy making his way across the dirt parking lot.

"Where's the fire, boy?" Elroy asked, easing the weight off his bad hip, moving slowly.

"No fire," Charlie said looking over his shoulder. As the door swooshed open, he spotted them in the back corner. *That's the fire right there.* Charlie ran his hand across the top of his head before throwing his hand into a fast wave. Abby's smile lit up the diner and caused his stomach to flip inside out.

"Well, good afternoon, Charlie. What brings you to my diner this fine day?" Jeremiah asked as Charlie made his way to the back.

"Your fries, of course," Charlie replied.

"Well, I will whip up some for you right now." Jeremiah's smile spanned from ear to ear. "You doin' all right today, Charlie?" Jeremiah said with a knowing look. He was a tall, lanky African American man with an inch-high afro and a voice smooth like silk. He always had some tidbit of wisdom to share with Charlie and a kind word for all his patrons. Miss Sally walked behind him, making her way to the cash register. Her hair rested in a small bun at the base of her neck. She wore a pale-yellow pencil skirt with a neatly pressed, short-sleeve white cotton blouse. Her blue gingham apron hugged her small waist and accentuated her full hips. She always looked neat as a pin. Her skin reminded Charlie of the Werther's caramels that his mama would slip in his hand during church from time to time. They were a special treat that Charlie savored the day after the offering plate was especially full.

"Hey there, Charlie. How are you today, young man?" Miss Sally smiled.

"I couldn't be better if there were two of me," he said, receiving a chuckle from her. He could feel Elroy approaching from behind, which made Charlie feel like an iguana shedding his skin.

He looked back at his daddy, who stood at the counter talking to one of the members of the church.

"Chaaaaleee boy. What's up?" Wes said, looking up with a mouth full of milkshake.

"Not much," Charlie said, watching Abigail's eyes following him. Her hair was pulled away from her face in a ponytail high atop her head. Her eyes reminded him of a sky filled with billowy white clouds.

"So, Charlie, are you going out for JV baseball this year or what?" Abby asked matter-of-factly.

"I don't think so. My daddy keeps me plenty busy," he said, not wanting to add that they didn't have the money for a uniform.

"Doing what? Your house looked like a tornado ran through it last time I was there," Wes said, stirring the thick milkshake in a circular motion.

Charlie reached across the table smacking the top of Wesley's unruly blond curls. Wes just laughed.

"Wes, you are just being plain mean."

"I'm not trying to be mean, Princess. You know that, right Charlie? I am just statin' the facts."

"Sure. I hate to say it, but you're right, man. No matter how much I do, it ain't never enough anyway. My daddy only likes preachin', grievin', or gittin' on me."

"Dang, Charlie, that sounds like a country song." Wes laughed, repeating the words with a melodic country twang.

Charlie chuckled, trying not to stare too hard at Abby. She seemed to get prettier every time he saw her.

Her eyes met his. "Well, you know what makes everything better?" Abby said, nudging his arm. "Chocolate."

Charlie swallowed into the flutter in his stomach. "That sounds good and all, but I think I'll stick with water today."

Before Charlie could respond, Abby was waving Miss Sally over to the table. "Oh hush, Charlie. When have you ever turned down a chocolate milkshake? It's your favorite."

She was right, but the few coins jingling in his pocket wouldn't cover it.

"Well, now. What can I get for you today, Charlie?" Miss Sally said with her hands planted on her thin, rounded hips.

"Sorry about that, Miss Sally. Abby got confused."

"I absolutely did not get confused, Charlie Nettles. Miss Sally, would you please bring him a large chocolate shake, and I'd like another, please."

The heat in Charlie's face was making it hard to speak.

Miss Sally smiled at Charlie and winked. "I got this one. It's on the house. Just consider it payment for helping me bring in those crates of vegetables last week."

Charlie exhaled and smiled back. "Thanks, Miss Sally. I really appreciate that."

"And before you leave, remind me to send one of my pecan pies home with you. I promised your daddy."

"Yes, ma'am. That sounds good." *Dinner.* As Miss Sally turned and disappeared into the kitchen, her little girl, Susan, walked up carrying a plate full of french fries. Charlie eased the plate from her tiny hands and placed them on the table. She was eight years old and small for her age. Her pale-pink dress with a lace collar reminded him of one of those perfect little baby dolls you buy in the box with the clear plastic. Braids shot in every direction, with little colored rubber bands displaying shiny little balls similar to lights on a Christmas tree.

"Thanks, Susan. You are a good helper," Charlie said, taking the fries from her small hands. She displayed a shy grin and skirted quickly back to the kitchen.

"So, what gives?" Charlie asked, biting a fry in half, shaking the heat from his fingers.

"I say we go fishin'," Wes said, shoving a bundle of fries in his mouth.

Charlie read the aggravation on Abigail's face. "I was thinking maybe we could ride bikes or see if we could go see a movie."

Wesley stopped chewing and cocked his head to the side. "What have you done with Charlie Nettles?" he said, leaning over the table and knocking on Charlie's forehead.

"Come on, man. You know nothing is biting today."

"Says who? I am seriously getting worried that aliens have taken away Chaaalie Boy."

Abigail smiled from behind her straw. "I think either would be fun."

"And what's up with you, Princess? You usually like to fish. I am seriously worried about you both," he said, sliding out of the booth. "I gotta pee."

As Wesley disappeared into the restroom, Abigail looked at Charlie while taking a slow draw from her milkshake. Charlie took a breath, rubbing the front of his T-shirt hoping that his heart would stop fluttering. It hadn't got the memo that she was one of the guys.

"You know you didn't have to do that."

"I don't mind taking one for the team."

"How did you know that I was spent on fishing, at least for a while?"

Charlie paused, wondering how her lips were naturally as pink as a piece of Hubba Bubba bubble gum. "I listen, that's all."

"Really?"

"Really. You said last time you were bored, and you never say that" Charlie said, smiling inside for paying such close attention. "I just knew it was time to shake things up."

"I have to say, you are gonna make some girl very lucky one day."

I want it to be you, Abigail Turner. "I guess." He was at a loss for words.

"No guessing about it."

Wesley slid back into the booth, spreading his arms along the top of the leather. "Don't ask. I realized when I got in there that I needed to drop the kids off at the pool," he said, laughing into his joke.

"Really, Wes. Gross. Oh no, don't look now," Abby said turning her eyes to her plate, whittling a french fry between her fingers. "It's Daddy, Wes. Oh, crap."

"Oh, crap's right. You are busted." Wes chuckled.

Reverend Turner approached the table. He was wearing a starched white cotton button-down and pleated pants that moved slightly as he crossed the restaurant, patting the backs of people and saying hello. Everyone in town treated him like a celebrity because the cable channels had picked up his revivals. At six foot four, Reverend Turner's presence filled any room that he entered, and he always carried an air of unmistakable charisma. There was no denying his effect on people. The women in town blushed when he spoke, and the men hung onto every word like he was one of the twelve disciples. Only Charlie felt a sense of unease when he was near, and now leaned onto his elbows, scraping a single french fry along the salt crusted onto the side of the white plate.

"Good afternoon, boys."

"Afternoon, sir," Charlie said, finding his posture and fixing his gaze on Abby, who anxiously twisted the edges of her napkin between her thumb and index fingers. He felt sorry for her. She never seemed to measure up in Reverend Turner's eyes, while Wes could do no wrong.

"Hey, Dad," Wes said as he looked at Abby and slurped the remainder of his milkshake.

"Hello, son." Pause. "Charlie." His face lacked the charismatic animation that he had displayed for the patrons of the restaurant only moments earlier. "Abigail, my understanding was that you were helping your mama at the church today."

"Yes, sir. I just stopped in for a minute to get something to eat."

"You know, Abigail, I have to say I am very disappointed." Reverend pointedly looked at his wristwatch and then to Abigail, who sat with tears filling her eyes. "Seems to me, if my calculations are correct, it has been at least two hours since you left the house. You enjoy spending time with your brother and Charlie? All of your girlfriends busy, I assume?" He leaned in with a whisper. "People love to talk, Abigail. I don't need them telling me you are spending time with boys."

"Lord forbid people see into our glass house," Abigail mumbled under her breath without looking up.

Reverend Turner cocked his head and smiled sideways, looking around. Charlie watched a tear drop land on Abby's arm as she stared at the table.

"Well, Abigail. I suggest you make your way to the church. Jeremiah should have my sandwich ready by now. Get your things, and I will give you a ride over there now. Your mama is expecting you." Reverend Turner patted Wes on the shoulder and tossed a $20 bill onto the table, looking through Charlie. "Here you go, son. This should cover it."

Abigail grabbed her denim wallet off the table and forced a smile. "I'll see ya later, Charlie."

"Bye, Princess," Wesley said with a grin.

Abigail cut her eyes at Wesley and fell in line behind her daddy.

His heart sank as he watched her amble behind Reverend Turner like a calf being led to slaughter. Wes continued eating his fries and started talking about some kid at school who got caught smoking weed in the boys' bathroom earlier that day. "Chaaalee boy, are you even listening to me?"

"Yeah, of course."

"Okay, so what did I just say?"

Charlie took a sip of his milkshake, trying to overcome the weight of Abby's absence. He'd planned on spending the day with them until Reverend Turner ruined it. "Ommm, you said that you like eating cow testicles for dinner every day."

They both laughed. Wes balled up his napkin and threw it, hitting Charlie on the side of the head. "What do you say we go throw the football around?"

"You know, actually, I'm gonna go home and get the house in order." Something about seeing that tear fall from Abby's eye had taken all the fun out of the day for him.

"Suit yo'self."

"I need to stop by the church, though, for a minute. I need to pick up something for my daddy real quick, or he will kick my butt." The lie burned his throat a little, but he needed to make sure Abigail was okay.

"All right then. Well, we just missed a perfectly good ride."

The dust was still settling in the parking lot from the wheels of Reverend Turner's shiny gray Cadillac, and Elroy was long gone.

"A walk will do us good," Charlie said, hoping to buy some time to come up with a legitimate reason for being at the church.

"Since when did you give two hoots about fitness? Heck, I have to practically pry you off the couch to go skateboard."

"Yeah, well, I don't have a skateboard, and the one you always loan me has the jacked-up wheel, remember?"

"Come on now, man. You know I can't have the ladies see me on my grandmother's skateboard." Wes laughed and punched Charlie in the arm as they walked out of the door.

"Ahhh man," Wes said, shaking his head. "Seriously."

"What?" Charlie asked as Wesley kicked the dirt and rocks under his feet.

"I knew I was forgetting something. I was supposed to go by and get some stupid sewing junk for my mama at the fabric store. Why don't you go pick up whatever you gotta get for your daddy, and we'll meet up later. I'm trying to stay in the good graces of the old man. Interims come out Monday, and well, we both know chemistry is not my thing, "Wesley said with a laugh.

"All right, man. Sounds like a plan," Charlie said, waving over his shoulder, jogging across the parking lot. Charlie made his way along dirt roads and shortcuts, finally reaching the church in twenty minutes. He was going to put a smile on Abigail's face if he had to stand on his head.

The church parking lot was empty except for the Reverend Turner's car. The sanctuary door was unlocked, so Charlie stepped inside. Met with a wave of cool air, he leaned into his armpits and sniffed quickly.

"Hello," Charlie said, but the sanctuary was empty. As he moved toward the door leading to the offices, he heard muffled voices. "Hello, Abigail, is that you?"

In an instant, Reverend Turner appeared with a strained smile, smoothing the front of his shirt down with one hand and his hair with the other. "Hey Charlie, what can I do for you?"

It was the same unwelcome response he got from his daddy when he knocked on his parents' bedroom door too late in the evening. He waited for Mrs. Turner to appear behind him, but all that filled the space between them was awkward energy that stuck to Charlie's skin like the adhesive from a Band-Aid. "I was hoping Abigail was here."

"No, she is helping her mama. Now you run along," he said, smoothing his shirt into the back of his slacks.

Something wasn't right, but Charlie couldn't put his finger on it. "Okay. Will you let her know that I was looking for her?"

"No need for that, son. You'll see her at school Monday," he said, ushering Charlie out the back door. Before he could respond, the door closed behind him, and the lock clicked. Charlie stood outside the sanctuary doors not sure what'd just happened.

—◦◦—

As Charlie stepped inside the front door, the sounds of metal tinkling onto the hardwoods were followed by a loud thud, followed by another. *What tha heck? Is he back already?* "Daddy, that you?" Charlie said, making his way into the kitchen to find Elroy standing at the back door slamming his fist against the door jamb.

"Whatchu lookin' at, boy? "Elroy said, turning to Charlie with a hammer in one hand and the other balled up in a fist. "I said, whatchu lookin' at?"

"Nothin', Daddy. I heard a banging sound when I came in the front door," Charlie said, reading the frustration in his daddy's face.

"Well now, you just go right on up those stairs and mind your business, you hear me?" Elroy's tear-streaked cheeks were glowing with the intensity of a branding iron. Turning away from Charlie, he removed a nail from his work apron and held it to the wood on the edge of the screen door before dropping it. Slamming his fist against the door jamb, he yelled, "Daggone arthritis don't let ya get nothin' done. A man of my age shouldn't be dealing with no old man's disease." With another failed attempt, Elroy started crying…the kind of cry that starts out low and works deep into a crescendo.

Charlie stood motionless, paralyzed by his daddy's emotion. As Elroy's cries turned into a low sputter, Charlie ambled over to him and carefully removed the hammer from his hand. For the first time ever, Charlie saw his daddy as just an ordinary man who was suffering, suffering from the loss of his wife, and suffering from the loss of his ability to handle his business as a man. The anger that had calcified in Charlie's chest cracked.

Without a word, he held his hand out and pressed the jagged screen against the wood. "I can help, Daddy."

"You barely have fuzz on your chin, boy. How are you gonna do man's work?"

"Well, I've gotten pretty good at woman's work since mama died, so maybe I can do it." Charlie watched and waited.

At that instant, his daddy's pursed lips released a strained laugh. "I guess you have gotten pretty good at it, haven't ya."

"Yeah, Daddy. I got this."

Charlie's laugh melted into his daddy's as Elroy handed him the hammer. It felt good to laugh with the man whom he felt like a disappointment to most of the time. Charlie worked his hands around the edge inch by inch with precision as Elroy supervised. His hand folded around the hammer as if it were another appendage while his daddy stood by guiding Charlie through until the last nail was planted firmly in the wood.

Charlie stepped back and inspected his work. *It looks good. Heck, better than good.* He wanted to grab the bucket of nails and go around the house fixing everything. Suddenly he'd found his sanctuary in the contrasting veins along the entrails of the wood.

He looked to his daddy, but Elroy's arms were crossed with his usual grimace. Charlie waited in silence for the criticism he knew was coming.

"You done good, boy." The hand that had only whipped him for months was cupped around his shoulder, squeezing lightly. Without a thought, Charlie wrapped his arms around his daddy, burying his face in his plaid flannel shirt. Elroy reciprocated without a sound, and they leaned into each other's pain. For the first time since his mama died, he didn't feel like an orphan.

It was a new beginning for them that day, one that ignited a passion in Charlie for working with his hands and one day becoming the man his mama always said he could be. Elroy's gruff exterior remained firmly in place, but Charlie knew now what was beneath it. Finally.

Chapter Five

The ground cooled, and the leaves turned multiple shades of red and orange. Life with his daddy had become easier but not perfect. Even so, he was grateful. Their relationship found its footing standing on opposite ends of a sawhorse as the smell of fresh-cut lumber filled the air. Charlie's favorite project was an arbor swing that they built together in the backyard beside the old magnolia tree. "Your mama always wanted one of these here swings. Now you need to sand this part right here extra smooth." Elroy's arms rested across his chest, cradling his bent fingers.

Charlie ran his hand the length of the wood, leaning in for closer inspection. He loved the aroma of fresh-cut timber. "I see. Can you hand me the sandpaper over there?" he asked as Elroy pointed to another rough patch on the wood's surface. Elroy supervised and let Charlie be his hands even though his proficiency had far exceeded Elroy's.

"Do you think of mama a lot?" Charlie dared to ask.

Leaning his forearm against the raw timber, Elroy looked down for what seemed liked hours. As Charlie was about the say "Never mind," his words sprang forward. "I think about your mama every day. I still picture her standin' there in her Sunday best the day we said our I dos. I ain't never gonna love another woman like her. She was my one true love."

Elroy stood glazed over for a full minute as Charlie eyeballed the wood, at a loss for words. He had expected Elroy to give him an abbreviated version of his real feelings. They rarely talked about his mama with much depth, just the occasional mention that left Charlie yearning for more.

"I miss her all the time. It's hard to believe she's been gone for so long."

"It ain't been that long," Elroy said, easing his hand along the wood Charlie'd just sanded. "To me it feels like yesterday. You finish up here. I got to get to my sermon notes." Elroy tucked a piece of sandpaper into his front shirt pocket and disappeared into the kitchen door.

If only they could sit around reminiscing about times they spent together when Charlie was just a boy. But Elroy simply would not engage in lengthy conversations about his mama, and Charlie figured the pain and grief would never allow him to be that open. Today he'd gotten more out of him than expected, so he would take what he could get.

Charlie stepped back and inspected his craftsmanship. "You would love this, Mama. If you were here, we'd come out here all the time and swing. We'd talk like we used to, and you'd pat my leg with that peaceful look on your face. I hope you like it. We built this for you."

Standing in the silence of his memories, he suddenly heard a branch crack behind him.

"So, you built this for me?" Abby said with a smile, offering up a sip of her Coke.

"Well, yeah, I guess I did build it for you too." His heart smiled as she sashayed toward him in a pair of loose-fitting jeans with a navy crew-neck sweater hanging lightly over her smooth curves. Charlie took in half of the Coke in a few gulps, handed it back to Abby, and stood back. "So, what do you think? You wanna be the first to try it out? We built it in honor of Mama."

"Sure," she said, sliding onto the seat. "This sure is nice, Charlie. Your mama would have loved it. You're really good. I've been telling you that forever though," she said, giving it the once-over and leaning against Charlie, roping her arm into his. They were as close as any two people could be. It was all Charlie could do not to reach over and pull her face to his for a kiss, but even as close as they were, he hesitated, determined not to allow his feelings to jeopardize the close friendship they'd built. Reclining into each other, they allowed their feet to graze the ground as they swung back and forth in silence.

"You know, Charlie. I wish I had something like this in common with my daddy, something normal."

"What do mean?"

"Building things, fixing stuff. You and Elroy, that's your thing. Hell, my daddy has been so busy all my life trying to shape me into the person he wanted me to be that he's missed the person I actually am."

A light breeze rattled the leaves in the trees hovering nearby, releasing a sheet of them onto the ground. "And who is that, Abigail Turner?"

Her smile was distant but warm. "The girl that can make a difference of her own, ya know? I've always felt like maybe I should join the Peace Corps or something. But of course, I could never measure up to the great Reverend Turner." Her smile faded at the mention of his name.

Charlie's heart leaped in his chest at the thought of Abigail moving away, so he quieted the response that felt honest. "Your daddy loves you, Abs. In his way."

"Yea, Charlie, his way. It's always been his way," she said bitterly.

"Hey, I think you are one cool chick. That's gotta count for something."

The aromatic scent of burning leaves floated in the air as they both rolled their heads inward, leaving their faces only inches apart. The irises of Abigail's eyes contrasted against her dark-blue sweater, so pale and clear. He could feel his heartbeat speeding up again.

"So, where is Wes?" Charlie asked, lifting his head forward.

"He had to help Mama load up the car with all of the stuff they're selling for the church fundraiser. He was so mad that I got to leave, and he didn't," she said, resting her head on the swing with her eyes closed. "I can't wait to go away to college. Charlie, won't you be glad to live in a whole new place? Somewhere that our folks aren't preachin' and people think we're so lucky, but they have no idea."

Charlie looked at her sideways. "What do you mean, Abs?"

"I just think it's funny how my daddy works so hard to build up everyone around him preaching the gospel, telling men how to lead their families and love them. He has all of this great advice and doesn't even take it himself. Where's the good in that? I will not be like him." Leaning into his arm and resting her head on his shoulder, she paused. "You, on the other hand, could change the world. I believe that."

"Really? Why would you think that?" An unexpected sense of pride rolled over Charlie, leaving him speechless.

"I mean you talk to the little kids in church, and you're so patient. It's like you know their language and they get what you're saying. Maybe you should follow in that long family legacy of yours, Charlie."

"Yeah, I come from a long line of conduits of the Holy Spirit, as my mama used to say." Charlie laughed, reminding him of what his daddy had just told him.

"Seriously, you do."

"I think I am fine with changing the world one birdhouse at a time. The ministry isn't for me, Abs. I wonder sometimes if Mama would still be here if my daddy had taken more time with getting her the help she needed rather than worrying about the church."

"You can't let your daddy be the reason that you don't follow your destiny." She paused. "Well, I know one thing for sure, Charlie. You have made a difference in my world. I can't think of anyone that can make me smile like you."

Cool air swirled around them as Charlie thought about what she said. His thoughts bounced between the idea of actually touching others with his words and, more importantly, touching her. Could he make a difference? Did he really have a legacy to fulfill? His mind raced as he became lost in the tendrils of blond hair cascading around Abby's face with the sweeping motion of his brand-new swing. In an instant, all thoughts of ministering dissipated as he fought the urge to take her face into his hands.

Chapter Six

Senior year was in full swing as Charlie enjoyed selling his custom birdhouses in Jeremiah's Diner. The cold bite of winter slipped away while pink blossoms covered the Bradford Pear in Charlie's front yard, welcoming spring. He yearned for summer, but this would do for now. The winter had yielded to an ice storm that knocked out power in town for a week, and two full-blown snowstorms, which was unusual for Sinclair. Charlie slipped a thin sweatshirt over his head and bounced down the stairs. He could smell bacon before he reached the bottom step.

"Something sure smells good, Daddy." Elroy stood at the stove with his mama's old pink apron on. Charlie stifled a laugh. "Now that is a sight."

Elroy pulled the peach preserves from the cupboard and handed them over to Charlie to open. "Well, we have reason to celebrate."

Charlie plucked a piece of crisp, brown bacon from the paper towel it was draining on and tore off a piece. "Dang, Daddy. This is pretty good."

Elroy smiled as he cracked an egg on the side of the pan with limited agility, dropping the yolk into the hot grease. "Your ole man hasn't forgotten his way around a kitchen. But it has been a while."

"So, what's the news?" Charlie plopped into the creaky old chair, combing his fingertips through freshly washed hair, and wondering where Elroy's newfound joy originated. "For you to pull out mama's apron and cook, it must be good."

"It *is* good." Bacon grease hissed as the incoming egg fell below the bubbles of heat. "I been talking to Reverend Turner, and he is gonna be stateside for a while. I been his backup for all these years, so he could spread the gospel with his crusade, but I think he is just worn out, wants to be closer to home. He thinks we need to do a series of good ole-fashion tent revivals. Warm weather is right around the corner."

Charlie hadn't seen the inside of a tent since before they moved to Sinclair, but part of him missed the transient excitement of that part of his life. "So where are you gonna do 'em?"

Elroy slid the perfectly fried egg onto a paper plate and placed it on the table in front of Charlie. A halo of grease formed around the egg as Charlie debated on taking a bite. Scrambled eggs were his preference, always had been.

"Dig in, boy. Me and the reverend haven't decided exactly how many yet, but I am gonna go up and down the coast and then round up with the last one here just in time for summer to wrap up. I don't expect you to attend all of them. I know you are practically a man now, and you deserve some freedom this summer 'cause once it's over, you either better be enrolled in school or makin' one heck of a living building those birdhouses of yours."

Charlie poked the center with his fork and toyed with the orange liquid oozing across his plate. His stomach turned. He moved his toast a safe distance from the egg and tore off a piece of bacon instead. "I know, Daddy. I am working on that." There was a pause as Elroy carefully eased into the seat in front of Charlie, rested his arms around his plate, and lowered his head to say grace. When finished, he flashed Charlie a half smile and proceeded to mix his eggs in a gooey pile, topping it off with pieces of bacon. Charlie swallowed hard and looked out the window to see Abby standing on the back porch.

"Good morning, Reverend Nettles. You are looking well in your apron this morning."

"Good morning, Abby. Why don't you pull up to the table and join us? I can make more eggs."

Charlie made a face and mouthed "no" behind Elroy's back.

"As much as I'd love to, we just ate. But thanks."

"Can I be excused?" Charlie asked.

"You barely touched your breakfast, boy."

"I know but my stomach is kind of queasy this morning," he said, quickly scraping his plate before Elroy could see how little he'd eaten.

"You think about what we talked about. You hear me?"

"Yes, sir. Will do," Charlie said, signaling Abby out the back door. When they reached the bottom step, Charlie stretched his arms high above his head and sighed. "Thank the Lord you showed up when you did. My daddy has cooked a total of probably three times in my entire life, and today was one. I am not a fan of fried eggs, that's for sure."

Abby smiled.

"Where's Wes?"

"He'll be by with the truck and the fishing poles in a bit, but I thought I'd come over early."

For a moment Charlie just stood with his hands still in his pockets studying Abby. She was his best friend. The one that didn't headlock him going down the halls at school or punch him in the arm with the veracity of a heavyweight boxer.

"I've got a birdhouse to finish for Jeremiah. Wanna help?"

"Sure."

Charlie rolled up the garage door, and Abby slid in behind him, moving immediately to the half-painted birdhouse.

"Charlie, this one really is beautiful. You outdid yourself this time." She ran her index finger along the smooth edges as she studied the levels of carved cedar.

"Thanks, Abs. I think it's beautiful too." At that moment she turned and faced him so close he could feel her warm breath on his face. "Just like you," he said before his nerve dissipated into the cool air that smelled of gasoline and fresh-cut wood.

Before he could second-guess himself, he placed his mouth over hers. To his surprise, she didn't resist, instead wrapping her arms around his neck and deepening the kiss. His adrenaline rushed as he tasted her for the first time. Her lips were pillowy and soft, damp with the remains of spearmint gum. Moving his hands around her waist, he fully engaged, easing her against the tall work bench.

Then he pulled away to study her glazed-over eyes.

"I didn't expect that," she whispered.

"I have been wanting to do that for longer than I can remember."

"Well, it's about time, Charlie Nettles."

He wondered how anyone could carry an ocean in their eyes. Easing his hands around her face, cupping it, he pulled her mouth back to his. Then he reached over and yanked the garage door shut. "We don't need to give my daddy a heart attack today."

They kissed deeply, teetering between frantic and calm until their mouths were fatigued. "You do know Wes will be here any minute now," Charlie said, wishing away the thought of this moment ending.

"All the more reason for one last kiss."

Her words resounded in Charlie's already ringing ears. The moment he'd dreamed of had arrived, and he wanted to explode and dance in circles all at once. Suddenly Wes's horn created a startled space between them. Charlie didn't want to relinquish her embrace, ever. "So, can we pick up later where we are leaving off?"

"I want you to know something, Charlie, and this is gonna sound crazy, so…" Abby looked at the ground.

"What? You can tell me anything." Her eyes met his as Wes's horn blared again.

"Seriously, what is it?" Charlie's breath hitched, hoping and praying she wasn't getting ready to let him down and tell him she'd made a mistake.

"Geez, this is harder than I thought."

Fear pressed into his chest. "For cryin' out loud, Abs. You're killing me, please. I can't take—"

"I love you, Charlie. Always have. There, I said it."

Charlie felt light headed as he shifted to fully engage his feet against the cold cement floor. His head was spinning, and the words sputtered to a halt before making sense.

"Well?" she asked as her cheeks flushed.

Charlie could not believe what he'd just heard.

"Oh no, I shouldn't have said…"

Charlie pressed his finger to her lips. "Abigail Turner, don't say a word." As she opened her mouth to speak, Charlie smiled. "Eh, eh. It's my turn." He took her face in both hands. "Do you have any idea how long I've waited to hear those words come out of your mouth? I can't believe my ears. Say it again so I can be sure I am not going crazy." The smile that breached his face almost hurt.

"If you're crazy, then so am I. I love you," she said, enunciating each word. "Is that better?"

"That's perfect." Lifting her into his arms, he swirled her into circles as she held on to his neck, laughing hysterically. "I love you Abigail Turner. I love you Abigail Turner!" They stumbled against the brick, dizzy but holding each other. "I need one more kiss before we go have the best day at Lake Jenson *ever*." Charlie pressed into the softness of her lips hoping once more that this wasn't a dream.

Chapter Seven

Charlie eased onto his back smiling to himself. The stars danced in the black sky, creating a display of beauty and tranquility as his heart puddled in his chest like melted butter. The months were rolling by with such velocity that he wished he could slow down time and magically revisit every single kiss, every touch since that first time in his garage.

"You know we gotta get back," he said. "Wes is expecting us to pick him up before going to the movie."

"Yeah, I know. It's just he's always with us, and we have no time to ourselves." Abby sighed, repositioning on her side, and propping her head up on her elbow. "Besides, I want to kiss you until my lips hurt, Charlie Nettles."

Charlie turned to her, feeling like all the stars in that dark abyss hanging over them had lined up for that very moment. He wanted to wrap his arms around her and explore her until the lights in the sky faded with the morning sun. Charlie rolled on top of her in one swift move, pinning her arms above her head and nuzzling her neck. "I am never gonna stop kissing you, Abs. You are my alpha and omega."

Abigail looked serious. "You shouldn't say that, Charlie. Isn't that kind of sacrilegious?"

Pulling back, Charlie returned her stare. "Well, I didn't think of it like that, Abs. I just meant that you are the ultimate everything to me."

"My daddy keeps telling me that we are getting too serious. He doesn't like 'us'," she said, making quotation marks with her fingers. "He would die if he knew we were alone right now. Thank goodness Wes has been covering for me. Dumb Dumb is good for something, I suppose."

Charlie flipped over, pulling her on top of him. "I will always make sure you come out on top. No pun intended."

"You are so bad. I swear you are gonna get me in trouble..." She paused, leaning over him, lightly kissing him from his forehead down the tip of his nose and stopping at his lips. "I just can't help myself with you." Abigail whittled her hands through his dark hair while kissing him slow and deep. Her body moved in a way that made his breath hitch. Her torso pressing into his was more than he could bear. His excitement was about to become evident, so he moved her onto the blanket beside him and took a deep breath.

"What's wrong, Charlie?"

Sighing, he nudged into her side facing her. "Nothin'. Absolutely nothing. I just cannot control myself with you on top of me like, that so I figured I better slow it down." His heartbeat thundered in his head.

"I love you." She whispered.

"I love you too. Always.

The hours eased by in a haze of kissing and talk of the future. Finally, Charlie folded the blanket up and slid it behind Abigail's seat. She was positioned in the crest of his arm as he eased his daddy's old truck into park. Landscaping lights showed majestically across the tall white columns, presenting a stately glow in front of Abigail's house. They owned the most impressive house on the block, where the business owners of Sinclair and the CEO of multiple tire plants resided. Charlie wondered how they could live so high on the hog when his daddy pinched every penny until it screamed. *No wonder Reverend Turner didn't want us together. I'll never be able to provide Abigail with a house like this.* He sighed.

"Where in the heck is that brother of mine? I swear, he will be late for his own funeral."

"I hate having to hide like this, Abby." Charlie leaned across the seat and pulled her face to his, not knowing where his lips stopped and hers began. His breath increased. "Oh, Abby." Pushing him against the seat, she climbed across him. "Are you trying to get me killed?"

"Well, at least we will die happy." She laughed.

Charlie knew the consequences if Reverend Turner caught them in the front seat of his car making out, and it wouldn't end well. "Seriously, Abs, if your daddy catches us out here with you in my lap and my hands all over you, he is gonna kill me for sure."

Her smile faded as she climbed off him. The moon's effervescent glow reflected off her cheeks, still flush from their kiss. There was a sadness that came over her as she gazed out the window at the oversized, white colonial home.

"What's wrong? You okay?"

Abigail looked ahead, crossing her hands in her lap in front of her. "You know, Charlie, I always thought college was my ticket to freedom. I could start out in a new place where no one cared who I was, where everyone didn't know my business." Abigail's eyes shifted to Charlie. They were filled with a sadness that made his chest cave in. "I just always assumed that it would be the three of us off somewhere at school. But everything has changed."

Charlie placed his arms along the top of the seat, resting his hand on her shoulder. "Oh, Abs, don't cry. Why are you crying?" Flustered, he reached into the glove box, got a tissue, and wiped it gently across her cheek.

"I love you, Charlie. Everything changed when I said those words. And now you're staying in Sinclair while Wes and I go off to school. I just don't understand. Why won't you leave with us?"

Charlie wanted more than anything to pack up and leave Sinclair with her. "It's just for a year so I can save up some money." In the midst of building birdhouses, he'd missed the deadline to apply, but he omitted that detail. Now he was faced with hurting the one person he loved more than anything or anybody. "I promise you, Abigail Turner, I will work my tail off this year and save every penny, and I will visit you every weekend. I promise."

"You'll drive that far every weekend?"

"Of course. It's not that far. What's a couple of hours to see my girl?"

They sat in silence for a moment with only the sound of cicadas filling the empty space.

"Charlie, can I ask you something?"

"Sure."

"Are you really staying because you feel guilty leaving your daddy alone?"

The words felt sideways to him as soon as she said them. *Could guilt and an obligation to his daddy be the real reason for staying? What was holding him back from starting a life of his own?* He sat quiet as his mind stirred.

"Charlie, did you hear me?"

"Yeah, I heard you. Heck, I don't know. Maybe a little, but that doesn't mean I'm gonna stay here forever."

"I know you've been helping out with the youth ministry at the church more, and I was just wondering."

"You can stop wondering, Abs. I am gonna do just what I said. My daddy just didn't save up for my school like your folks. And I want us to be able to start our life together without a bunch of bills."

Her eyes danced as she leaned in and kissed him. "You know that's the first time you've ever talked about our future. Like that anyway. You wanna marry this girl, huh?"

Charlie pulled her down onto the seat holding her arms above her head as he kissed her neck. "You bet I am gonna marry this girl. And when I do, nothing is gonna keep us apart, not school, not your daddy, nothin'—"

At the tapping on the window, Abigail jolted up, knocking Charlie into the dash.

"Open up. Hurry."

Charlie leaned across Abigail and unlocked the door. "Man, you scared the life out of me."

"Scooch it over, Princess," Wesley said breathlessly. "Sorry, it took me a minute. I was in the middle of a video game."

"Dude, you scared the crap out of me. I thought you were your dad."

Wesley shot Charlie a look. "Na, man. If that was my old man, you would be dead right now."

Charlie eased down the block before switching the headlights on. He bantered with Wes as Abigail bounced in her seat to the radio. Cruising along Main Street past Jameson Pharmacy and Jeremiah's place, he wondered how this drive would feel when the summer was over and the seats beside him were empty.

Chapter Eight

Charlie tried to tiptoe across the living room, but footsteps were descending the stairs before he was halfway across.

"Last time I checked, your curfew was twelve o'clock," Elroy's voice cut across the dark.

Charlie was exhausted and in no mood for his daddy's toying. "I'm really tired, Daddy. I am sorry. I lost track of time."

"You know the rules. You can't abide by them; you need to get a job and find your own place."

"I'm not trying to test you, Daddy. I am just worn out."

"We both know the movie got out two hours ago. Son, you do realize that her daddy pays our bills, right? You realize that taking this relationship to the next level could be a real problem here, doncha?"

The heat rose in Charlie's neck. He knew where this was going.

"You go and get the senior pastor's daughter pregnant, and we gone have a real problem here."

Charlie puffed his chest out as his anger grew. He would not allow anyone, including his own daddy, to badmouth Abigail. "You hold it right there, old man. It ain't like that."

Elroy's lip twitched as he leaned onto his good hip. "Now I have always liked Abigail, but I see the way she looks at you, boy, and you at her."

"Daddy, she's not like that. I love her, and one day I'm gonna marry her."

Somehow these words just made Elroy look sadder. "Charlie, you listen, and you listen good. Reverend Turner will never let you marry that girl. He talks about her marrying a doctor or lawyer someday. You are my boy, and it makes me mad as fire that he wouldn't think you were good enough, but that is just who he is, son. You need to realize it sooner than later."

"I hope you aren't telling me to break up with her, 'cause that ain't ever gonna happen." Hot tears pooled in his eyes as he looked away. "I love his daughter, and that should be enough. I love her with all my heart."

Elroy's tone softened as he read the pain on Charlie's face. He placed a hand on Charlie's shoulder and said, "I know you do, boy, and I wish it wasn't so, but she is leavin' for school soon, and things change, son."

Sadness welled up in Charlie like crude oil bubbling to the surface of his soul.

"Bottom line is this, boy. I won't say nothin' about your relationship with Abigail as long as you keep it pure. If I find out otherwise, son, you gonna have hell to pay. Not just with Reverend Turner but me. You hear me?"

"Yes, sir," Charlie said, swallowing the pool of hot liquid under his tongue, remembering where his hands had been only thirty minutes earlier.

"Finally, you gone be at that last revival, boy. You ain't been to one yet, and this is your legacy."

"But, Daddy, I am good with my hands. That is what I feel like I am supposed to do."

Elroy paused and looked straight into Charlie's eyes. "Son, working with wood ain't much different than workin' with people's hearts. You start out with this beautiful piece of wood, raw and natural just as the good Lord made it, and you help it find its shape and the beauty hiding inside." Elroy paused, "Now go git some rest."

Upstairs Charlie lay in his bed poring over his daddy's words. *That is the most profound thing my daddy has ever said.* But soon all thoughts of his future were replaced by Abigail's porcelain skin glowing in the moonlight, her smile, and her eyes that held enough love to fill a thousand oceans. Charlie pulled the sheet tightly under his chin as the words *I got this, I got this, everything will be fine,* played in a loop in his head until he fell asleep.

Chapter Nine

Charlie awoke to the sound of his daddy's voice echoing up the stairs. "I'm gone run in town for a bit to pick up a few things, then go by the church. I'm gonna be out for a couple a hours. When I git back, you better have your feet on the floor and that room picked up."

Charlie pulled the sheet over his face.

"Ehhh, boy. You hear me?"

"Yea, Daddy! I hear you!"

"And don't forget we need to leave this afternoon in plenty of time to git to the revival!"

Charlie rolled over, dreading everything about the day. Suddenly he heard footsteps on the stairs.

"What did you forget, Daddy?" he mumbled into his pillow.

"Well, I can honestly say calling me Daddy is a bit weird, but if it's your thing…"

Charlie bolted upright.

"Hey, I hope you don't mind me coming up."

"Course not." As he watched her standing above him with a smile reserved only for him, a part of him hoped that this would be that moment, the moment when they finally took their physical relationship to the next level. But his resolve kicked in as he sat up and wrapped his arms around her waist, resting his face in her abdomen. "You drive me crazy; you know that?" he said, filling his lungs with her scent.

Abigail combed her fingers through his hair as she spoke. "I don't know what I ever did to deserve you." Reaching down, she took his face in both of her hands. "I love you, Charlie. I will love you forever and a day for added measure."

"Stop, Abs. Don't say another word." Elroy's words reverberated in his head, "We need to talk about something."

"What's wrong, Charlie? Why are you so serious all of the sudden?" Abigail slid onto the bed beside him, resting one hand on Charlie's leg. "Talk to me."

"Before I say this, I want you to know that nothing is gonna change. It is just on my mind, and I need to get it off my chest."

"Okay."

"I was talking to my daddy last night. He said some stuff, Abs, that really bothered me."

"Okay, what did he say, Charlie? Tell me."

"Basically, he said that your daddy would never accept me, that I would never be good enough for you."

"It's not you, Charlie. It's any boy. No one will ever measure up in my daddy's eyes, especially not me." She sat beside him and let him wrap her in his arms. "I just keep trying to make it right with him, ya know? Maybe one day I will. Or I'll find the courage to stand up to him. But for now, let's not mess this up or let him get in the way, okay? He doesn't think we're serious, so he's not all that concerned." Her face, which had been tarred and feathered with hurt only moments ago, turned softer as she looked at him. "Thank you for believing in me, Charlie."

"I love you so much, Abs. I love your forehead," he said, kissing her forehead. "I love your nose." As Charlie worked his way around her face and onto her shoulders, Abigail melted into him. He could feel each kiss removing another piece of the painful puzzle Reverend Turner had created in her heart. Her body welcomed his as she raked her fingers along his hairline and met his gaze to kiss him.

"You feel that, Charlie?" she said, placing his hand over her heart.

"Sure, I feel it," Charlie said, catching his breath at the warmth of her flesh beneath his fingers.

"This is where you are no matter what happens. This is where I will keep you forever."

Charlie fell into her gaze. He closed his eyes and inhaled her presence. He opened his eyes and studied the smooth bridge of her nose just before the slight tilt lifting up as if her face was smiling. They kissed again, this time deeper. He wanted to drink in every moment with her as he sank into the tenderness that was reserved for her. Charlie swept his hand along her shoulder, followed by his lips, savoring the warmth of her skin. Desire crashed over him in waves, leaving him breathless as she lightly circled his back with her fingertips.

"I love you so much," Charlie said, holding her face in his hands as if it were a bubble that could dissipate at any moment.

Abigail leaned her forehead into his and whispered, "It's just you and me, we were made for each other. We love each other, Charliebody. How could this be wrong?" She said moving his hands slowly down her sides onto her hips.

Charlie pulled her body flush with his and held her. Their breath merged. He had to trust that this was their moment and that nothing would change. His spirit conveyed one truth but his body another as their kiss deepened, leaving no room for doubt. "We don't have to do this."

"I know, but I cannot imagine this with anyone but you."

Charlie held her gaze, searching for the air. Every touch made it hard to breathe. "I love you so much, Abs. I love you. This is perfect. You are perfect. Are you okay?" Charlie stopped and whispered.

Abigail paused to look at him, her eyes soft. "Just shut up and kiss me," she said, pulling his mouth on top of hers.

He moved across her body like a silk scarf, kissing and touching her in rhythm with her breath. Charlie could barely control the train thundering through his body as they surrendered to what felt natural.

Afterward, Charlie fell onto his back, breathless. He could taste the salt of their union on his lips. "I think you are the most beautiful girl in the world." He could feel her smile radiating through her cheek resting on his bare chest.

"Charlie?"

"Yeah?"

Abigail stared at him with a glazed-over smile. "I need to know that no matter what, you will always know how much you mean to me."

"I promise."

And with that they kissed until everything else was drowned out—the future, their fathers, and all their fears.

———<∘>———

Two months passed in what felt like hours. This was their last day together before she and Wes left for school. She and Charlie had spent the day languishing in the shelter of their favorite oak tree on Lake Jenson talking about everything except her departure the next day. Charlie drank in every second with her. Finally, they stood in his driveway, Abigail leaning against the side of the truck. Charlie pulled her into a long kiss. A flicker of sadness and uncertainty flashed in Abigail's eyes as he pulled away.

"Hey, what's going on? We can't have this."

"Charlie, I'm scared."

"Of what?"

"I don't know." Her cheek rested against his chest as he rubbed her hair in long strokes.

"I wish I could come over in the morning and say goodbye one more time."

"You know my daddy, Charlie. It's just best this way. I'll call you as soon as I get there. You can come next weekend and stay in Wes's dorm with him. It will all be fine…right?"

He kissed her once more, leaning into her hair, which smelled of lilac, as they tried to prolong this time together. "God, I love you, Abigail Turner." Thirsty for her eyes, for that connection, Charlie pulled back. "I love you with all my heart."

"I love you too. And Charlie, you *are* my heart. I'll love you forever." She stopped. "And a day, for added measure." Her eyes pooled, but she smiled. It was faint but enough to allow him to ease the truck door shut.

She rolled down the window, inviting him to lean in for one more kiss. Their lips parted, and Charlie watched her pull away in a cloud of dust until her taillights disappeared from sight. If he'd known that was the last time he'd see her, he would have never let her go.

Part Two

Chapter Ten

The wheels screeched along the tarmac, jolting Charlie from a blank sleep. Adjusting in his first-class seat and shifting from his hip, he pushed the plastic shade up, revealing the twinkling lights of the Atlanta airport. His body felt heavy as the captain came over the intercom system thanking them for flying Delta. His brand-new Cartier watch, an anniversary gift from Marianna, revealed that by the time he arrived home, his son Chandler's fourth birthday party would be close to, if not, over. One delay after another had left him feeling emotionally ragged. He couldn't imagine missing his little Chan blow out the candles on his fireman themed birthday cake.

Charlie stretched his arms high above his head, shaking his hands in front of him hoping the fatigue would magically leave through his fingertips. Before the wheels had lifted into the belly of the plane in Nicaragua, Charlie had fallen into a deep sleep. He wondered if his snoring annoyed the other first-class passengers. *It wouldn't be the first time,* he thought, and if he kept up this pace, not the last. He felt a perpetual fog on his brain. In the previous months, he'd racked up more frequent flyer miles than he cared to discuss between conferences, speaking engagements, promoting his first book, *Living God's Dream*, and scouting for potential new locations around the globe and stateside. He often wondered if he'd bitten off more than he could chew, but he still felt the calling that he had answered when he was eighteen years old, and that hadn't changed. His daddy had told him that God's work wasn't a full-time job. It was a twenty-four-hour job, and if he couldn't handle it, he was in the wrong business. And his daddy was right. The business of ministry was taking a toll on him. Charlie felt like a bunch of balloons that someone had overfilled with helium and released, flying in a million directions, just waiting to burst apart.

He stood with the others and retrieved his bag from the overhead bin, grateful that he'd mastered the art of one piece of carry-on luggage, no matter how long the trip.

"Pastor Nettles, we are so honored to have you flying with us today," the copilot said, on the verge of awestruck. "Any time I fly through Atlanta, I try to make one of your services. Or I listen online. And your podcast series on finding love in a fast-paced world changed my life. I met my wife not long after that and attribute it all to you."

"Thank you so much for sharing that. I'm glad it made such an impact on you," Charlie said genuinely.

"Oh, man. You have no idea," he said, taking Charlie's hand in his clammy grip.

"Nice to meet you, man," Charlie said, pulling his hand away, casually slipping it into his jacket and rubbing it along the soft lining of his pocket. "Stop by and say hi after the service next time you're in town." As the words escaped his lips, he pictured this guy and his wife front and center at the next service ready for an hour-long post-service conversation.

Charlie made his way through the airport and was sliding behind the wheel of his new black Chevy Tahoe in record time. As he tossed his bag onto the back seat, Chandler's car seat caught his eye. There sat his gift—perfectly wrapped in bright-blue paper with fire engines all over it and a large red bow with streamers that flowed across the top. He would have kissed his assistant, Lily, right then and there if it wouldn't have been completely misconstrued. She'd remembered to pick up the fire truck and have it wrapped and waiting in his SUV so that it would appear that he'd not forgotten to pick it up himself, which he had. A wave of guilt rolled over him as he dialed Marianna's cell phone.

"Hello," she said with a note of irritation.

"Hey, Honey. I just landed. But I'm in the car and heading your way. How's the party going?"

One sigh was followed by another before she spoke, "Well, Charlie. I guess it's fine. We just cut the cake."

"I'm so sorry, Marianna. I feel terrible. Where's Chan?" The noise level increased as Charlie listened to Marianna making her way to Chandler. Her muffled voice told him that his daddy was on the phone as she held it to his ear.

"Doddy, I mith you."

"Hey, buddy. Daddy will be home real soon. Hey, and guess what?"

"Whut, Doddy?"

"I have a special present just for my birthday boy." A rustling sound replaced the silence. He could hear Marianna telling him to talk to his daddy over the shuffling of the receiver.

"Ok. I gotta go. Wuv you, Doddy."

His heart sank in his chest as he waited for Marianna to get back on the phone, but instead it went dead. Charlie tried to focus on the lights along the interstate as he listened to the fifteen voice mails that had accumulated on his phone during the flight. Everyone needed something from him. He felt like a Stretch Armstrong doll being pulled to his limits.

As soon as Charlie passed through the gate of their community, though, he felt relief. They'd been fortunate enough to score one of the larger lots in Chamford Estates, and their brick-and-stone house was tucked back nicely into the woods. Charlie would have been fine staying in the modest brick ranch in Buckhead that they'd bought just after their honeymoon. A foreclosure in need of major updates. Charlie had done all the work himself, building the vanities for the bathrooms on the weekends and completely remodeling the kitchen one cabinet at a time. When the finishing touches were complete, Charlie glowed with pride. Even so, Marianna insisted that they needed more privacy, which was code for closet space and room to entertain. Finally, Charlie gave up the fight and put it on the market. But sadness rolled over him the day he closed on the house. It had felt like home.

Two cars lined the driveway. One belonged to Wes and the other to his pretentious new neighbors who'd adopted them into their circle mainly because of the notoriety that Charlie carried.

Charlie opened the car door, securing the gift under one arm and his carry-on in the other. His body felt heavy and old, not like a thirty-three-year-old man should feel in the throes of success. The constant traveling, nonstop planning, working, and preaching pushed a long sigh from deep in Charlie's belly.

Murmurs came from the kitchen as he opened the front door. A squeal worked its way to him as Chandler raced toward him yelling, "Doddy! Doddy!" Chandler, with dark curly hair that fell carelessly on his shoulders, was small for his age. Chandler's button nose and rosy cheeks had always reminded Charlie of a cherub, which was fitting since Charlie knew he was a blessing straight from God. Charlie placed the gift and suitcase on the floor and scooped him into his arms, burying his face into the remnants of white icing on Chandler's collar. His heart swelled. Chandler pulled away and placed his tiny hand over Charlie's nose. "Doddy, your nose is code."

Charlie chuckled as he nuzzled behind Chandler's ear into the mound of dark swirls, tickling him simultaneously. "Well, now maybe Daddy can warm it right here."

Chandler squirmed and howled in high-pitched hiccups. "Do it again, Doddy. Do it again."

"Okay, Buddy. One more time," Charlie said, pretending to bite Chandler's neck while growling.

"My man!"

Charlie shifted Chandler onto his hip. "What's up?" Charlie said, greeting Wesley as he and his wife, Donna, made their way across the living room. Wes was still tall and lean with a crazy mop of blond mane. His clear blue eyes had entranced many girls in college until he'd met Donna, a petite blonde with perfectly wide-set eyes and porcelain skin. She'd been approached in school to model locally but, at a mere five three, wasn't tall enough to take it further. She was a good fit for his best friend, and Charlie loved her like a sister.

They shook hands and pulled in for a shoulder bump. Wes stepped aside as Donna leaned up, kissing Charlie on the cheek. "Well, you are just a sight for sore eyes," she said with a wink.

"I know. I am so beat right now," Charlie said as Chandler wiggled his way past Charlie's leg, scurrying back to the kitchen, where the murmurs continued. "Where's Mar?" Charlie asked, sliding his black leather jacket off and laying it on the back of the large tan sectional sofa that spanned the center of the living room.

Wes looked over his shoulder and leaned in. "She's in the kitchen with those crazy neighbors of yours. How do you put up with those two?"

"I know, man. It's like Ken and Barbie on steroids with a touch of pretentious jerk. I don't know. Marianna seems to get along with Piper pretty well, so I tolerate Dan, basically. I have been gone so much since we moved in that I didn't want to rock the boat. Not crazy about Piper's influence, though."

"I don't blame you," Donna said with genuine concern. "I've reached out to Marianna a good bit in recent months, but she's always with Piper. I guess I don't fit into Piper's Pilates-and-Botox-obsessed crowd. Just know I've tried."

"Honestly, I don't see why Marianna is spending so much time with her, but what can I say when I haven't even been around lately. I guess she's just trying to fit in now that we own these fancy digs." Charlie smiled and left it at that. He didn't want to get into it about the bottle of diet pills he'd found on the bathroom counter before he left for his trip or mention her having some filler injected around her mouth to soften her smile lines, as she put it. Charlie loved her just the way she was.

"Well, I guess my wife is a bit miffed since she hasn't made her way in here. Let's go see what's up. Maybe a piece of cake will wake me up."

Piper's deep, throaty laughter met Charlie as he entered the kitchen, where Chandler was circling the adults with a small plastic airplane, making zooming noises. Charlie approached Marianna, who looked up with a strained smile. "Hey, stranger. Glad to see you could make it."

Tension filled the air as Charlie leaned down, kissing his wife on her cheek. Vanilla filled his sinuses. He longed to pull her to him and linger against her. He'd missed her terribly. But her body stiffened as he rested his hand on the small of her back. "I'm sorry, honey. It's been crazy."

"I know. This is our life, I suppose."

Irritation welled up in his chest. Why did she have to be snide in front of the biggest gossips in the neighborhood? Couldn't she wait for everyone to leave? He was fiercely protective of his private life since social media loved to rip him to shreds given the opportunity.

"I'm just glad I made it in time before Chan crashes, which from the looks of it won't be long." Charlie watched as Chandler flew his plane into a cabinet.

"What's up, my man? You been out there saving the world? Good for you," Dan said without extending his hand, instead wrapping it around his wife's ultranarrow hips.

"So how was your trip?" Piper asked, tilting her head to the side and adjusting a stray piece of bleached blonde hair that had melted into her pale pink lip gloss.

"Exhausting but good."

"So, I guess your boy, Wes, here holds down the fort when you're out there saving the little orphans and sinners."

Charlie felt his jaw constrict as he turned to Wes, who stepped forward.

"Yep, we are the superheroes of the free world. And on that note, I think we are gonna take off." Wes pulled Marianna in for a tight hug. "Thanks, lady, for a great time. We appreciate the invite."

Marianna's response was a weak "Thanks" as she turned her attention back to Piper.

"Let me walk you guys out," Charlie said, following them to the door. Lowering his voice, he said "Man, I am sorry. Has she been like this the entire time?"

"Actually, no. She's been pretty normal."

"So, she basically shifted gears when I got here."

The apologetic expression on Wesley's face said what he didn't.

"I'll see you tomorrow. Why don't you sleep in? You've had a pretty busy couple of weeks."

Charlie paused. "Nah, man. I have so much catching up to do." The words almost lodged in his throat. A day of lying around the house in his boxer shorts mindlessly channel surfing was overdue but not possible, as far as he was concerned.

"All right," Wesley said with a concerned grimace. "You know you are burning the candle at both ends."

"I got this. I'm good. Really." The lie didn't sit well as he said it. "You guys are the best. Thanks for coming. I know Chan was glad. He loves you both."

"Well, we adore that little guy," Donna said, hugging Charlie.

As Charlie watched them make their way across the yard, he felt grateful that Wesley had remained his best friend. Their relationship allowed Charlie to navigate unchartered waters with confidence, most of the time. The few instances during his ministry he'd floundered, Wesley was there reaching down into the abyss pulling him back to sanity.

As he closed the door, Marianna was hugging Dan and Piper goodbye, and then she disappeared upstairs with Chandler's limp body draped over her shoulder.

"You know," Dan said as Charlie held the door open, "I can make that money of yours grow. Still waiting on you to stop by and let me work my magic."

Well, you are going to be waiting a long time. "Good to know. Thanks for coming." Charlie had already had his fill.

Piper pulled Charlie in, air kissing both of his cheeks. "She's really having a hard time with you being gone so much, Charlie. Maybe you should cut out some of this travel. Family first."

Did she really just say that? "I'll keep that in mind, Piper. Good night." Charlie urged them out the door, closing it behind them before they had a chance to respond. He wanted to tuck Chandler in and talk to Marianna.

Charlie cut off the downstairs lights and made his way upstairs, where the dim glow from Chandler's turtle lamp spilled onto the hardwoods in the hallway. Charlie leaned against the door jamb watching his little boy sleep. It was what he'd longed to do since he boarded the plane. Guilt washed over him like a frigid rain. *If only I'd seen him blow the candles out.* Now he'd missed tucking him in as well. He felt like a zero on a scale of one to a thousand. Charlie eased across the room and rested his hand on Chandler's head, watching his little eyes move behind the lids. What could this amazing little person be dreaming about so peacefully? He stood over him and thanked God for his little boy before he leaned over and kissed his tiny forehead, lingering a bit longer than usual, inhaling him.

As he walked into their bedroom, Charlie could hear the shower running. His clothes were off before he even made it halfway across the room. Hopefully Marianna had forgiven him and would welcome him into the shower. Steam rushed out of the bathroom, meeting his senses with warm vanilla sugar body wash. He loved rolling into the mounds of dark hair blanketing her pillow each night and making his way to that spot in the crevice of her back, allowing her fragrance to filter through him.

"Shut the door, please. You're letting out my steam." Her tone was a clear indication that this, too, would be a night of showering alone.

"Sorry, honey." He stepped in quickly and pulled the door closed behind him. He hoped she would take pity on him and allow him to get lost in her warm, tanned body, escaping to that realm of ecstasy that had numbed his pain so many times before. Their physical attraction had allowed them to forgive and forget more times than he could even remember—until recently.

"Why would you think it's okay to roll into town late for our son's party, as you have been late for everything else important lately, and then try to join me in the shower?" she said, looking directly at the hand covering his now-disappearing erection.

"Honey, I'm sorry. I can't help it. This is our life right now. And I'm doing my best."

"I didn't sign up for this, Charlie. And neither did our son, for that matter."

Anger rose in Charlie as he grabbed an oversized white towel from the hook hanging outside the shower. Steam covered the mirror, preventing Charlie from seeing the vein he could feel bulging from his neck. He took a deep breath and turned to face her, leaning against the countertop with his arms crossed. "You know, Mar, there was a time when you and I were in this together, one hundred percent. There was none of this you against me. It was us."

Marianna continued lathering her hair without looking at Charlie. "Charlie, when we started this ministry, I felt like it was something we created together." Running her hand down her thigh, she shot Charlie a look. "Now it's *The Charlie Nettles Show*."

Charlie clenched his fist down on the counter, determined to maintain his stance. "Did you really just say that? I mean, who are you anymore? This has never been *The Charlie Nettles Show*, Mar, and it's not *The Charlie and Marianna Show*. This is about bringing people to Jesus. Plain and simple. Where is this coming from, Mar? This doesn't even sound like you."

As she turned the water off, opened the heavy glass door, and stepped onto the fluffy gray rug, Charlie could not help but feel that attraction welling up in him. She was beautiful. Her Latino roots provided her with ample curves in all the right places that contrasted her tight stomach and taut thighs.

"What are you trying to say? I am being brainwashed or something?" She laughed under her breath, cutting Charlie.

"Well, yeah, I am, or at least influenced. Ever since we moved into this house and you've been hanging out with Piper, it's like this ministry that we built together has taken a backseat to shopping, nails, and wine parties. That, I might add, you never cared about before, or at least not like this."

"I am going to pretend you didn't just say that. Nails and wine parties…really."

Marianna stood naked, towel drying her hair before slipping her red camisole nightgown over her head. *Torture, plain and simple. Are you toying with me now?* The red nightgown had always been reserved for those special nights they'd shared before their relationship became strained. To make matters worse, her body was tighter than ever since she'd hired Piper's personal trainer to work with her five mornings a week.

"Honestly, Marianna." Charlie's stare heated as she stood at the counter slathering lotion along her arms.

"I am just not in the mood, okay?" she said with a vague smile.

"Marianna, we used to make love all the time. What's happening? When we'd fight, that's how we reconnected, honey."

Marianna paused and turned to Charlie. "It's just not enough anymore. I've felt this way for a while. I am tired of being lonely."

Charlie cupped her smooth arms in his hands. Crushed beneath the weight of her words, he exhaled and said, "Listen, I will slow down. I promise. I need you, Mar. I love you." Her eyes met his with an unfamiliar emptiness. "Please don't give up on us."

"I'm tired, Charlie."

"I can go in late. You can skip your workout, I'll make the three of us breakfast, and we can talk, really connect."

Marianna stood silent looking at him.

"Talk to me," Charlie pleaded.

"I'm too tired to talk, Charlie. I want to go to bed. Please let this go. I have to be up early. I can't cancel my workout. My trainer is expecting me. Plus, I already paid for the session."

Charlie watched her leave the bathroom with the same emotion she exhibited when picking out a grapefruit. Charlie turned on the shower hoping it would wash away the sting of their conversation. But by the time he climbed into bed, he was only more convinced that his life was spiraling. He was on a runaway ministry train growing by the minute, and he was losing his wife and missing his son's childhood. *Something has to give.*

Chapter Eleven

Charlie pulled into the parking lot of the main campus. Mom's Morning Out had been canceled and Marianna didn't want to miss her workout, so Chandler was in the backseat watching a Mickey video on the player in the car. The employee parking lot was already full, escalating Charlie's stress level at the thought of everything on his plate.

"All right, buddy. We are here. You ready to go say hi to everyone?"

"Yeth, Doddy. Yeth," Chandler said with enthusiasm.

"Okay, then."

As he opened the door, Chandler's sippy cup fell to the pavement, cracking the lid in half. "Well, that's just great," he muttered as he picked it up, shaking the apple juice from his fingers.

"I want soda like you dwink?"

Charlie chuckled. "But don't tell Mommy. Daddy might give you a can all to yourself today."

"I like sprite, Doddy."

"I know what you like," Charlie said, dumping the remaining juice in a nearby patch of grass. "Okay, let's get you unbuckled." Charlie hoisted him out of the seat and put him on the pavement. He took his hand, and they walked toward the building, Charlie going over his schedule in his head. As he scanned his card through the reader on the door to the offices, Lily's face appeared in the glass. She opened the door and scooped Chandler up as he wiggled in her arms with excitement. "Oh my gosh, Chani Poo! Have you grown? You are almost as tall as your daddy."

"Yeth, I am a big boy now."

Relief flooded through Charlie as Lily took over. "You know you are my favorite, right?" Charlie said in a hushed tone with a wink.

"I've known it all along, Pastor C," Lily said, bouncing Chandler on her hip. Lily's brown, almond-shaped eyes were always filled with contagious excitement. He'd hired her as an intern and offered her a full-time position a week after she received her Bachelor of Arts degree from the University of Georgia, swearing he'd been lost without her. She was very type A but with a "go with the flow" attitude, and the members of the church loved her. Lily always showed up when Charlie was in a pinch, relieving the pressure of his job.

"So, Marianna is picking up Chan in an hour. I have a meeting with the staff at nine o'clock, right?"

"Actually, nine thirty. Wesley's on a conference call that's running over."

"Okay. Has anything been added to my schedule that I don't know about yet?" Charlie asked.

"Nothing earth shattering. Just a couple of items that we can talk about once I'm done with my little monster man here!" Lily tickled Chandler, and he let out a piecing scream of excitement.

"Okay, buddy, see you in an hour," Charlie said as he made his way into the pit, as they called it. Everyone looked up from their cubicles saying *hey*, some fist bumping and high fiving him as he passed.

Charlie scanned his card to gain access to his office and tossed his bag onto the plush brown leather sofa against the wall. He used it more for meetings than the two leather wingback chairs sitting in front of his dark mahogany desk. Many hours were spent on that couch napping after preparing for sermons into the wee hours. Pictures documenting groundbreakings for the various locations as well as plaques his staff had presented him lined the walls. His favorite was the award for the Most Likely to Change the World. His staff had presented it to him after the ground-breaking ceremony for the fifth campus. As Wesley handed him the award among all the church leaders, employees, family, and a large number of the members, his daddy appeared from the crowd. An unexpected surprise but a memorable one.

Elroy made his way slowly to Charlie's side and looked at Charlie with tears in his eyes, saying he'd become the man that he and his mama had always dreamed of. Tears rolled down both of their cheeks as they hugged.

His desk was bare, with only two framed pictures, one of him and Marianna on their wedding day and a family picture taken on Edisto Beach when Chandler was two. It was windy that day, creating waves of hair around them, but it captured the happiness of his family unit.

Waiting for his computer to boot up, his eye gravitated to a picture of him and Wesley during their eleventh-grade summer, his arm slung carelessly over Wesley's shoulder, his smile reflecting the affection he felt for Abigail as she fiddled with her new camera in utter confusion. Her laughter rang in his ears as his office door swung open.

Wesley fell onto the couch holding a legal pad. "I see you made it in."

"Yeah, did you see Chan?"

"Of course! Are you ever gonna cut his hair? He's starting to look like the kid in *The Jungle Book*. I mean it's cute and all, but—"

"I am not even opening that can of worms with Mar. I am trying to get *out* of the doghouse, not add an addition to it."

"Nah, man, not my intention. You make peace after we left?" he asked, twirling his pencil like a baton across his fingers.

Charlie hmphed under his breath. "I offered it, but she just didn't accept it." Leaning onto his desk, Charlie rubbed his chin stubble.

"Has she put you on a shaving restriction as well?"

"No, smart aleck. I figured I could go one day. Give myself a break. You know I hate shaving," Charlie mused, scratching both cheeks. "It does kind of itch, though."

"What's up with you, man? I know you're tired. Is there something else?"

Charlie paused and pushed himself back from the desk, crossing his arms in front of his chest. "You ever wonder what it would be like if Abs hadn't left?"

"Where is that coming from? Yeah, all the time. I miss her."

"I love Mar, you know that. I just can't help but wonder sometimes, ya know? I still don't get it. To this day I don't know why she left like she did."

"Dad swears she just felt the calling to ministry. I only asked Abigail once when we were on the phone, and she danced around it."

"Dude, she left and never came back. You don't find that odd?"

"Yeah, but what can I do? Charlie, it's been years. It's time to let it go."

Part of Charlie wanted to reach over and smack Wesley for implying he wasn't over it, but the truth was, he never got closure. As much as he loved Marianna, Abigail still lingered in his thoughts from time to time.

"I let go of it a long time ago." Charlie pulled himself to the desk and tapped out his password. "Ok, now, what's on the agenda for today's staff meeting?"

As Charlie detailed his ideas for the new series, his mind wandered between his flailing marriage and Wesley's statement that he needed to let it go. He loved his wife with all his heart and would never leave her even if Abigail reappeared, so why was it so hard to let it go once and for all?

As the staff meeting wrapped up, Charlie paced back to his office and checked his email. Marianna was running over an hour late and hadn't called. He shot her a quick text message and took a hearty gulp of the piping hot coffee Lily placed in front of him. An email titled "Important Message" appeared on his screen.

The message read as follows:

Mr. Nettles (because you don't deserve the title of pastor),

I am really disappointed in your convoluted version of God's word. You stand on that stage so high and mighty while you live in contradiction to HIS will. Everyone knows you used your followers' hard-earned money to buy that fancy house of yours and that brand-new Tahoe. How many hardworking people does it take to keep the senior pastor of the church in the latest clothes, cars, and luxury homes? I could go on, but it sickens me, so I will simply state my disdain in a few simple words. You are a disgrace, and everyone sees straight through your humble beginnings story of starting out in a dorm room with one dollar in your pocket. What, do you want a reward for living the life of a poor college student like the rest of the population? It's pretty obvious you saw a business opportunity and ran with it.

Charlie paused as his adrenaline pelted the vein in his neck. Lily always filtered his emails so that he didn't have to deal with these types, but somehow this one had made it through. Charlie knuckled across his beard and continued reading...

As for that facade of a family, how about you tell that wife of yours to find some pants that don't hug her body like a second skin, leaving little to the imagination? She reminds me of a trashier version of that gold-digging fraud Victoria Osteen. I will have to say, though, if ole Victoria is skirting around on Joel, at least she's being discreet. Again, hypocrites! Well, I'd say I have vented enough for today. I am sure you'll get to my email somewhere between buying a Rolex and taking retirement from old ladies.

Signed,

Reality Check

Charlie's fingers took on a life of their own as he started typing. "*F- you!*" he wrote, then stood up, taking a deep breath. That definitely didn't fall in line with how a man of God would respond. He thought he'd become immune to such blatant lies, but sometimes the sting kicked in, leaving him breathless. Why couldn't people see his heart for ministry? Wasn't his love for Jesus evident every Sunday when he delivered his message that he'd prayed over and agonized over for hours? He stopped himself from taking this out on Lily, though he wanted to scream at her for not being a better gatekeeper. He needed his team to isolate him from this kind of crap that served no purpose. It was too mentally and physically draining to address the haters, and nothing was ever resolved. At least this one didn't threaten his life, but it did shred his character to pieces along with Marianna's. And what did he mean by the "skirting around" comment? That had never even occurred to him. *Liar.*

"Hey."

Charlie looked up, and Marianna, wearing black yoga pants and a fitted pink zip-up hoodie, was standing in the doorway, her hair piled on top of her head, a few pieces framing her makeup-free face. Charlie stood, walked over to her, and kissed her forehead, which left a salty taste on his lips. "Hey, honey. How was your workout?"

"Good," she said as Chandler ran in behind her and wrapped his arms around her leg. "Hey, baby," she said, patting the top of his head. "You have fun with daddy today?"

"Yeah. I've been playing wif Lily."

Lily peeked her head inside the door. "Hey, Marianna. I'm heading back to my office, Pastor C."

"Ok. Thanks for helping out."

"Yeah, thanks Lily," Marianna said with a faint smile.

"So, what do you have going on today?"

"Well, I have some errands to run. He's going to be with Nicole."

Charlie wondered why she was picking up Chandler just to leave him with their part-time nanny.

"I thought you gave Nicole the day off since it's Mommy's Morning Out Day. You usually hang out with him."

Chandler bounced in circles, running a Matchbox car along the wall.

Marianna stared at Charlie like he had a third eye in his forehead. "So now you're telling me how to parent?" she said in a low hiss.

"No, that's not it at all, Mar. I just thought—"

Cutting him off, she took Chandler by the hand. "Yeah, you just thought."

This was worse than he'd imagined. "Whoa, Mar. I'm not the enemy here."

"Well, it sure feels like it. Come on, Chandler. Tell Daddy bye."

Charlie stared at her, hoping for a retraction, but she stood her ground, so he bent down on one knee in front of her and pulled Chandler's body to his and held him tight. "I love you, buddy. I'm so glad you came to work with Daddy today."

"I wub you too. Can I have my Sprite, Doddy?"

Charlie could feel the heat of Marianna's glare. "Sure. Maybe Mommy can get you one on the way out?"

"I sent apple juice, which is a *treat*. You know I don't like him drinking soda, Charlie."

"I broke his cup getting him out of the car. I figured it couldn't hurt."

She threw her hands up, and Charlie watched her make her way through the pit without a single word to anyone, which was out of character for her. He could tell everyone picked up on it.

He pulled his laptop from his briefcase and pulled up the pages of notes for his next meeting.

What is with this blank stare she gives me now? Where is my wife? Maybe I should take some time off, work this out. Divorce will never be an option. Don't even think it, Charlie. I am the leader of this church. That won't happen. Ever. He'd go without sex if he had to, but separation wasn't an answer. The words hadn't come out of her mouth, but he knew her well. She was not one to stay unhappy. If she didn't like something, she changed it. Hence the three dining tables in the last nine months.

Charlie collected the papers from the printer tray and glanced at the clock on his computer. Another late night if this meeting ran even the slightest bit over an hour. Closing his eyes, he asked for the strength to be a good husband, father, and messenger. Waves of peace disintegrated with the boom of Reverend Jacobs's laughter getting closer by the minute. Charlie took a deep breath and opened his office door. With a smile pasted on his face, he muttered to himself, "I got this."

Chapter Twelve

Light and sound thundered amid the sea of people with hands raised high. Standing at the foot of the stairs leading to the stage, Charlie moved in sync with the bass line, swaying back and forth as a volunteer worked vigorously to attach his mic pack. Closing his eyes, he thanked God for the opportunity to serve, ignoring the gnawing in the pit of his stomach. Speaking in front of people had never come naturally, and if he could prerecord every sermon from his office, he'd be happy. But the occasional beta blocker slowed down his heart enough to allow sound to come from his mouth when his nerves took him hostage.

The music faded as a young Adam Levine look alike led everyone in prayer. Ready to ascend the stage, Charlie looked at the front row. It was empty.

Midway through his message she appeared, taking her seat with Piper in tow. Without looking up, Marianna retrieved her cell, snickering and showing Piper the screen. In an instant, Charlie's mind went blank. He stood for a moment to collect his thoughts before glancing down at the floor monitor. As he continued to deliver the message, his wife continued to whisper back and forth with Piper. In all his years of ministry, he couldn't recall ever being so rattled or angry while onstage. His wife was acting like some inconsiderate teenager surfing the net in the front row.

As everyone stood for the closing prayer and bowed their heads, Marianna and Piper eased out of the aisle toward the back exit. Not only was she leaving early after arriving late, she was now parading down the center aisle instead of slipping out the side exit. Charlie felt as though he were having an out-of-body experience and barely managed to pull the words from his constricting throat.

As the service ended, Charlie asked Lily, who was standing backstage talking to a volunteer, to go find Marianna. Within minutes she reported back that they were in the atrium talking to some people but looked like they were getting ready to leave. Charlie ripped the mic pack from his body and slammed it into the hand of a wide-eyed volunteer. "Sorry, man," he said and made his way to the atrium. He waded through the masses, trying to smile and seem normal. As he stepped into the parking lot, he spotted Marianna sliding into the passenger side of Piper's black Hummer with large chrome wheels. Charlie jogged to the vehicle and stopped Marianna's door as it closed. Breathless, he didn't know what to say.

"Hey, can you get Chandler from class? We're trying to get a quick Pilates class in," Marianna said, applying lip gloss in the lighted drop-down mirror.

"Are you freaking kidding me, Mar? What's with strolling in late, surfing the net, and then slipping out? Seriously. Are you trying to publicly humiliate me or what?" he asked through gritted teeth.

"I'm sorry. We were just running late."

"Yeah, the line at Starbucks was off the chain and I needed my latte," Piper said, resting her head on the steering wheel. Marianna appeared somewhere between embarrassed and irritated with Piper's flaky remark but remained silent.

Charlie's look of dismay shifted from Piper to Marianna. He couldn't believe what he was hearing. He leaned back, running his hands along his hairline and scanning the parking lot to ensure no one was watching even though the greeters were no more thana hundred yards away. Marianna sat quietly looking ahead.

"Mar, what has gotten into you? I could see if you were legitimately running late. Fine, I get that. But the whole latte thing, and well, it's your attitude."

"Oooh, you better watch out. Someone is gonna hear you, Pastor C." Piper giggled.

"Knock it off, Piper," Marianna said.

Charlie paused, pushing down the irritation. "Piper, I really need you to just give us a minute. Could you do that, please? Maybe let me talk to my wife?"

Piper's eyes widened as she turned her head.

"Mar, what is up? Seriously, this is driving me crazy. You can't imagine."

Marianna held her hand up as he spoke, cutting him off midsentence. "Enough, Charlie. We can talk when I get home. This is not the place."

A sarcastic chuckle escaped without warning, "Oh, so we're worried about decorum now? Really? After you, my wife, one of the figureheads in the church, giggled and Facebooked her way through the message today?"

"I wasn't Facebooking."

"Oh, my bad. Let me retract that. Texting. Right, Mar? Is that it?" Charlie realized his volume was escalating as a couple walked by staring at him. "Okay, enough. We'll talk when I get home. You need to come back after Pilates and get Chan. You know he doesn't need to just linger in Toy Town all day."

"Okay, Charlie. I got it. Will do." Her flat words made it hard for Charlie to breathe. He could feel hot liquid in his cheeks as he turned away. It was like a bad dream where you're trudging, to no avail, through a tar pit with an ax murderer on your heels. He hated feeling so powerless in his marriage, and he hated the tone he'd just taken with Marianna. This was not who they were; cattiness was never part of their dynamic.

"Fine," he said, turning and moving hastily back inside the church. Charlie forced a smile as he passed the greeters and paced to the back of the church where the offices were located. Hurt settled in his chest as he slipped into his office, closing the door behind him. Charlie flopped on his back and, staring at the ceiling, replayed the last year.

They'd just moved into the house, and Marianna begged him to go with her furniture shopping, but his schedule didn't permit it. As he prepared for a new year and the planning of another location, Charlie didn't notice the house gradually coming together room by room as their connection began to fray in tandem. Instead of snuggling together on the couch watching TV at night after Chandler went to bed, he became engrossed in social media and YouTube videos while Marianna flipped through a magazine or worked out in their new gym in the basement. Charlie needed the mindless distractions to unplug, so he'd settled into a routine that was not conducive to the intimacy of his marriage.

This is my fault .I am the reason that she is so unplugged. Charlie swung his feet around. If he hurried, he could make it home to talk to Marianna and be back before the next service. But then he realized Marianna was at the gym. Making his way to the parking lot, he decided to go to the gym and find her. He needed to apologize. He'd been exactly what he never wanted to become—a hypocrite, just like the email said.

As he pulled into the parking lot of Buff Fitness, he spotted Piper's Hummer near the door. He slammed his Tahoe into park and made haste across the half-empty lot. Self-tanning lotion permeated the air as he passed the tanning bed spa and was greeted by a young man with a broad chest and an even broader smile.

"Hey, my wife is in Pilates. I need to talk to her. Can you point me in the right direction?" Charlie scanned the landscape of free weights and various types of equipment. Piper, with her platinum-blond hair and bright-pink workout bra, was easy to find on an inverted board across the room. But he didn't see Marianna. Charlie weaved through the row machines and past the ellipticals as Piper unhooked her feet and swiveled off the board. The color drained from her bronzed face as he approached. "Hey, Charlie."

"Hey, I thought you guys were doing a class. Where is Mar?"

"I'm not sure," she said, blotting her face with a makeup-stained hand towel.

"What do you mean? Is she here or not, Piper?"

"She wasn't feeling good, so I dropped her by your house."

OK, to the house I go.

A few minutes later as he rushed through the front door he was met with silence. "Marianna, you here honey?" he called, bounding up the staircase two steps at a time. "You here, Mar?" You could hear a pin drop as Charlie looked through every room yelling her name. Something felt very wrong. As he dialed her number, a text came through.

Had to run to store. Started my period at gym. And why are you checking up on me, Charlie? SMH.

Charlie read the text in disbelief and responded; *Piper said you were sick. Thought you were home. Checking up on you? I came to apologize to you. I am really sorry for the way things have been, Mar, and I want to make it right.*

We can talk later. I'll go by and pick up Chandler in a bit.

I'm confused by all of this. What's going on?

Charlie waited for a reply. Ten minutes passed before a reply came through.

> I can get Chandler. See you tonight after 6:00. Piper got her signals crossed. Will explain later.

Charlie paced along the top of the staircase, reading through their messages again and again. He felt numb and didn't really know why. Something was out of place.

Chapter Thirteen

Howling laughter met Charlie as he opened the front door. Marianna sat cross-legged on their large sectional with Chandler cradled in the center of her lap reading Dr. Seuss's *Green Eggs and Ham*. Charlie shook off the chill, pulled his jacket off, and tossed it on the wingback chair beside the couch. Chandler hopped out of Marianna's lap, landing in Charlie's arms with an excited thud.

"Doddy, Doddy. Mommy is weeding me a book. I wuv Doctor Thuse. He's da best." Chandler pulled in tight, rubbing his cheek against Charlie. "Ouch, Doddy."

Charlie leaned back and smiled. "Ouch is right. Daddy needs a shave, huh?"

"Yeth, very much so."

"I love it, and I love you, buddy. So much," Charlie said, glancing over at Marianna, who was watching. "Something smells yummy."

"I went ahead and fed Chandler. I left yours in the microwave."

Charlie studied her expression. It had softened, and her tone was less vague. "Okay. Thanks. I got here as soon as I could. The construction downtown held me up. I did my best. Really."

"I know you did," she said, uncrossing her legs. She collected the books sprayed around her, piling them neatly and placing them in a neon-green backpack. "Hey, Chandler, would you mind taking these up to your room and putting them away for me?"

Charlie released Chandler, and he bounced over to Marianna, pulling the backpack onto his narrow shoulder.

"Good job, Chan, my man," Charlie said, easing onto the couch beside Marianna. "We need to talk, Mar. This thing going on between us is crazy. I'm dying inside."

"I agree."

Charlie turned his head to the side, releasing a deep breath. "Really, Mar?" he asked, not sure of her response.

"Really."

Chandler bounded down the stairs and plopped on the couch between them. "Doddy, take me to de birdhouse."

"You got it, and then it's bath time." Charlie looked to Marianna for confirmation before scooping him up and walking out the back door onto the concrete patio with Chandler high in his arms.

"Shhhhh…look, Doddy. She der, wight der."

Charlie eased to the far edge of the patio without stepping onto the grass. A multicolored birdhouse sat high atop a painted two-by-four, speckled with bright yellows, oranges, and reds. Six months ago, Charlie and Chandler put the finishing touches on it. Chandler had a natural affinity for building and working with his tiny hands, which made Charlie proud. Working side by side with his son was a gift that could only come from God.

A large cardinal with hues of red coloring her breast sat perched on the landing of the birdhouse, pecking at the feed just inside the hole.

"See, buddy, she's back to visit us. And you thought she'd forget about you."

"She's becoming a wegular."

"That she is. You know you did a really good job on that house. Daddy is really proud of you."

Chandler pointed his tiny finger as he gave the birdhouse a once-over. "You sthee thot, Doddy? I painted it awww my own. I picked da co;ors."

"I think it looks awesome. You are very talented, son. You know some people say that when you see a red bird, someone is thinking of you in heaven."

"Your mommy is an angel, and so is Gwanpa Roy."

"They sure are, buddy. I loved them very much."

Charlie felt a slight lump in his throat thinking of his parents. He could still hear his daddy's words as he gazed down at Chandler for the first time. "Pure love. God's gift from heaven," he'd said with a tear in his eye.

"Yep. They loved you so much." Chandler nestled into Charlie's shoulder.

"I know." Chandler shoved his middle and index fingers in his mouth, suckling like he had from the day he was born. They'd tried on numerous occasions to discourage him, afraid he'd look like a buck-toothed cartoon character, but Chandler simply wouldn't stop. So, they gave up and figured he'd outgrow the bad habit, and if not, they'd buy braces for him when he was a teenager.

After a warm bath, Charlie and Marinna tucked Chandler in. As they pulled the door closed, Chandler yelled, "I wove you bofe." They laughed as they said it back in sync.

Charlie followed Marianna down the stairs and into their bedroom, where she sat with one leg tucked underneath her thigh as the other dangled off the side of the bed. Her eyes were clear but sad. Charlie eased onto the comforter in front of her.

"So," he said before she cut him off.

"No, Charlie. Let me speak. Please. I have a lot that I need to say to you."

Worry filled his chest as he watched her struggle for words. "Okay."

"When we moved to this neighborhood, I was in a bad place. Emotionally, that is. You were traveling a lot with the ministry, and then we bought this big house."

"I know, Mar. I—"

"Let me talk, Charlie. If I don't say this now…anyway, I was lonely, and between taking care of Chandler and all the expectations of the church, our life felt like it was spiraling. Just like I was living in a dream in a fishbowl all alone."

Charlie's heart ached with guilt as he sat quietly listening.

Pulling her other leg underneath her, she took a breath and continued. "I know how important the growth of this ministry is, and I knew coming into this marriage that you would build a church that would reach the masses. I just never imagined, Charlie, that it would grow like it has. I felt like I was being swallowed up in this world, this life we created together. I felt so alone, all the time. I couldn't tell you to slow down or do less. I see so clearly now that the way I responded was…" Marianna hung her head and sobbed. "It was wrong, Charlie," she said, meeting his confused gaze with raw pain. "When I met Piper, it was sort of a relief. I mean, she was there. I guess she's been like my lifeline." She pulled a pillow into her abdomen and continued to cry.

Charlie's heart ached with every syllable of every word. When he placed his hand on her shoulder, she held hers up as if to say no.

"I don't deserve that, Charlie. I don't deserve your comfort."

Charlie retreated as if she were a bubble that would burst with the slightest movement.

She wiped her eyes and looked at Charlie. "You know I haven't connected with the women in the church. I just haven't, and Piper was so different, but just really easy to talk to. I didn't feel like she was going to turn around and gossip, ya know. And as you know, we've become very close." Marianna began to cry again as Charlie's mind raced in panicked circles. He inhaled, waiting for the next sentence. *What the heck is going on here?*

"Charlie, I've been someone that I don't even recognize. These last six months, I've been trying to climb out of this well of confusion that I fell into. I was in denial until I saw your face in the parking lot. I could see the hurt. I guess it all just came to a head for me, and I started lashing out."

"But Mar, you haven't been acting that different. I mean, I know we haven't been having sex, and I miss you, Mar. I miss the way you feel in my arms."

She wiped her eyes with the sleeve of her gray crew-neck sweater and continued. "I know, and I'm sorry. I need to make some changes. I didn't have headaches. That was just an out for me."

Charlie felt a pang in his chest. *She doesn't want me.* He shifted on the bed as she struggled once again for words. A look of certainty covered her face as she spoke, "I have made some mistakes, some of which you are going to have a hard time with, but I will take my punishment. I will do whatever you want."

"What…what have you done, Mar?" The words felt like golf balls in his throat.

"I need to collect my thoughts some more, and I need to do something. Can we please just talk again tomorrow night, Charlie? It took a lot for me to even say this."

Charlie pressed into his knees and tried to process the pain on his wife's face. He had a bad feeling, but pressing down on her for more answers might push her away again, so he forced a smile. "Okay, Mar. I can wait," he responded as his heart searched for an extra pint of blood in his chest.

"I love you, Charlie. I do. Please forgive me for all of this. Please." Sliding to Charlie, she placed her hands on both sides of his face. "I need you, Charlie. I need to feel you, touch you."

Passion rushed through him as he took her face in his hands pulling her mouth to his. The familiar warmth of her lips, her breath, easing her shirt over her head as she worked the button on the front of his jeans. He didn't care what had happened. He needed this as a man, as her husband.

"Forgive me Charlie."

The room became a blur as he spiraled into a hypnotic haze. Nothing she'd said could steal this moment. He'd yearned for her touch these last months, and nothing could destroy the connection they shared, so he pushed her recent behavior to the far corners of his mind.

Curling onto his chest, her dark hair blanketed him. "I love you, Charlie. More than you'll ever know."

Chapter Fourteen

The week flew by in a haze of meetings and work. A night hadn't passed since their talk that they hadn't made love. Even so, she'd not revealed what she'd done. She said she needed more time, time he was willing to allow. It was hard to resist her warm, tanned curves and tender kisses, so he didn't press her. Besides, nothing she could say would change his mind. He was committed to her and the marriage that they'd built together. Each day he'd delegated one more task at the office to free up more time for his family, and he'd decided to shelve his next book idea and postpone his trip to Canada for a month or so to regain the footing needed to sustain his marriage.

Sunday morning arrived, and Charlie looked over at the clock on the bedside table. Six a.m. came way too early, he thought as Marianna rolled onto her side opening her eyes slowly.

"Morning, handsome," she said with a hazy smile.

"Morning, beautiful," he said, sweeping a strand of hair from her cheek.

Her arms pulled him to her as their bodies became tangled in the same heat that they'd experienced the night before. Breathless, they looked at each other and laughed.

"We are having some crazy good love makin' going on here, huh?"

"That would be an understatement," Marianna said as she slid a gown over her head.

A light tapping on the door brought a lazy smile to his face. "Good timing," Charlie said, watching Marianna slide off the bed and pad toward the door.

"Who is it?" Marianna asked, leaning playfully against the door.

"It's me, Mommy."

"Who is me?" she said, smiling back at Charlie.

"Your baby boy, Mommy."

Marianna eased the door open, peeking around as Chandler popped inside. Marianna scooped him up, galloped to the bed, and tossed him lightly onto the mounds of down.

"Chan, my man. You sleep good, buddy?"

"I dreamed of buttafwys. Big ones with big blue wings."

Charlie buried his face in the top of Chandler's head, talking through ringlets of dark hair tickling his cheek. "Man, that sounds awesome. You ready to go to church and learn about Jesus?"

"Yep. And Lily has a supprize for me."

"You gonna wear your Mickey pajamas?"

"Oh no, Doddy. I'm a big boy. I gonna wear my new sweatshirt Uncle Wes and Aunt Donna gave me for my birfday."

Marianna eased back under the comforter, sandwiching Chandler between them. Chandler rested his tiny arms behind his neck and closed his eyes. "Dis is heaven. All we need is my buttafwys and miss red bird, of course."

Charlie rested his arm across the two people who meant the most to him as the buzzing of the alarm clock continued, reminding him that he needed to get up. He wanted to review his sermon notes one final time before delivering the message, and he needed a minute alone to prepare his spirit, but he just could not pull himself from the warm mound of love in his bed.

—◁∘▷—

What a day, Charlie thought a few hours later as God's presence filled the room. He'd powered through each of the messages without missing a beat. Many Sundays, he found himself pushing through the final service of the day mentally exhausted, but this day he felt re-charged.

As he invited anyone looking for redemption down to the front, his mind wandered to the day ahead with Marianna and Charlie. Mondays were like his Saturday, but in recent months, he'd found himself working right through to Tuesday. But tomorrow the plan was to start with ice-skating, which Chandler was picking up quickly, according to Marianna, and then to dinner at Mama Rosa's Italian Bistro.

The energy surged like a vortex through the room as people young and old made their way to the foot of the stage praying with the volunteers. He could feel the change that had come from one simple decision—family first, always. Now he was being rewarded by the miracles God was working in and around him.

"Everyone, I just have to say one thing before we wrap up. I have been finding it difficult to maintain my focus tonight because of one very special lady sitting in the front row." Color filled Marianna's cheeks as he said her name, covering the smile on her face. "Come on up here for a minute, honey."

Marianna smiled as everyone clapped. Crossing the stage, she shrugged, teasing the crowd. Pulling her to him and kissing her on the top of the head, Charlie felt a clarity that could navigate them through whatever they faced.

"This ministry…our ministry…would not be where it is if not for the love and support of this woman, my wife, Marianna Nettles. She supports me and our family, and I just wanted to take this opportunity to say…" Charlie turned to face her, holding both of her hands. "I love you so much, Mar, and I just want to thank you for being you."

Tears fell down her cheeks as he folded her into his arms amid a sea of "awes" and claps. He held her, savoring the warmth of her embrace. *How did I get so lucky, to be so blessed with this woman? Thank you, Father.* Charlie motioned for the roaring applause to quiet.

"Now she is embarrassed." Pulling her into his side, he smiled. "Let us close in prayer." Bowing his head, Charlie conveyed the love and gratitude that filled him. His life felt full circle.

As they stepped off the stage, a volunteer worked to remove his mic pack and earpiece. Marianna stood close by. "You okay?" Charlie asked, touching her cheek.

"Of course. I have you," she said as her smile faded.

"You sure?"

"Yes. We have a lot to talk about tonight, and everything has been so good between us. I'm just afraid I'm gonna mess that up."

Charlie took her face in his hands with a certainty in his eyes. "There is nothing you can tell me, Mar, that will make me love you any less. We'll get through this, I promise." He held her gaze until she agreed.

"Good night, Pastor Nettles," said Roger, the head of their security team. "Security is getting ready to head out. You need an escort to your car?"

Charlie didn't waver. He patted Chandler's back, who napped as he sucked on his fingers contently, resting on Marianna's shoulder. "I got this, Roger. I think we'll be fine."

A chill met them as they stepped onto the sidewalk. Marianna pulled Chandler into her body. "You did a really good job in there tonight, Charlie. You brought a lot of people from darkness to light," she said, smiling over Chandler's mounds of dark hair.

Charlie placed his hand on the small of her back. "I couldn't do it without you—"

A dark figure stepped from behind Charlie's Tahoe, arms extended, pointing a gun at his chest.

Without a thought Charlie stepped in front of Marianna and Chandler.

"Don't move, honey. Stay behind me," Charlie said, standing his ground. He pressed his hands onto the front of his jeans to eliminate the involuntary shaking. "Look, man, I don't know what's going on here, but we can work this out. Just put the gun down. We don't want anyone getting hurt here today." Out of the corner of his eye, Charlie watched as Roger swept along the perimeter of the bushes in front of his Tahoe. Charlie had to protect his family, and holding this guy's attention was all that mattered. "Look, we can talk about this." His heart thudded as he estimated how many steps it would take to knock the gun from his hand if Roger grabbed him from behind.

Hang in there, Mar. I got this. I will not let anything happen. Bridging the gap was a risky move, but it would prevent this lunatic from hurting his family. His mind calculated the attack as sweat dripped down his sides.

The barrel of the gun trembled as the gun man took a step back. "It's just time, man. Time to make this right."

"If you do this," Marianna's voice trembled, "it will never be right. Just turn and leave. We won't tell anyone. I promise."

His laughter spewed sarcasm. "Really? I think we're past that. Now you move that way," he said, angling his gun toward the church. "This is between him and me."

Marianna took a step back and began to cry. "You don't want this, I promise. There is a good man inside of you, one that would never hurt anyone."

Just be quiet, Marianna. I got this. I got this. The gunman glared at Charlie, unmoved by Marianna's words, but his hand shook violently as he worked to maintain his grip. This was not an experienced shooter.

Charlie held his hands up in front of him as adrenaline pounded into his chest, forcing the air into his lungs. "She's right. I am sure you are a good man," he said, working to maintain eye contact as Roger knelt behind a dark-red pickup truck only feet away from them. Charlie prayed that Roger's time in Desert Storm had prepared him well for combat. They'd need to work as a team, reading each other's body language. He surveyed the area looking for anything that he could use as a weapon.

Roger eased into position like a cheetah closing in on its prey, and a prayer of courage raced through his mind as he eased his legs apart, establishing his center of gravity. *I got this. I got this.* In an instant, Roger's short, heavyset body lunged onto the assailant, pulling him into a choke hold with one hand and working to gain control of his left hand clutching the gun. They spun in place as Charlie looked for his opportunity to lunge. The gun waved wildly, sweeping across the starless sky—

It all happened so fast. Two gunshots echoed through the night air. His ears rang as he turned to see Marianna and Chandler on the ground, blood seeping through the back of his boy's Mickey Mouse shirt.

"Oh, God no!" Charlie screamed, reaching them in a single sprint. Blanketing their bodies with his, he could only hear scuffling and banging into cars as the two men fought. Within seconds, pounding feet were fading into the distance as Roger pursued the gunman into the nearby woods. "Someone call an ambulance!" He didn't recognize the primal cry that came from his chest as he lifted Chandler's limp body onto his lap. "Son, please! Are you breathing?" he begged, lowering his ear to Chandler's chest.

Blood was pouring out of a ragged hole in Chandler's chest as someone from behind handed him a wadded-up T-shirt. Pressing it on the gaping wound while reaching over to feel Marianna's neck, he screamed, "Oh, God! I don't think he's breathing!"

Wesley was suddenly there, kneeling down beside Marianna, starting CPR as he spoke. "Help is on the way. I got her." Turning to the half dozen people that had remained in the church, Wesley yelled, "Somebody, make sure that ambulance is on the way!" He pulled his shirt off, balled it up, and pushed onto the well that was bubbling out of Marianna's chest. "She's still breathing, but she's losing a lot of blood."

Sirens squealed into the parking lot as seven police cars blanketed the area, led by an ambulance. The EMTs were on the pavement and easing everyone out of the way within seconds.

"Charlie, they need to stop this bleeding. Let go, buddy. These guys need to check them," Wes said, holding Charlie's shoulders.

Charlie could barely catch his breath. His head felt like it was floating up and away from his body. He struggled to relinquish his hold on Chandler. Two firemen stepped in, and Charlie moved to the side. Neither Chandler nor Marianna appeared to be breathing.

"We have a pulse," said the fireman assessing Chandler.

Charlie cried out in relief watching Chandler as CPR was being performed on Marianna. The echo of sirens blended with the ringing in Charlie's ears. The rest was a blur of panic and tears.

Chapter Fifteen

Beads of sweat dampened Charlie's hairline as the morning sun landed squarely on his face. He was usually the one to close the two-inch white wooden blinds each night before bed. The gray keyhole-patterned panels on the window framed the light in front of him, slowly taking focus. Within seconds the morning air turned heavy. He closed his eyes, pulling his knees into a tight fetal position, holding Marianna's black silk robe to his cheek along with Chandler's footed pajamas. He inhaled both, exhaling a low sob.

His head was swimming from the Ambien he'd taken, and he barely remembered Wesley driving him home from the hospital. Rolling onto his back, Charlie raked his fingers through his hair. The smooth white ceiling took on their faces as Charlie played the day before over and over in his mind. None of it made sense. Why would someone do this? If only there hadn't been a struggle, if only he'd let Roger walk out with them, if only he'd acted quicker. A thousand *if only* spitted his mind.

He stumbled up from the bed and turned on the shower. It nearly scorched him, but he didn't care. He wanted to burn, to feel more pain. If only he could swirl around the drain and disappear like the water at his feet. As he watched the blood wash off his skin, he didn't know where his tears ended, and the water began. His cries echoed against the tile floor and wall, but the water couldn't wash away the shame he felt for not saving his family. Was God testing him in a way that he'd never imagined? After all, he was anointed to do His will. There was never a reason to believe he wasn't protected. He'd walked past men with assault rifles in the Congo without being harmed.

Charlie leaned against the dark tile clasping his hands together, eyes closed. Depleted, he prayed. *God, please take this from me. I have served you and honored you, but I don't know that I can do this. My wife and my baby boy…gone. How is this right? I have given my life to you and honored you and brought people to you. I know you say you won't put anything on us that we cannot handle, but this, Lord—this is more than I can bear. I have always tried to do what's right. Living in your will, raising my son to be a Godly man. I was doing everything that I promised you. Growing this ministry, bringing people from darkness to light. All for you. Are you punishing me, Lord? I know why you took Abigail away from me. We didn't do things right. I thought that pain would last a lifetime. I thought I'd paid my dues, Lord. I loved her so deeply with every ounce of my being, but I made myself take up the cross and step into your will 100 percent. Was I a bad husband? Was it that I didn't spend enough time with Chan? Should I have done more? What was it? What did I do that made you so angry that…*

It occurred to Charlie that he'd spoken with many people in the past with broken hearts, who wondered if they were being punished. He would lean in and speak softly. "We serve a loving God who wants the best for us. Things happen in this lifetime that we cannot always explain, but it always comes from a place of love."

He opened his eyes. There was nothing left to say, no changing the finality of his situation. Charlie stepped onto the rug sobbing, pulling an oversized, fluffy white towel off the brushed nickel holder on the wall. Wrapping the towel around his waist, he went into the bedroom and reached into his bedside table. The worn leather of the Bible that his daddy gave him the day he graduated from high school greeted him with hope for answers. Charlie thumbed through the book of John before crumbling into a pile on the bed. He had nothing.

—◦◦◦—

Wes's voice woke him. He'd dozed off clutching his Bible.

"Hey, man, wake up. There are two detective's downstairs to see you."

Charlie rolled onto his side. "I thought we'd covered everything at the hospital. I answered all of their questions."

"Come on, man, get dressed. I think they may have caught the guy that did this."

A rush of anxiety pelted Charlie in the gut as he sat up. "Okay, tell them I'll be down in a minute."

"Will do," Wesley said, closing the door behind him.

I can't wait to face this son of a bitch. He needs to know whose lives he ended. I will take pictures of Mar and Chan and make him look in their faces, see the goodness he stole from this world.

Standing in the middle of the living room were Wes and two detectives.

"Hey, Charlie Nettles," he said, extending his hand to the first, then second detective before retreating back with his hands in the front pockets of his jeans.

"Sorry to be meeting under these circumstances, Pastor. My name is Detective Lyons, and this is Detective Snellgrove."

"Have a seat, gentlemen," Charlie said, inching into the corner of the sectional while Detective Lyons took a seat in the middle with Detective Snellgrove standing nearby. Wes sat in the wingback chair across from them.

"Pastor Nettles, we feel certain that we know who committed these crimes against your wife and son."

Charlie leaned into the adrenaline, trying to read the blank expressions on their faces. "Okay. So, he's in jail?"

"Not exactly," Detective Snellgrove said and cleared his throat.

"I'm confused. What do you mean?"

"Pastor Nettles, do you know a man by the name of Jonathan Myers? He's a trainer at Buff," Detective Lyons said. He removed two Tums from a paper tube in his jacket pocket, shoved them into his mouth, and crunched into them with a low cough.

Charlie thought for a moment. "No, but that's the gym where my wife works out—or used to…" His stomach contracted with the realization that she was no longer a member at any gym. "Wait a minute. I think that guy was her trainer."

"Pastor, were you aware that your wife was in a relationship with Jonathan Myers?"

Charlie's mouth filled with warm liquid. "What…what did you say?" Charlie looked at Wesley, who was shaking his head with disbelief.

"Pastor Nettles, we received a 911 call from his mother," Detective Lyons said.

Charlie's ears rang as if he were walking out of a Metallica concert.

Detective Lyons continued, "At eight a.m. this morning, we received a call that there had been a suicide. When we arrived on the scene, the victim's mother was in possession of a letter detailing the victim's relationship with your wife."

Charlie stood up, raking his hair with both hands. "Okay, so let me get this straight. My wife was having an affair with her trainer, and he shot them. Am I following? I mean this is all so crazy. There must be a mistake. I mean Mar would never cheat on me, cheat on our family."

"Pastor Nettles, there were no signs of foul play, and the victim's mother stated that she was aware of the relationship," Detective Lyons said.

Charlie looked at a wide-eyed Wes, who was covering his mouth. "Okay, wait a minute. This makes absolutely no sense. Are you saying that she was just blatantly having an affair in the open, and I didn't know?"

"It seems that the deceased…"

"Okay, stop right there, Detective Lyons. This Jonathan person is dead?" Charlie asked, trying to process this new information.

"Yes, Pastor, he is."

Charlie's heart raced. He wanted to punch something and cry at the same time. He felt light headed as he sat lightly on the edge of the couch. "This makes zero sense, Detectives. My wife was not a cheater. We had a good marriage. I mean, we were going through a rough patch, but every marriage has its moments, right?" Charlie pressed his hand into his face. The venom of betrayal stung his heart. He would not cry in front of these men. *I got this.* Charlie took a deep breath and paused. He needed the facts. *Get your thoughts together, Charlie.* "Okay, so when did this affair start?" Charlie asked with an evenness of tone that surprised even him.

"According to the letter, it started six months ago. Apparently, your wife met with Mr. Myers yesterday morning to break it off. Mr. Myers stated that he could not live without your wife. His intent was to shoot you and then take his own life. When he shot your wife and son, he went back to his apartment, where he wrote this letter, texted his mother, and shot himself."

Charlie couldn't get rid of the image of Marianna's face looking him straight in the eyes and lying. "So, this was never about my ministry? It was all about my wife?"

"There was no mention of your religious affiliation being the motive. He stated clearly that he was in love with your wife and wanted the three of them to be a family. With the realization that this was not going to happen, he snapped. His intention was not to shoot your wife or son."

Charlie sat quietly, trying to clear the static in his head. *None of this is true. It's all a big lie.* "I need time alone, I need to think," Charlie said, standing up. "If we're done here, gentlemen, I'd like you to leave now."

Wes stood up and shook the detectives' hands, thanking them for their time as Charlie stood stoically, extending his hand to both.

"Here's my card, Pastor. Call me if you have additional questions," Detective Lyons said with warmth in his voice.

As Wesley closed the door behind them, Charlie slammed his fist into the wall by the fireplace. Rage and hurt throbbed in his fists.

"So, who all knew about this, Wes? Did you?"

"No, Charlie. I would never keep something like that from you. I am so sorry. That was not what I expected."

"This just makes no sense, man. Mar wasn't that kind of person."

But the look on Wesley's face said she was.

"If his mother knew, God only knows who else knew. She betrayed me, man. My wife cheated on me with her trainer. I am a freakin' walking cliché."

"I don't know what to say, Charlie. I didn't think this whole thing could get any worse. What do you need, man?"

"And to think…" Then it dawned on Charlie. The most unimaginable thought. "Wes, she's the reason our son Chan is gone. She did this, man." Sobs filled the raw air in the room as Charlie fell to his knees. "Why, how could she do this to our family?" Charlie shook his fist in the air and wailed. He was broken.

Wes gently helped a limp Charlie to his feet and eased him onto the couch. "Come on, man. Sit down. What do you need?"

"I need for my wife to not be a cheating bitch, that's what I need!" His words were replaced by regret as he held his face and cried.

"You don't mean that. There has to be a reason, man. None of this makes sense. None of it."

"What am I gonna do, Wes? I can't handle this. I felt like I was breaking in two before, but this…"

Wes placed his hand on Charlie's shoulder. "I know you feel weak, brother, but you aren't alone."

Charlie paused and immediately thought of Chandler. His sweet smile, contagious laugh. He wouldn't experience either again except in his mind, and his very own wife was the cause. He'd never felt more alone.

Chapter Sixteen

The following months were a blind of tears. Still, the sun rose, spraying golden hues along the jagged branches of the crepe myrtle in the back-yard. Charlie's breath coated the glass as his forehead rested against the cool surface. He'd been staring at the birdhouse for over an hour waiting for Miss Red Bird to appear. But she'd not made an appearance since Chandler died. It was as if he had taken her with him, leaving behind the dream that had once been high atop the hand-painted roof line.

The colored shingles seemed dull and lifeless as Charlie stepped barefoot onto the tile patio leading to the backyard, inhaling the morning air. No sound greeted him. No birds basking in the morning's glory singing in the trees. The walls of his home were closing in on him and had been, little by little since the funerals. Only feet from the birdhouse, Charlie had placed one of their patio chairs, and he'd sit for hours staring into the sky, hoping for a miracle, a sign that his life had a purpose, but so far nothing. Falling into the thick, cream-colored cushion, Charlie angled his face toward the cloudless sky, transfixed.

Miss Red Bird had to come back. He needed a sign. A sign that he was not going to die from the mass of gummy anger and sadness that had formed between his chest and stomach. He wasn't ready to forgive enough to grieve her. Not yet, and he wasn't sure when that day would come.

"God, I know that I am supposed to be a pillar of strength, counting on you, walking by faith, but right now I am still so broken. My marriage was a farce, and…my son…" Charlie's voice shook with emotion. "My son has been taken from me, and he's never coming back, and you see, I get that you sent your son, and he died for me, but this pain…" Charlie clutched his chest. "How did you do it, Lord? How did you watch him die? See, I should have been a better husband. None of this would've happened. None of it. She needed me, and I was not there. I was doing what I thought was the right thing, and now I'm second-guessing everything. All this time I thought you had my back. Where did I go wrong? What did I do that made you decide I needed to be tempered like a piece of glass, shaped into a better version? I am just Charlie Nettles. That's it. That's all I got, and you have adequately removed any traces of the life I created here, while all I ever wanted to do was build your kingdom."

Charlie leaned on his knees, rocking back and forth before pushing off of the chair. Anger surged through him as he looked toward the gray hues weaving across the sky. Clutching his head, he said, "Why did you take them, and disgrace me, making a mockery of me, of my life, the life I built with her?" His teeth clenched as he stood up and paced around the birdhouse. The more he paced, the angrier he became. A haze of tears welled over his eyes. Clenched fists pressed into his eyes before taking on a life of their own, waving and shaking in the air above his head. "Maybe I have reached my shelf life. Maybe it's time for you to take me out, too!" Charlie shouted.

He ripped the birdhouse pole up, the house falling to the ground, and smashed the pole into the deck. Bright-red blood dripped onto the thick pad of zoysia grass as he continued swinging into the rage. As he raised his foot to stomp out the house itself and the remaining memories, Chandler's tiny voice echoed in his head. *Why'd you do dat, Doddy? Now where is Miss red bird gonna wiv?* Charlie fell to his knees clutching the cracked roof line against his chest. "I'm sorry, Chan, so sorry. Daddy didn't mean it. I am so sorry, buddy," Charlie cried, collecting the pieces, clutching them tightly to his chest, and making his way toward the house.

He flipped on the garage light, lay the pieces on his workbench, and glanced to the far corner of the garage. Draped in a black cover was an old friend that he'd missed terribly—his Harley-Davidson Heritage Soft Tail Classic that he'd bought to ride with Marianna in their spare time before the responsibilities of ministry and parenting weighed in. Charlie turned his attention back to the space that would never serve its true purpose. This birdhouse was the only product from this garage equipped with an assortment of tools. He and Chandler had built it the weekend after they moved in with the intention of tinkering around, teaching Chandler how to use his hands to create beauty with wood. And the only project they'd completed was this birdhouse that now lay in two pieces, cracked, and removed of the joy it brought him.

Charlie picked up the roof and flipped it onto its back—exposing Chandler's thumbprints. Air rushed into his lungs with a gasp as Charlie stifled a sob.

Charlie recalled smiling as he had asked. "Hey, buddy. Whatcha-doin'?"

Chandler had kept inspecting his handiwork before leaning back with pride. "I am leaving my the fumbpwint on the birdies."

"Buddy, how did you come up with that?"

"You said it, Doddy. You said you were going to leave your fumpwints all over this church bringing people to Jesus. Rememba? I heard you tell Mommy," He said, looking up at Charlie nonchalantly.

The memory washed over Charlie as though a blanket filled with sand spurs were covering his body, resting heavily over his heart. *No second chances, Charlie Nettles, none that will ever make this right.*

The table in front of him looked unused with no signs of carpentry. The metal box that had once been filled with nails of all shapes and sizes was as empty as Charlie's chest. *How am I supposed to fix this with no nails?*

Within minutes, Charlie was pulling into the Lowe's parking lot.

—◦—

The warm rays of dusk filtered through the garage window as Charlie placed pieces of roofline from the birdhouse together tapping a small nail into it. He felt a pain-free glimmer of pleasure as he lightly sanded along the edges, trying to preserve the original paint job. His hands ached, and a dizzy haze reminded him that he'd not had a bite of food all day. Tonight, after dinner he'd add touch-up paint, and at first light tomorrow, he'd place it high upon the original pole. A smile eased over his face as he swiped the sandpaper easily back and forth with a familiar gritty sweep.

Chapter Seventeen

Charlie knelt beside the post staring up at the freshly painted birdhouse. The integrity of Chandler's work was at least somewhat present. But Miss Red Bird was still nowhere in sight.

He pondered how he'd let the months pass without any intention. *Maybe the lack of connection with the church and God is the new me.* No matter how much he prayed, anger crept into his prayers, leaving him feeling like a petulant child. He remembered having these very emotions as a boy scanning the landscape of their backyard for a switch after talking back to his daddy. He knew not to pick the skinny, spindly branches because of the sting they provided and the lasting red welts with each swipe. Big was definitely better. Charlie could not see the "bigger branch" in his life.

So, he piddled around the house analyzing what he needed to take his next step. He was determined to take a step today no matter how small. As he paced along the area rug in front of the stone fireplace in the living room, he sorted through the questions that remained.

Within minutes he was pulling his Tahoe onto a circular driveway, past a massive water fountain spewing a stream high into the air. Their wealth wasn't the reason Charlie disliked them. It was simply their unadulterated lack of gratitude and humanity.

Charlie threw the SUV into park. He drew a breath as he stepped onto the porch going over the questions that only Piper knew the answers to.

The doorbell boomed throughout the foyer, and the sound of clicking heels grew closer. Piper opened the door with a sad smile. Her blond hair was cropped close to her head, and without makeup, she didn't remind him of a cheap version of Barbie. She looked more subtle but tired. Minus all the ado, Piper had a natural beauty, and her clear blue eyes shimmered with what Charlie assumed were tears, but he knew better. Piper was pretentious and self-centered.

"Hi, Charlie. How are you?" she asked, holding his gaze.

"I'm making it, I guess." Charlie shoved his hands into his front jean pockets and forced a smile. "Piper, I was hoping you would answer some questions for me."

"Sure, come on in. It's just me," she said.

Charlie nodded, stepping into the vast foyer of shiny white marble. He was relieved that Dan wasn't home. One of them at a time was about all he could take.

Piper led him down a hallway lined with boxes. The wall behind the desk was covered in mahogany built-ins, creating a contrast to the light-gray walls. Rich navy textured drapery panels flanked a large window overlooking their perfectly manicured side yard. Boxes were stacked on every surface including the vast mahogany desk. The two leather wingback chairs in front of it were the only empty spaces.

Piper waved her hand as she sat gently on the chair. "Have a seat, Charlie. This is the least messy area."

"So, you guys finally making that big move you talked about so much? I know Dan said the walls were literally closing in on you guys here. I can only imagine," Charlie said, pushing down the sarcasm in his voice.

Piper crossed her pencil, thin legs, resting her hands in her lap. Her expression was fragile beyond recognition. "Actually, Charlie, we're splitting up. I'm divorcing him."

Many scenarios would have crossed his mind, but this was not one of them. They were the perfect, over-the-top "me meme" couple paired together like an Alma Rosa Pinot Noir and a burger with way too much cheese. "I have to say I'm surprised."

"Yeah, well, I was too. I was especially surprised when I found out that Dan had been keeping a mistress up in New York. You think this is nice, you should see her apartment overlooking Central Park. Makes this place look like a hovel."

Charlie craned his neck back in disbelief. "Wow, not what I expected to hear. I am so sorry."

She responded with a tight smile.

After a brief pause, Charlie transitioned into the purpose of his visit. "So, Piper, I need to talk to you about Marianna."

She swallowed. "I figured this visit would come. Just surprised it wasn't sooner. I want you to know, Charlie, how sorry I am for everything."

Charlie studied her expression. The pretentious air that she had once worn like this season's Christian Louboutin's was gone. She looked broken. "Piper, I need some answers, and I feel like you are the only one that has them. Can you help me with this?"

"I will tell you whatever you need to know."

Charlie took a breath. "So, you knew about her affair?"

Piper shook her head, looking down at her fingers entwined in her lap. "Yes, I did."

Charlie leaned onto his knees and into the involuntary pain radiating through his heart. "So, I want to know when they met, how long they were together. I want to know it all."

Piper looked up slightly, wiping a tear from the outside of her eye. "He was my trainer. He's the reason I have a backside you can bounce a quarter off of."

There she is. I knew you were in there.

"I'm sorry; that was inappropriate." She cleared her throat and met Charlie's gaze. "She kept complaining about having never lost her baby weight. He'd always been a bit flirtatious, but I figured he was just that way with me. I am truly sorry. I just…well, never mind that. I really thought I was helping her out. At first it seemed normal, nothing out of the ordinary until she told me they'd gone for coffee and sat in her car outside of Starbucks talking for over an hour."

Charlie's heart stung. "So, when was that?"

"I guess about six months before she died. Basically, Charlie, they started out as friends. She didn't tell me until they'd been seeing each other for over a month."

He swallowed hard, as his throat dried with every syllable she spoke. "Can I have a bottle of water or something?" he said, coughing into his hand.

"Here you go," Piper said, handing him a bottle of Evian from the mini fridge by her desk. "Are you okay, Charlie?"

Charlie gulped half of the bottle, freezing his throat. *God don't let me hyperventilate.* He nonchalantly wiped the moisture from his brow with the side of his hand.

Piper placed her hand on his shoulder. "Do you need a bag or something?"

"Okay, I'm fine. This is just tougher than I thought. Where were we?" *I cannot have a panic attack in Piper's office.*

"Honestly, I think she regretted it. I think he just took advantage of her vulnerability. She tried to break it off multiple times, but he said he loved her. He was very intense about them having a future together." Piper's voice trailed off. "And then the morning of the shooting, she said she went over to his apartment and told him that if he didn't leave her alone, she was going to get a restraining order and that she needed to do the right thing. She said she begged him to just let it go."

Charlie looked out the window at the gray sky. "Did she love him, Piper? Did she tell you that?" He held his breath. Reading Piper's expression was like finding color in a manila envelope. She stared ahead without a sound. "Well, did she?"

"I think she cared for him. I do. But love, no."

Charlie exhaled into the chair, rubbing the tension out on top of his legs. "So, what exactly was it?"

"I don't know. I think he just filled a gap. Maybe an escape."

Charlie's elbows pressed into the tops of his legs. "I am just broken, Piper. I am broken from the inside out. I don't know how to recover." Vulnerability pressed into his resolve as he continued. "I'm trying to just make sense of this. I miss my family. My wife, my boy."

Piper shook her head, eyes welling with tears. "I know, Charlie. I know. I miss them so much."

Suddenly, he was exhausted. "Thank you for taking this time with me."

As he stood up, Piper leaned up and grazed his cheek with a kiss. "I hope you find peace, Charlie. You didn't deserve this."

Chapter Eighteen

Charlie watched the midday sun in the distance flex its muscles. The temperature was already an unbearably humid ninety-seven degrees and climbing. By all estimates this would be the hottest summer in many years. But today was the day he needed to move the mountain of sadness out of the way.

The doorbell rang, and Wesley walked in carrying two large sweet iced teas. "So, how are you feeling today? You are looking good. Showered, I see. That is always a plus," he said with a hearty laugh. "But dude, not sure about that beard."

Charlie smiled. "Thanks, man," he said, running his hand along the bottom of his chin. "This thing is the least of my worries. I'm glad you came by. I have something that I need to run by you." Charlie eased onto the couch and sipped the super sweet liquid. "Dang, I think they need to add some tea to this sugar."

Wesley flopped onto the chair beside the couch, crossed his legs, and leaned into the down cushion. "Just like I like it," he said with a gulp of tea. "I figured you needed a change, shake things up a bit. Starbucks wasn't on the way so, ya know."

Charlie wasn't sure what to say next. He only knew that he would summon the strength to press on. He wasn't sure what that looked like though. "Well, first and foremost, I want to thank you for holding down the fort for me, man. I don't know what I would have done without your support and the support of the church. I mean everyone has really rallied around me," Charlie said, rubbing the pale suntan ring that remained where his wedding band once was. He had taken it off the day of the funeral and missed twisting it around his finger when he was nervous.

"You know I am here for you. And this sounds eerily like a speech that doesn't have a happy ending," Wesley said. He drank his tea and rested the cup on his leg.

"Yeah, well about that. I don't really know what that ending is at this point."

"What do you mean?"

Charlie reflected back on the months of emotional turmoil, his lack of faith, his prayer life that felt like a shirt with too much starch, the days waking up to a perpetual emptiness, the disconnect he felt to everything including himself. Charlie swallowed hard into the hurt. "Wes, I need something, and I can't quite figure out what."

Wesley stared at him for a moment. Charlie could see him struggling for a response.

"I don't know that ministry is truly my calling anymore. I can't believe the words are coming from my mouth, but it's true, Wes. You are the only person that I could say that to. You see these other pastors that suffer great loss, and they lean into the pain, man. *They* make beauty from the ashes. All I have succeeded in doing for the last few months is growing this beard," he said, running his hand over it and scratching the itchy patch under his chin.

"Come on now. You *are* the sexiest pastor alive. If Facebook says it, then you know it's true. In all seriousness, this is just a blip on your spiritual screen." Wesley paused and shook his head. "That didn't come out right. I'm trying to lighten the mood and just stepping in it big time. I am not downplaying what you are dealing with, but I do know this: ten years ago, the Lord planted a seed in you that has grown to bring thousands and thousands to HIM. That was you, Charlie. No one else was given that, and you have built so much. Think of the schools that we are funding, the churches we are building right now, as we speak, in Nicaragua and Australia. I mean, that is big. And you did it. It took a lot of people, but it was your vision. That's where it all started. Now is not the time to just walk away. You have a responsibility, man."

Charlie sat quietly. Wesley was right. He knew that Elroy would have been sitting right beside Wesley stoking the fire in his son, urging him to do God's will no matter the cost. Suddenly Charlie pictured Chandler as a young man. He would've been tall with wavy dark hair and the same infectious laugh that still echoed in Charlie's ears. His eyes would have conveyed kindness as he navigated life with a gift for ministering to others just as he did with building Miss Redbird a home. He'd have a heart for the Lord and a love for Jesus that would never fade. Chandler would've been strong because his daddy had raised him that way. Chandler wouldn't have been a quitter…

Charlie gasped as tears came to his eyes. He knew what he needed. The answer slammed into him with an unexpected shock wave, and it was clear to him, finally. "Wes, this is what is going to happen. At the service this Sunday, I am going to open. I owe them that much."

"You sure, man? This week?"

Charlie shook his head through the uncertainty, but it was a decision.

Wesley smiled and threw his hand over his head. "Well, hallelujah! The preacher man is back."

"I have a lot of thinking to do, but just carve out a few minutes for me at the beginning, okay?"

"You got it, man."

The parking lot was already full when Charlie pulled his motorcycle onto the church campus. His mind was clear as he maneuvered into his space designated by a sign that read Pastor Nettles. His heart began a gradual climb as he stepped onto the pavement and swiped his pass at the office door. He was relieved that no one was in the employee lot on the side of the church walking inside with him. Maintaining a calm composure was going to take some work. *You got this, Charlie, you got this.* His watch said eleven thirty. He could hear the music playing in the distance as he opened his office door. His desk had a few papers scattered along the surface, the way he'd left it the day everything changed. Thumbing through them, they were sermon ideas he'd printed out with the beginnings of what would have been the following week's message. A silver frame with the word *family* held the last family picture of him, Marianna, and Chandler. They were sitting in a grassy field with a barn in the background. Chandler's mouth was agape with laughter. Charlie had just goosed him in the side to provoke a real smile. Charlie lifted the frame to his chest and closed his eyes while a surge of pain worked through him.

"I'm making the right decision," he said aloud, placing the picture back in its place in the front center position on his desk.

Charlie scanned the room without touching anything else. Resting his hands lightly on the back of his leather desk chair, he closed his eyes and began to pray. "Please, Lord, help me find my way back. Give me the strength to go out there today and lay my heart out. Help them understand that I am doing the best that I can do. I feel so broken, Lord, and weak. I just don't know anymore. I just don't know."

As he made his way through the building, everyone he passed shared a smile, welcoming him back. The auditorium was quiet as Wesley led a prayer. A young African American man with long dreadlocks and an inviting smile handed Charlie his earpiece and audio pack. No words were exchanged. Charlie's heart thundered in his chest, and his ears were ringing as he heard the words "Let's welcome him back!" Adjusting his earpiece, he stepped onto the stage to roaring applause. Everyone stood, some holding their hands high, others visibly emotional at his return. This response tugged at his conscience for what he was getting ready to do. He wondered how these people who'd loved and supported him would be affected. Charlie took a breath and forced a half smile.

Wesley met him halfway with a hug. "Welcome back, buddy," he said, squeezing Charlie's shoulder.

Charlie moved to the center of the stage. The room was packed. Even the balcony seats. Wesley must have shared that he was going to be there. The outpouring of love he'd experienced from his church, and even strangers all over the world, made this moment intensely emotional.

He wiped a tear from the top of his cheekbone and raised his hands. "Thanks so much. Please, please everyone, have a seat." As the applause diminished, Charlie tried to collect his thoughts. He'd not prepared for today like he would have for a message. The words would come. He did have faith in that much. Taking a deep breath, he looked out at the sea of faces. Most smiling, some wiping away tears. These were his people, and he owed them more than what he could give them.

"First and foremost, I want to thank each and every one of you for your support." Charlie paused and cleared his throat, still pushing down his emotions. "As most of you know, I lost my wife and son just a little over six months ago." Charlie paused. "It's been the hardest thing I've ever been through." Charlie paused again and looked down before he pressed into the emotion. "You know in my ministry I have walked many individuals through death and tragedy but never fully understood it. Not until now. I wish that I could say I am okay, that I could stand before you today as a leader strong with conviction and strength." Charlie looked over at Wesley, who stood arms crossed on the side of the stage with a thumbs-up. He drew a breath and continued. "I wish I could say that I have been faithful and prayerful, coming out on the other side of this as an example to each of you, but right now I can't." His attempt to keep his emotions in check was brittle as his chest caved into a sob. "I'm sorry," he said, turning to the back of the stage and squeezing his eyes shut with his fingers. *I got this. I got this.* As Wesley stepped forward, Charlie waved him back. He had to do this alone.

Charlie turned around to a sea of red noses and audible sniffs. "I am really sorry. I am trying to hold it together." He paused and then looked up as a smile covered his face. He pinched the end of his nose and drew another breath. "You know this season in my life reminds me of a precious memory with my son, Chan. We'd just removed the training wheels from his bicycle." Charlie smiled, lost in the memory. "The little guy was bursting with excitement until he realized what it all meant. So, his little face went from smiles to frowns as I removed the training wheels from his little blue bike. He kept saying, 'Doddy, Doddy, I'm skeered.' That's how he said it too," Charlie chuckled. "So, I put his helmet on, snapped the strap under his little neck, and eased the bike out of the garage. Meanwhile, he was on my heels telling me how afraid he was. So, I took a knee beside him, looked him squarely in the eyes, and said, 'Chan, I am right here, buddy. I am your daddy, and I promise I won't let you fall.' His little face scrunched up with more concern than a little one should have, and he said, 'Are you sure? Are you positive? 'Cause if I fall, it's gonna hurt real bad.' So, I placed my hands," Charlie said with his hands on two imaginary shoulders, "on those tiny shoulders, never losing his gaze for a second, and said, 'I will be beside you every step of the way.'"

Charlie wiped away a tear, holding one hand over his heart. "And I was. I never let him fall, even though he continued questioning me as I ran along with him. I never left his side." Charlie paused, pushing his hands into the front pocket of his jeans, looking for strength in the gray concrete beneath his boots. He looked up and with an even tone said, "It wasn't long before he was riding that bike like a champ. He just needed to know I was *there*, and I *was*, because I am his father."

This was the hard part. "I've made a decision that I hope you will all support. I am taking some time away."

Audible sighs danced throughout the auditorium.

"I am not sure what that looks like right now or for how long, but you will continue to be in good hands. I wish I could say that I had answers, but I don't. I just know that I am in a place where I have to find a way to trust and forgive enough to remove *my* training wheels. See, I know He is there," he said, pointing up and then patting his heart. "Always has been because He is a good Father. When I figure out how to be the leader that you all need and deserve, when I am flying solo again with no training wheels, I promise you I will come back and share my journey."

Wesley stood on the side of the stage with a puzzled expression on his face. Charlie knew that Wesley would be upset that he'd not discussed this with him and the board, but he knew Wesley would forgive him and have his back no matter what.

Charlie looked back across to every corner of the auditorium and said, "I know this comes as a surprise not just to you but to the leaders in this church as well, and this is not a decision that I've made lightly," he said, noting Wesley with his arms crossed swaying back and forth. Charlie could tell he was miffed. "I believe in this church and its leaders. I ask that you, too, support any and all decisions they make regarding the future of this church for they, too, love it just as I have from the very first meeting in my college dorm room. I will be off the grid for a while, but I will keep in contact with Pastor Wes, who will, in turn, provide you with updates. I want you all to know how grateful I am for your support these last months." Charlie paused. "This church—these very walls and the walls of every single location—have housed so many people as they stepped from the darkness into the light. This church will always serve as a reminder of God's goodness and grace. The mission of this church has always been to minister to and serve those in need and cultivate a love for Christ, and that mission will continue."

He surveyed the room one final time, noting the view from where he'd stood so many times. He wanted to remember the hum of energy around him, the heat from the lights above, the feeling of all eyes on not just him but Jesus. Charlie untucked his hands, braiding his fingers together in front of his chest. "From the bottom of my heart, I love this church, and I love you. Thank you so very, very much."

The silence that followed was expected. They had every right to be angry and confused. And then, one by one, they stood—erupting into applause, shouts of love filling the air, and a piece of Charlie's broken spirit found its way back into their forgiveness.

Now he just had to recover all the other missing pieces.

Charlie stood at the door of his office again. It was cluttered with so many memories. He felt overwhelmed packing it all away. He'd not thought to bring any boxes, making it that much harder. Silence filled the room.

"So, what's next?"

Charlie turned to see Wes, red-eyed, leaning in the doorway.

"Well, I rode my bike for the first time in longer than I can remember. It felt good. I have to get out of this place for a while. I need to retrace my steps and see what God has planned for me. And I have to find forgiveness. I lost something, man. I gotta get right, right with myself and the Lord."

"So, where are you going?"

Charlie paused. "I'll let you know when I get there."

"Really?" Wesley asked with agitation.

"Really. I promise. I will call you in a few days when I settle in," Charlie said, collecting the framed picture from his desk. "I need to leave today, so I won't be able to address our staff members here or the other campuses. I will put together an email when I get settled."

"Then I guess this is it. What about your office and all of your things?"

"Well, I guess if I decide to come back, with the support of the church, I will have an office. Otherwise, you can box it up and put it in my garage. You know where I hide the extra key. If you wouldn't mind, go by the house every so often and just make sure it's still standing. I'm probably gonna put it on the market at some point, so it needs to be in okay shape." Charlie looked around. He could feel the walls that once housed his passion closing in on him. "All right, so I will call you in a few days, okay?" Charlie said, opening the door.

Wesley pulled him in for a hug. "Man, take care of yourself. I will be praying for you. You know that, right?"

"Yep. I got this, man. Really," Charlie said, forcing a smile and turning to leave. "Oh yeah, and don't get any bright ideas about my chair. You been eyeballing it since I bought it. I plan to be sitting in it somewhere."

Wesley laughed. "Yea, that couch is nice too."

Charlie smiled, knowing he was going to miss Wesley. One more loss, one more moment of saying goodbye to someone who encompassed his world through years of memories.

Part Three

Chapter Nineteen

Within moments of pulling out of the church parking lot, he knew where he needed to start. I-75S bustled with life as Charlie looked over his shoulder and merged left toward Macon. Lost in thought, he wondered if his life would have been different had he not gone into ministry. What if he hadn't decided to build a church that touched millions across the globe? What if they'd started a small church in a small town and left it at that? Would his wife and son still be alive? *Most likely*.

Before long he was passing the sign reading Sinclair 10 Miles. He inhaled and tightened his grip. It was time to pick at the edges of this band-aid of ache and pull through the stickiness before ripping through the stinging pain. Somewhere in the tiny town that he had called home for the first chapter of his life was the salve he needed to put his life back together. He wasn't remotely sure what that looked like, but it beat withering away in his gated community.

Cornfields spanned as far as the eye could see on both sides of the road. The population had grown from twelve thousand to eighty-five thousand, allowing for a Publix grocery store and a Walmart super-store, but it still felt like the edge of nowhere to Charlie.

Over the years, Main Street had morphed into a handful of bou-tiques, a shoe repair shop, a bakery with outdoor seating, a sports bar, and a handful of that retail stores that sold everything from knick-knacks to leather goods. Before turning off of Main Street, he passed Jeremiah's Diner on the left. He would definitely stop in to see his friend as he'd done during his visits in the past. Jeremiah always updat-ed Charlie on the changes over a plate of french fries.

Charlie stopped at his daddy's mailbox, taking in the place that housed so many memories. Giving the bike just enough gas to bump over the curb and onto the driveway, Charlie inhaled a combination of fumes and sadness. The old house hadn't changed much with its black shutters and small front porch stoop. For the last five years, Charlie had paid a landscaping company to keep up the yard. But they'd ob-viously missed him this month and maybe last month as well, as the grass was just above his knees.

He'd felt the pull to put the house on the market several times in recent years before remembering that his mama took her last breath there and the walls were saturated with her memory. He could also sit on the back stoop and see his daddy handing him a Pepsi after they had worked together on a project in the garage. The bricks of that house built the foundation for the life that he'd loved and lost.

Charlie slowly made his way to the back of the house and parked in front of the garage, which was home to a thick layer of English ivy, no longer revealing the cracked bricks beneath. He turned off the engine and removed his helmet, his riding boots firmly planted on the tall brush. He removed the bungee cords holding his duffel bag in place and made his way to the rickety screen door, taking the stairs deliberately. "This place is a freaking mess," he muttered, scanning the backyard before retrieving the spare key from under the weathered black rubber mat.

The old screen door creaked open, and Charlie took a breath, plac-ing his bag and helmet on the tiny kitchen table. The light switch was buried behind a stack of moving boxes. The sides read Elroy Nettles Room 333. Charlie grazed the words with his fingers and sighed. *Why am I even here?* Sadness pulled at his throat. "There is no way I am dodging these for Lord knows how long," he said, and he collected the boxes one by one and placed them in the storage space just beneath the stairs.

Now Charlie flipped the switch, but nothing. He made his way around the house, and each switch revealed no light. *Seriously*, he thought as he took out his cell phone. He dialed Southern Electric and Gas and opened the blinds, coughing as dust billowed from them. Charlie eased his jacket off with one arm while clutching the phone against his shoulder. A nasally operator finally said "Hello," reminding him of an episode of Charlie Brown. She proceeded to tell him that they'd not received a payment from him in over six months.

Six months. Had Marianna meant to stop paying for the upkeep of this place to spite him? Or had she just forgotten? Another question he would never have the answer to.

He slept late from the long journey the day before, and when he woke, he knew the first place he would go was Jeremiah's. A tall glass of cold iced tea and some good conversation was long overdue.

Charlie eased off the gas pulling into a space at the front door. The pristine awning and fancy letters spanning the glass reading Jeremiah's Diner evoked a mix of emotions. The majority of his youth had been spent within these now-expanded walls. When Abigail and Wesley were busy, he'd sit at the bar and talk to Jeremiah about the best wood to use for whatever project they were working on. They shared a mutual love for building and creating beauty with their hands. Jeremiah always took time to marvel at every single birdhouse that Charlie brought to him, asking questions and thanking Charlie before strategically placing it on one of the shelves in the corner of the restaurant.

Jeremiah was an example of the man that Charlie aspired to be. He shared a kind word with everyone who stepped over the threshold of his diner. He was a loving husband and father, and he gave back to Sinclair with every opportunity that presented itself. Whether he was donating his famous pecan pies to the women's auxiliary or mowing a disabled veteran's lawn, he was always giving. When Charlie butted heads with Elroy, it was Jeremiah who helped Charlie make sense of his daddy's temperament. He often wondered if his mama took Jeremiah aside before she died and asked him to look out for her baby boy. If she had, Jeremiah more than kept up his end of the deal.

The familiar aroma of fried chicken welcomed Charlie as he turned off the engine. Heat clung to him like a swarm of gnats as he pulled off his helmet. Charlie looked over his shoulder at the heat rolling across the pavement and shook his head. Sitting outside was as inviting as dipping his body in honey, but Charlie eased off of the motorcycle and made his way to one of six black wrought iron tables. A young couple with a little boy about Chandler's age walked out the front door and smiled at Charlie as the dad slung the boy high atop his shoulders. He smiled back at them, searching for his breath. When would he stop feeling like someone had punched him in the stomach at every turn? *How am I ever going to feel normal again?*

He looked out across the parking lot at the awnings on the other side of the road, marveling at the growth that had taken place. The distraction allowed him to catch his breath and push the hurt back to its proper place.

"Hello there, old friend."

Charlie opened his eyes as Jeremiah hobbled out of the door carrying a menu against one of his crutches. Charlie stood to help him, but Jeremiah motioned for him to take his seat. Their hands met over the table with a familiar shake.

"Jeremiah, what happened to you?" he asked, looking at the blue cast starting at his knee and working its way to his ashy brown toes.

"Well, this old man decided to climb up a ladder and take a short cut back down," he said with a laugh.

Charlie smiled. "Please, sit down," Charlie said, motioning for Jeremiah to take a seat.

Jeremiah leaned his crutches on the wall behind them and hopped to the seat gingerly. "You do know we have tables inside, right?" he asked, rolling the back of his hand above his brows.

"Not ready to run into anyone just yet." Charlie rested one arm on the table, leaned back in his seat, and ran his middle finger in tiny circles against his thumb. Distractions allowed him time to get his emotions in check.

Jeremiah broke the silence. "Just in the nick of time," he said as a twenty-something girl with sinewy limbs and short dark hair placed two iced teas on the table in front of them. "Thank you, Allison."

She smiled, clasping her long, thin fingers together at her chest, exuding awkward charm. Her dark, pouty lips revealed perfectly straight teeth and the smile of a shy cat. "Can I get you something to eat?" she asked, her gaze dancing between the two men.

Charlie looked at Jeremiah with a knowing nod of the head.

"He'll take a cheeseburger all the way with two sides of fries," Jeremiah said, and Allison turned with a curtsy, opened the door, and disappeared into the low hum of people. "I've been meaning to follow up with you since…you know…you lost Marianna and Chandler. I left a couple of messages for you but wasn't sure if you'd even gotten 'em. I was at the service for them, but you were bombarded with people, so I slipped out intending to make another trip to pay my respects. But then I had to go and do this to my driving foot," he said, patting his right leg.

Charlie coughed into his hand to buy more time before he spoke. He had to let the wave pass. "I don't remember much of the funeral or the days right after. I do appreciate you being there, Jeremiah."

"Hasn't been a day since it all happened that I haven't remembered you in my prayers."

Charlie's teeth ground his bottom lip. "Thank you. I appreciate that," he said hoping, the conversation would shift to mindless banter. "I need all the prayer I can get. It's been hard."

"I know, Charlie," Jeremiah said with a pained look. "So, you just taking some time to catch your breath, get away from the big city?"

"Something like that, I suppose." Charlie shifted in his seat, willing away the urge to break down.

Jeremiah sensed his struggle and spoke up. "Without sounding trite, son, God will work with you in the midst of this pain you are feeling."

Charlie shook his head as anger welled up. "I'm sorry, Jeremiah. I'm just struggling."

"Well, son, struggle is natural right now with what you've been through…but we serve a mighty God, one that would never leave or forsake us."

Charlie shifted in his seat as tears welled up in his eyes. He looked up at Jeremiah, searching for the words to transition out of the heaviness that was wrapping around him.

"You know, Charlie, days like this you should cool your heels in the lake. There's just something healing in the waters." Jeremiah paused and looked into the distance. "I swanny, time sure does fly. It seems like yesterday you kids were coming in my diner smelling like lake water with the glow of summer all over your faces. Or you with one of your birdhouses under your arm."

Charlie cleared his throat. "I don't know that I have ever thanked you for putting them in the diner and selling them for me. Times were pretty lean when Mama died, and the money came in handy. Why anyone bought them is beyond me. Especially that first batch when I was figuring it all out." They laughed. "You probably had to give them away as departing gifts to people leaving the diner," Charlie said, feeling at ease.

"I thought you did a mighty fine job. Heck, I still have a few of them scattered here and there. They remind me of the young man that carried my wife's groceries in the back door of this old place and the kids that started a firestorm among the church ladies with that sardine stunt." They both laughed aloud. "I thought I would never hear the end of that one the following Sunday at services. Those ladies were just beside themselves and couldn't understand how my Sally managed to have a clear tailpipe," Jeremiah said, eyes gleaming.

"Yeah, I had to pick a switch after that one for sure. The good Reverend Nettles was none too happy," Charlie said, reflecting back to rolling with laughter as he, Abigail, and Wesley watched through the tall reeds of grass. "Those were some good times, Jeremiah, for sure."

"Yes, they were. You know we have to hang onto the good times to get us through the bad. Amen."

"Amen."

"You know, I always knew you was gonna do something big. You were too big for this little town, Charlie."

"I don't know about that. But I also don't really know why I'm here." Charlie took three long gulps of the sweet tea, savoring the cold against the lump of emotion in his throat. "There really isn't anything left for me here anymore. No offense."

"None taken." Jeremiah smiled.

"I think the walls were just closing in on me at that house, and well, I needed to either get out of there or lose what little bit of sanity I have left."

"I know that feeling," Jeremiah replied with kindness in the crinkles of his eyes.

Charlie paused. "You know I am so sorry I didn't make it back here for Miss Sally's funeral. I was in Europe on church business, and by the time I got back, it was too late. I hope that you at least got the card and flowers that I sent. I am really sorry. She was one special lady."

"I did, Charlie, thank you, and yes she was something special," he said, glazing over for a brief moment. "You hadn't lost your daddy much before. No apologies here, my friend."

It was his turn to lift the mood. Charlie took a sip of tea and shifted in his seat. "So, I hear ole Judge Alford's place is on the market. Boy, you talk about getting in some trouble. We were always sneaking over there."

Jeremiah laughed. "It's been on the market for about six months now. His estate is gonna make some money if they ever sell that place.

His family is trying to sell it in the shape it's in. Fancy that. I will say, though, there are some nice houses around the lake now. It's really built up."

"The last time I was out there, he'd added a dock, but there was still a lot of woods. Place hadn't changed much."

"I don't think they believed in change, that's for sure. I have a feeling it's going to be on the market for a minute, green Formica countertops and all. The value is in that land and that beautiful view of the lake."

They continued to talk about everything from the weather to how long it took Jeremiah to build his new workshop, and they settled into what felt like the first normal meal with another person Charlie had eaten since his family died. It was well needed and overdue.

He waved goodbye to Jeremiah, slipped his helmet on, and watched his old friend hobble back inside. As he pulled out of the parking lot, he looked to the clear blue sky above him filled with white, billowy clouds and mouthed, "Thank you." For the first time in a long time, it felt right.

As his daddy's neighborhood approached in the distance, Charlie decided to take a quick detour, and within minutes he was pulling onto the old dirt road adjacent to Judge Alford's property.

As he walked to the water's edge and stripped down to his boxer briefs, the lake glistened with a thousand diamonds. The water was just cool enough to remind him why so many summers were spent in its midst. He floated on his back, soaking in the majesty of the sky above and the muffled quiet. This day was turning for the better. He floated and swam until dusk, savoring the peace that he'd found, allowing his mind to wander into an abyss of blank thoughts.

Chapter Twenty

The garage door rolled open and creaked to a stop. It smelled of oil and dust. The workbench that Charlie'd hovered over in his youth, lost in thought, crafting birdhouse after birdhouse, was cluttered with dirty old rags. Parkinson's disease had stolen Elroy's meticulous nature, leaving him scattered much like the tools littering the various surfaces in the garage. Charlie placed a hammer on a hook that extended from the bare pegboard on the wall. His eyes analyzed the boxes labeled Christmas on the wooden shelves along the walls. Dust covered his fingertips as he ran them across his mama's cursive handwriting. *If only*, he thought, brushing his hands across his gray V-neck T-shirt.

Just as he turned to pull the tattered tarp from his daddy's truck, something caught his attention out of the corner of his eye. A black yard debris bag. "I'll be," Charlie said, easing the bag off to reveal the roofline of Abigail's birdhouse. How had it gone unnoticed for so long quietly tucked away in a corner?

Charlie shook out a dusty cloth and wiped away the years of dirt that had collected. The familiar sound of her voice rang in his ears. Her eyes, the tone of her skin in the golden light of a summer dusk so clear in his mind, all taking him back to another hurt. Suddenly the betrayal times two flushed him with a rush of heat. "I loved you both, and this is what I have to show for it," he growled.

His answers were not in Sinclair after all. He should've known better.

Within the hour he was back with a flatbed full of mulch, a power washer, paint, and brushes. Cardboard boxes lay flat, tied together with twine. It was time to pack up his past and haul it to the closest Goodwill. The sooner he cleaned it all out and prepared it to sell, the better. He'd start on the outside and work his way in. The exterior wood around the windows and fascia boards below the roof line needed a good painting—white with black shutters. First, Charlie retrieved the garden hose from the side of the house and plopped it onto the grass beside the garage. He'd start by pressure washing it.

Sweat poured down his cheeks as the sun raged high in the sky, but adrenaline didn't allow him to slow down. Before dusk, he'd pressure washed the house and the garage, the driveway, and the front porch, along with the stoop at the back door. This was his job now. Packing up and leaving the past behind.

⊂○⊃

Light filtered through the dust particles floating above Charlie's face as the electric clock on the bedside table read six a.m. Charlie tucked the checkerboard quilt under his chin and stared at the louvers spanning the closet doors, listening to his heart thudding in his ears. The previous night's blank slumber had turned into a dream about Marianna just before he woke up. It was the first time he'd dreamed about her since she died, and her image was so vivid that he could still smell her perfume. His heart yearned with anger. She was telling him that she had never loved him and that she was taking Chandler and leaving him to be with Jonathan Myers. In the dream, Charlie was screaming "I hate you" with such veracity that it stole his breath.

Until now, Charlie wasn't curious about Jonathan Myers. The pain of loss was greater than his desire to learn more about the man who changed his stars. He would not allow Jonathan Myers to be anything more than a common criminal. But post nightmare, he wanted answers. He wanted to know more about the monster who had stolen his life. *What made you snap, Jonathan Myers?*

Charlie reached over and took his phone from the nightstand. Before he could second-guess himself, he touched Search and held his breath. He scrolled past the links to the murder; that wasn't what he wanted. He clicked on Facebook, then to Jonathan's page. He scrolled through his friends. No Jonathan. He clicked on Piper's page next. Her last post was before the murders. When Jonathan's name appeared, Charlie swallowed into the urge to vomit. His finger tapped the name. Charlie stared at his profile picture. Jonathan Myers stood with both arms flexed and with a wide smile. His tank top was plain and white. "Wow, you are a super cheeseball," Charlie said, touching the photo section.

Fitness memes and random quotes filled his feed. "If you ain't first, you're last," Charlie said aloud. "What a walking cliché you are." Charlie continued scrolling. "A video. Hmm." Charlie sat back down on the bed and tapped the start icon. It revealed Jonathan Myers at the gym in the midst of a set of squats with what Charlie could only estimate as around a total of four hundred pounds resting on both sides of a weight bar. Testosterone and ego oozed from Charlie's phone. The video stopped, leaving Charlie perplexed. If he'd imagined whom Marianna would cheat with, it would not be this muscle head. He continued scrolling down the page through more pictures of Jonathan either flexing his arms or taking full-body selfies. "What were you thinking, Mar?" he said in a whisper.

Charlie held his phone up, fighting the urge to slam it to the floor. Instead, he closed the screen and turned off it off. "I've seen enough," Charlie said, grabbing his duffel bag and slipping on a pair of athletic shorts. He barreled down the stairs and out the front door and was met by a sticky heat. The street was quiet with the early-morning sun glistening off the dew-covered grass. Within seconds Charlie was easily clocking an eight-minute mile. Images of Marianna and Jonathan played on a loop as he pushed into the pain, houses and trees rolling into a blur meshing with his wife's face. *God, help me. I have served you and done your work. How could this happen? How could she betray me like that?* Charlie ran harder, Jonathan Myers's voice ringing in his ears. He wanted to scream and flail. "How am I ever going to reconcile this? You took away my opportunity to confront you, you narcissistic jerk! You forever changed the way I see my wife; you soiled my marriage, you killed my boy…" Charlie lost control and sobbed, heaving for air. He stumbled to a stop leaning on a lamppost, sweat and tears pouring down his face. He wanted to die.

"Son, you, okay?"

Charlie turned around, wiping his brow with the back of his hand. An elderly gentleman stood on the sidewalk wearing matching light-blue pajamas and a blue plaid robe tied loosely at his waist, clutching a folded newspaper to his chest. His calm eyes creased with goodness. "Son, are you okay?"

Charlie hung his head, shaking it as he cried. He wasn't okay. The man shuffled toward him slowly.

God, help me. God, help me, please.

The warmth of his crepey hand rested on Charlie's shoulder. "Are you okay?"

Charlie met his strangely familiar gaze only briefly before hanging his head again. Unrelenting pain extended from his heart like another appendage. He was too lost to speak.

"I don't imagine you want to talk right now, but if you don't mind, I'd like to pray over you, son."

"I'm not worthy of prayer," Charlie whispered.

"Well, I am going to disagree with you on that one. There isn't a problem or mistake bigger than our Lord." The old man gripped his shoulder with the same tenderness Charlie'd gripped Chandler's with, assuring him that he would not leave his side. His words were a symphony of praise and worship overflowing with compassion, humbling

Charlie to his core. The tears fell harder at times as the old man's voice shifted between fervor and faith. One moment morphed into another, allowing Charlie to absorb the kind words of this stranger who felt unmistakably familiar. Finally, he lifted his hand from Charlie's shoulder but not before giving thanks with a soulful amen.

Charlie's eyes remained closed as he rested in the bosom of peace. In that moment he felt closer to God than he'd felt since he lost his family. He wiped the remnant of a tear from the corner of his eye and lifted his head to thank this man for his kindness. Never had he been the recipient of such unbridled compassion.

He anticipated meeting the old man's kind eyes with a thank you—but he wasn't there. Charlie turned a complete 360 surveying the street in both directions. Nothing.

He continued turning in every direction. Where did the man go? Surely, he would've heard him shuffling along the sidewalk making his way back toward one of the houses nearby.

He cradled the back of his head with both hands, trying to make sense of what had just happened. He looked around, and the only movement was a pair of squirrels scurrying after each other up the base of a pine tree. He was dumbfounded.

Renewal filled the summer air. He wasn't sure what had just happened, but he was certain that Divine Intervention had played a role.

⸺◦⸺

The months unfolded as the leaves changed colors, and the air danced, morphing into another season. Charlie's days were spent reading his Bible and working on the house. His spirit had changed colors just as the leaves had swept across the front lawn with deep hues of orange and gold. He still struggled with forgiving, and that ache was not subsiding in God's word, but the house was freshly painted with new hardwoods, and every room was packed up except his mama and daddy's.

With the house completed and ready to be put on the market, Charlie realized that it was time to move on. To where he didn't know, but the rest would play out however God saw fit.

Wesley was acting as senior pastor, but not in a permanent capacity, he'd told Charlie. The board said they were taking this time to reevaluate the direction of the ministry, but Wesley said they were really holding out hope that Charlie would reconsider coming home.

The puzzle of his life had been laid out and pieced together over the months as he swam in the lake, spent his meals with Jeremiah, and silently prayed for peace. But there was still one single piece missing. Maybe it was forgiving. Maybe he needed to truly release Marianna from her transgressions and say those words. But they were lodged in his throat and prying them out with prayer hadn't worked.

Charlie grabbed his coffee from the kitchen counter and stepped outside the back door as it clapped shut. The cool breeze carried on its back the smell of burning leaves. Charlie slid onto the swing admiring the work he'd done to refurbish the arbor. He inhaled, took a sip, and allowed the warmth to fill his chest as he surveyed the house, admiring the work that he'd completed. All new shutters, fresh paint, additional box shrubs lining the garage and backside of the house, and his sanctuary, the very swing he sat on. He knew in his spirit that God was healing him, one day at a time. He'd worked diligently to transform debilitating pain into a new life, one that would remember his son with smiles and not tears.

The beautiful blue skies above him were turning gray, so Charlie decided to head inside and finish packing up the house. The door of his parents' room creaked open. It smelled musty, unlike the rest of the house, and he could feel electricity in the air as he opened the windows.

Charlie grabbed a box from the hallway and placed it on the bed. He opened the half-full closet and began folding his mama's dresses neatly and placing them in the box. He'd forgotten how many different colors and fabrics she owned of the same style of dress. One in particular caught his eye. It was a pale lavender covered in deep-purple flowers. He could still see his mama sitting with her hands folded in her lap watching his daddy intently. Her eyes followed him as he moved around the dusty old tent sharing his special brand of fire and brimstone. Every so often her hand would land on top of Charlie's as if she knew that his anxious heart was stirring to get up and escape. Charlie held the dress to his chest as a smile parted his lips. He remembered just how pretty she was with her hair twisted into a perfect bun at the base of her neck. *I would give anything to see you in this dress again, Mama. You would've known exactly what I needed to hear to find my place again. You always knew.* A tinge of ache stung his heart as he placed the dress in the box.

Within an hour Charlie had packed up the closet and the chest of drawers. The wind was picking up outside as a blanket of darkness hid the few remaining clouds and a gust whipped in, blowing a film of colored leaves onto the bed and floor. Charlie rushed to close the windows. He wished he'd bought screens. He knew that he'd forgotten something.

A large raindrop landed on the outside of the window, closely followed by another until they were pelting the window ledge with light pops. Charlie found the smell of a fresh rain intoxicating. Every ten or fifteen seconds, lightning roared across the sky in bright, jagged bolts. By the looks of the deep-gray sky and the trees bending and contorting into unnatural positions, Sinclair was in for quite a storm.

Charlie might have forgotten the storm windows, but he was ready for something inside him to be washed away.

Chapter Twenty-One

Charlie awoke to "It Is Well" softly playing in his ear buds, which aligned perfectly with his mood. His heart was filled with a mission today. This was the day that he was going to place the final piece back into the puzzle of his life that had been so scattered for months. He lifted himself off the couch, opened the back door, and surveyed the damage. A plethora of leaves and tree limbs peppered the yard. But the air was cool and still.

Within twenty minutes he was fully dressed and climbing onto his motorcycle. The sky was a palette of pale blue with only smudges of clouds. Charlie knew that the motorcycle wasn't the safest idea with possible limbs and debris scattering the road, but he yearned to feel the air, still pulsing with energy, pressing against his body. There were a few downed trees and a lot of leaves everywhere, but for the most part, Sinclair seemed okay.

Charlie carefully maneuvered his way along the road to Lake Jenson, which greeted him with iridescent twinkles. He squatted on a mat of wet leaves, resting his forearms on his knees. The lake invited him into her cool waters, but today his agenda was closure.

Charlie inhaled. Renewal was in the air. He observed the play of light on the waters surface, enjoying her show. He picked up a smooth rock and ran it between his fingers, thinking. Finally, he stood up and walked to the water's edge. His body warm with intention, he skipped the rock along the glassy water's surface. "Thank you, Mama, for helping me find my way. I am so grateful for the way you always believed in me. You and Daddy made sure that I knew where I came from," he said, smiling softly. He marveled at the beauty of the sky and water melting into each other. "It's time," he whispered.

"Mar, it feels like a lifetime since we spoke." Charlie paused with an unexpected swell of emotion that he allowed to roll over him. "I've just been so angry, Mar. I still don't understand what made you do what you did, but I realize now that what happened, well, somehow, I had my part in all of it, a big part in it. I'm sorry that I wasn't the husband that you needed, and I am even more sorry that I didn't press you to talk to me and open up. I knew something was heavy on your heart, and I just tried to pretend we were going to be fine. I wish I'd done things different." Charlie lowered his head, tucking one hand in his front jeans pocket. He closed his eyes, took a long breath, and held it for a few seconds. "I forgive you, Mar. I forgive you for everything." His breath hitched. "Even Chan." A low sob filled his chest. "I know how much you love him, and you were always a good mom."

Charlie lifted his head to the sky and closed his eyes again, breathing through the hurt. "I take comfort knowing that he is with you and the Lord. I pray with all my heart that you are at peace knowing that I am at peace. I love you, Mar. I will never let what happened overshadow our life together. Not anymore. I am done with the anger." He took a moment. "Done." He paused. "And do me a favor. Pull Chan in real close and bury your face in those dark curls and kiss him for his daddy. Tell him how much I love him and that I will be counting the days until I see him again."

Charlie wept, allowing the anchor of hate hanging onto his heart to fall away, drifting into the darkness that had imprisoned him.

Charlie gazed up at the sky. "Lord, thank you for restoring my peace. Thank you for never giving up on me."

A shift had taken place within him, and Charlie was finally ready to accept the life he was in now, at this very moment. Today he would clean up the debris from the storm around his house and take the remaining boxes to storage, but not before stopping by the diner for one last piece of Jeremiah's pie to say goodbye to his dear friend.

Charlie sat on the motorcycle and slid the helmet over his head, but he could not take his eyes off the water, the light bouncing and twinkling. Charlie swept a tear away and hit the ignition. The combination of the lake, fresh air, and rumble of his motorcycle reminded him what it was like to feel again. More good memories than Charlie could recall had been made at Lake Jenson, in this very spot.

Charlie inhaled the cool air laced with fragrance and remembered the lazy days on its banks and the easy nights staring at the stars lighting her surface. It held many secrets, most of which would remain in the corners of his mind. He smiled remembering the times he and Wesley cannonballed from her banks to see who could create the bigger wake. Then Abigail's face appeared, reminding him of the tenderness that her blue eyes had evoked more times than he could recall. He wondered if she was happy and living a big life. She would always be part of the history that had led him to this moment and every moment before that. For the first time since she left Sinclair, he felt grateful for the part she had played in his life, and he forgave her as well.

"Thank you, God, for it all," he said aloud. "I'm sorry that it took me so long, but I know what you have in store for my future is beyond what I can imagine. I trust you, Lord, with all my heart."

Buried in the many years of his ministry were stories of redemption and forgiveness, but until now, he'd never fully grasped the unmistakable peace that accompanies it. The shift in his spirit was unmistakably beautiful.

When Charlie pulled up, Jeremiah was hanging a Closed sign on the front door glass.

"What gives, Jeremiah? You closing early?"

"Charlie, you have perfect timing." Jeremiah's forehead was creased with worry.

"What's up?" Charlie asked, removing his helmet.

"It's the church, Charlie. That big ole oak gave way last night in the storm and fell slap through the middle. That storm was a doozy."

"That's terrible, Jeremiah, but you file insurance and rebuild. Pretty simple."

"It would be simple if that crook of an accountant hadn't emptied the discretionary funds and let the policy lapse."

"That's crazy, Jeremiah. How could that happen?"

"He was way too smooth for my taste, but the church council voted to hire him, and well, here we are. We're gonna meet and talk about how in the world we are going to make this happen. You wanna come along? After all, it is the church your daddy loved."

"Sure, of course."

Within minutes they were pulling up in front of the old white church that Charlie was raised in. Sure enough, a large portion of the oak that had sheltered him, Wes, and Abigail from the sun on many Sunday afternoons was now penetrating the rooftop. He and Jeremiah sat in quiet disbelief as a group of people mulled around inspecting the damage.

"What in the sandhills are we gonna do, Charlie?" Jeremiah asked, leaning back and running his hands along the rim of the steering wheel.

Charlie couldn't believe his eyes. If his daddy were here, he'd be devastated. "Come on, Jeremiah. Let's take a look."

They both got out of the truck, still in shock by the destruction in front of them, moving into the group of people standing quietly. He could hear whispers of condemning it and everyone going to the big, new church a few counties over. Memories washed over Charlie. This church represented the foundation of his faith, and there was no way he'd let it be torn down and forgotten.

Jeremiah pressed his hand down on Charlie's shoulder. "You coming to the meeting tonight?"

Charlie could feel his plans to leave Sinclair today changing. "Wouldn't miss it."

Chapter Twenty-Two

Charlie stepped inside the double doors of the townhall amid chatter and people milling around. A long arm waved above the crowd. Jeremiah stood tall at the front of the room, guiding him to two empty seats in front of the podium. Charlie smiled politely as he made his way down the center aisle. It felt reminiscent of the many Sundays he'd stop and chat with people after finishing his message. Before the pressure of ministry pushed him straight to his office afterward, he had loved this time with the members. It provided him the opportunity to plug into the community and minister to those in need. It had been months since he had been in a setting like this, and it felt surprisingly good as everyone greeted him kindly.

"Hello, my friend. Come, have a seat. They're about to get started," Jeremiah said.

Charlie settled into the metal chair and folded one leg on top of the other. "Man, it looks like all of Sinclair is here, huh?" The room was packed, with people lining the walls and spilling into the hallway.

"Yes, sir," Jeremiah said, swiveling around and surveying the room as more people filtered in, lining the walls in the back and along the sides. "This town loves that ole church. It represents so much more than a building to the folks of our town."

"I have some pretty good memories of it myself, except for when I was stirring up trouble." Charlie chuckled. "I definitely shocked this place with my decision to go into ministry instead of landing in jail."

"You definitely gave it a go back then."

"I did, and that's why we have to come up with a plan."

"Well, I think it's going to boil down to money, my friend, and even if we all pooled our resources, I don't know if this town can raise what it would take. Enlightened Church is just one county over. I guess everyone could go there in the interim. Heck, maybe people want those big churches nowadays." Jeremiah paused. "No offense."

"None taken."

Pastor Dalton walked to the podium and greeted everyone with a warm smile and a prayer. Charlie lowered his head as his mind wandered to those formative years, and his heart raced as he pictured that land without the church on it. *Surely the people of Sinclair will find a way.* Charlie imagined all the people who had given their lives to Jesus in that church. He thought of the families who'd raised their kids in the very pews that were now damaged or broken. His heart ached for that little church in a way that was surprising and unexpected.

Charlie listened as people raised their hands and made suggestions for fundraising, while others suggested migrating to the other church until a decision could be made. Charlie read the pain on Pastor Dalton's face with each suggestion that they migrate to the other church and demolish the remaining structure. Voices escalated as opposing solutions volleyed back and forth. Charlie swept his hand along his neck, rubbing out the heat. It was becoming apparent what direction this meeting was moving, and he wouldn't allow it, not as long as he had air in his lungs.

Just as the energy spiraled into a heated debate, Charlie stood up waving his hands in the air. "Everyone, please calm down," He said as

Jeremiah shook his head at the dissention in the room. "Please listen, everyone. Please, this is not the way it should be." The room quieted, and Charlie took a breath. "My name is Charlie Nettles, and I grew up in this church."

There was an appreciative murmur around the room. They knew who he was.

"My daddy served as the associate pastor when I was a boy and moved into the senior pastor role before he retired." Charlie paused. "My mama and daddy loved this church, and even though as a boy I didn't appreciate it, as a young man I found healing within its walls. It was here that my passion for ministry was ignited, that I finally saw what God's will was for me. It was from my roots in this church that I was able to grow my own ministry. I am forever thankful for that. And that is just my story. I am sure each of you has your own testimonies and stories of faith. How can you just allow that to die?"

Charlie stopped and looked around, searching for support. "I know I haven't been back in Sinclair long, but I want to protect the history of this church out of respect for my mama and daddy and all the folks that were blessed within its walls. Can we all just explore the idea of rebuilding ourselves? That would eliminate some of the costs. And I am sure that with the generosity of this town, we can make this work. There is always a way when God is involved." His words resonated so deeply that he needed to take a breath. This was his family's legacy and, more importantly, God's. "Please, everyone, let's put our heads together. To start, where could services be held during reconstruction?" Charlie asked, hoping they would follow him down this path.

A young woman raised her hand. "I know that the gym at the high school is under construction, but how 'bout the cafeteria?"

Pastor Dalton responded, "That's a good idea. What else, folks?"

Charlie felt the energy shifting as people spoke up, making suggestions. He was about to ease back into his seat when a man spoke up from the back of the room.

"Where are we even supposed to get the money from, Mr. Mega Church Pastor?"

A low rumble filtered through the air. Charlie was surprised by the underlying hostility in his voice. He took a breath and turned in the direction of the voice, but the man had sat down. "My church didn't start out as a megachurch, sir. It took time and the kindness and generosity of the members to build it up one brick at a time. Right now, I think we need to consider what options are available to continue to worship. That is what is most important. I don't have all of the answers, but I am here willing to commit all of my resources to be part of rebuilding."

Charlie peered into the eyes of the people in the room as a heavyset woman with readers resting on the crown of her head spoke up. "We can all agree that this church is our home, but it doesn't change the fact that our church is broke. That thief took away our ability to make that choice," she said with tears in her eyes.

Charlie felt the solution stirring in his soul. An unmistakable clarity washed over him. "I've seen a lot of loss in the last year, and one thing I know for sure is that even when you feel broken, God is working to put you back together. And this church is no different. As some of you may know, I lost my wife and son this past year. It's been the hardest season of my life." Charlie cleared the debris of words from his throat. "But I have to believe that from such a horrible tragedy, good can come, that purpose can arise from the deaths of my wife and son. I need to believe that I can still raise beauty from these ashes." Charlie paused. His words were lost in the emotion he was trying to bridle until he looked at Jeremiah, whose kind eyes encouraged him to keep going. "It would do my heart good to work alongside you fine people and rebuild the church."

Charlie had one final plea as he searched the faces in every corner of the room. "If we give up because of money, the enemy wins. Let's at least lay our offerings at the feet of the one that gave it all for us and see what he can do with it. Can't we just trust Him to provide?"

Silence filled the room.

"Absolutely, Charlie," Pastor Dalton said with emotion.

Charlie pulled his shoulders back, looked up, eased the wallet from his back pocket, and retrieved a blank check. Jeremiah pulled a pen from his front pocket and handed it to him. Charlie turned to the banquet table in front of the podium and leaned down. Without hesitation he wrote a check to the church, giving them the remainder of the insurance money, leaving just enough to sustain himself until he could sell the other house. *This is for you, Chan.* Charlie looked around, grabbed a basket that was on the table, folded the check, and placed it in the basket. "I prayerfully ask that you all search your hearts and ask the Lord what He would have you do to rebuild the church and, further, His kingdom. It may take some time, but we serve a mighty God," Charlie said as he handed the basket to Pastor Dalton.

"Thank you, Charlie. I agree—we do serve a mighty God, and I believe in the generosity of this community. Would you all mind bowing your heads so that we can go to the Lord in prayer?"

Charlie languished in the familiar energy of the Spirit moving around the room, changing hearts and minds as Pastor Dalton's words drenched his soul, satisfying his thirst for prayer. He allowed the words to weave through and saturate the fabric of his spirit. A calm energy worked its way through the room. Humbled, Charlie swiped a tear away with an amen.

Pastor Dalton passed the basket around, and when that spilled over, a few gentlemen removed their hats and passed them around until they were spilling over with checks and cash as well. When everyone had made their contribution, Pastor Dalton gathered the collections and placed them on the front table as Charlie took his seat beside Jeremiah. God was present, and it had never felt better.

"You did a good thing here tonight, Charlie," Jeremiah whispered in his ear.

When the meeting adjourned, Charlie stood up, smoothing out his jeans. His head was swimming with ideas. After the offering and prayer, they'd strategized how to get the church built. Charlie was prepared to work.

⸺◦◦⸺

The following week consisted of cleaning up the debris, removing the tree, and taking the church down to the studs. They would leave the old foundation and add on for the newer spaces. The number of volunteers varied each day but averaged around fifteen. It reminded Charlie of the many hours he'd spent at each of the locations with a hard hat on, inspecting the progress. It was like adding brick and mortar to the part of God's kingdom that wasn't visible to the naked eye. Blanketed in satisfaction, he walked over to the water cooler and poured a small cup. Out of the corner of his eye, he saw a tall figure approaching. He turned to a welcoming grin as Wesley held his arms wide.

"You know I couldn't let you have all the fun."

"Dude, you are the last person I expected to see," Charlie replied with an embrace.

Wesley looked around with surprise. "Man, I didn't anticipate all of this. I mean, this really is a total rebuild. I had no idea."

"Yeah, it's going to be pretty amazing when we finish. So, where's the tool belt, man?"

"I definitely plan to dedicate some time to help for sure, but…" Wesley took a breath. "My old man is sick. I came home because Mom says he's not doing good."

"I'm sorry to hear that. I thought they were in Florida, though."

"They have been. But Dad suddenly wanted to come home. Then apparently yesterday Dad had some kind of health crisis and passed out at the house. Don't know the details, but it doesn't look good. I wanted to stop by here real quick because the good reverend will want a progress report, I am sure."

Charlie watched the pain on Wes's face and wished that he felt something other than a dull anger. Reverend Turner was one of those dark spots on his spiritual record that had been hard to erase. He'd never gotten past the way he had treated him when he was devastated about Abby. He'd held her location hostage for months while Charlie felt like he was dying a slow death.

"So, how long are you here for?"

"Don't know. I kind of left that up in the air."

"How's your mom holding up?"

Charlie listened as Wesley described her struggles, all the while hoping he would bring up Abigail, but he didn't.

"You're welcome to crash at the house with me. I could use the company."

"I may do that. Mom insisted on sleeping at the hospital. My room at the house hasn't changed a bit. Pamela Anderson is still on the back of the door."

"The fact that she never made you take that poster down proves that she never went in your room."

"She was probably afraid of what might jump on her."

They laughed.

"So, I guess I'll let you get back to it. You look good, Charlie. This church building looks like it's feeding your spirit. I can see a bit of the old Charlie again. I'm glad for you, man."

"Thanks, Wes. I feel like I have been to hell and back. I am definitely better, but I have a ways to go yet."

"You got this, man," he said, placing his hand on Charlie's shoulder. "I believe that with all my heart."

Watching Wesley leave to take care of his father took Charlie back to the last time he had seen *his* daddy alive. Inhaling deeply, he faced what was the foundation for a new beginning. Charlie knew in his heart that Elroy would be right there beside him, working as his hands to rebuild the church one piece of wood at a time.

At that moment, Charlie realized what was missing.

"You ready for a full day of church building, son?"

"Jeremiah," he said, glad to see his friend, "yes, sir, I am."

Jeremiah studied Charlie. "You okay?"

"I was just thinking…how do you think this town would feel about a series of good old tent revivals? The kind my daddy and Reverend Turner had?"

"You know, son, that might be just what this town needs right now," he said with a smile. "And quite frankly, I don't think that big ole church that we've had to attend is this town's cup of tea anyway."

Ideas rushed over Charlie.

"I say we run this by Pastor Dalton and see what he thinks," Jeremiah said, waving to get his attention. The pastor put down a two-by-four and joined them. Charlie excitedly shared ideas that he felt would resonate with the members young and old. Pastor Dalton agreed only if Charlie would partner with him and, instead of doing one, they had them every Sunday until the church was finished. Charlie's heart leaped. This would honor his mama and daddy like nothing else.

Wesley showed up at the door a few hours later with a pepperoni pizza in one hand and a liter of Pepsi in the other. "Dinner is served," he said, setting the box of pizza on the coffee table.

"Nice. Smells good," Charlie said, waiting for Wesley to give him an update. Charlie took the Pepsi into the kitchen, poured two full glasses, and grabbed a package of paper plates from the cabinet.

"So, what's the story with your dad?" Charlie asked, pulling a piece of pizza apart, leaving a string of cheese hanging in the air before sweeping it into his mouth.

Wesley shrugged and took a bite. "I don't know. He seems fine. They're running more tests, but so far nothing has come up."

"Well, I guess that's good news, right?"

"I had a feeling that Mom may have been looking for some quality son time."

"Well, in that case, shouldn't you be with her?" Charlie said, taking his last bite of the crust. "Man, that's good pizza."

"All her sisters are there, I had to clear out. Realistically, I need to get back home. We're starting a new series this Sunday and I feel like I need to be there."

Charlie listened intently as Wesley talked about the series and how he and the other teaching pastors were approaching it. He felt like he was standing in a train station watching everyone he knew pulling away leaving him behind.

"I think your approach will really resonate in the messages." Charlie struggled for a response. "So, it sounds like you guys have it all under control," he said, standing up and taking his plate to the trash can.

"Man, I'm sorry. I didn't mean to talk around you. I'm just pretty on fire about this series. Been working on it with the team for weeks tweaking."

Charlie fell into the chair in front of Wesley unsure of how he felt. "Nah, you don't need to tiptoe around me. I made a choice, and I'm working on my stuff. It is what it is."

Wesley leaned onto his elbows. "You know you can come back. The door hasn't been shut for good. I mean, you started the church, Charlie. You are just as much a part of it as you have ever been."

"I do have some cool news to share." Charlie smiled.

"Do tell."

"I'm pretty sure that we are going to do a series of tent revivals while the church is being built. Pending the committee's approval, of course."

Wesley cocked his head sideways. "No way. Actually, I think that's a great idea. And right up your alley. You do tend to go all Pentecostal from time to time."

They both laughed.

Suddenly a muffled ringtone vibrated from Wesley's pocket. "Hmmm, that's Mama," he said, and then, low, "Hello."

"What's up, man? Everything okay?"

"Actually, no. I gotta run. Apparently, Daddy took another turn. I need to head back to the hospital."

"What can I do? Let me grab my coat," Charlie said with genuine concern.

"I appreciate it, but let me go see what's happening, and I'll give you a call as soon as I know more. Mama may be overstating again, but she sounded upset."

Charlie followed Wesley to the front door. The question rose in Charlie's throat before he could stop it. "So, will Abigail be coming here?" He felt embarrassed before finishing the sentence. *Where did that come from?* "Never mind. I don't even know why I asked that." Shame flushed in his cheeks.

"I doubt it, Charlie. She and my old man haven't spoken since she left."

Charlie felt like Wesley knew more than what he was saying, but now wasn't the time to press in. "I guess Africa is pretty far to come anyway." Charlie waited.

Wesley looked at the ground and then met his gaze with an expression mixed with equal parts sadness and what looked like shame.

"Charlie, you and I need to talk, but now isn't the time," he said, stepping onto the front porch. "You've done a great job on the house. It looks good."

"Thanks, man. Let me know what I can do."

"Will do," he said with an embrace and a pat on Charlie's back.

An hour passed as Charlie wrote pages of ideas for the tent revival series that he couldn't wait to share with Pastor Dalton. He was completely lost in thought when the phone on the coffee table startled him.

He was met with a low sob. "Charlie, my daddy is gone."

Charlie sat up immediately. "I'll be right there."

By the time Charlie reached the hospital, he had reconciled enough with the lingering animosity of the past to focus 100 percent on Wesley and his family. As he approached the nurse's station, he spotted Wesley huddled in the hallway with his mother and a few people he didn't recognize. Wesley looked up with bloodshot eyes and walked toward him. They embraced. Wesley's mother, Ellen, eased over to Charlie greeting him with warm hug, speaking quietly in his ear. "It's good to see you, Charlie." His heart ached for her. "It's been way too long." A sad smile inched across her face. "And I hope you received the card and flowers we sent to your wife's service. I've kept you in my prayers."

"I did. They were beautiful. Thank you, and I'm sorry for your loss," he said with sincerity.

Ellen had always been kind to Charlie, but her loyalty as Reverend Turner's wife never wavered or allowed for her to share information about Abigail. Even after Charlie married and started a new life, the Turners treated the subject of Abigail's absence as taboo. *Could this be a turning point? Will I be able to find out where she's been and why the big mystery? What I did that was so wrong that I needed to be permanently shut out of the one person's life that I absolutely loved with every ounce of my being?*

"Again, I'm so sorry, Ellen. Is there anything that I can do?"

"No, I just appreciate you being here."

With that, Charlie left not sure what to feel.

Chapter Twenty-Three

The day started out a chilly forty-three degrees but climbed to an unseasonably warm sixty-eight degrees by lunchtime. Charlie peeled off his flannel shirt, revealing a long-sleeve Henley. Fatigue weighed on him as he watched the construction team begin to rough in the plumbing.

"I'm surprised to see you here," Jeremiah said, approaching Charlie and handing him a sweet tea in a Styrofoam cup. "Here, I brought an extra."

"Thanks; I need that about now. Why surprised?" Charlie asked, and he took in a mouthful of the sweet liquid.

"I just figured that you would be with Wes and the family."

"I went to the hospital last night. Wes let me off the hook today. Sorry, that came out wrong, but they are planning the service. Let me ask you something, Jeremiah."

"Okay, whatcha got?"

"What would you do if you'd prayed for answers to something that had weighed heavy on you for a really long time, but you finally tucked it away, just decided to move on. And what if you felt like those answers were at your fingertips, finally, and you were scared out of your mind to go there?"

Jeremiah looked at him sideways with a knowing smile. "Well, I'd say where's that big faith of yours, Charlie? I don't believe in accidents. I'd say when the time is right—and you'll know when that is—you'll be ready. There are no mistakes, son," he said, squeezing Charlie's shoulder.

Charlie smiled, but his stomach was flopping like the Brim he and Wesley would catch in Lake Jenson and throw into the bottom of a bucket half full of water. "I know. You're right," Charlie said, reciprocating with a squeeze to Jeremiah's shoulder.

"Well, we best get to it. This church here ain't gonna build itself," Jeremiah said, striding toward the commotion.

He wanted to know the truth as sure as he was standing in front of the church that had shaped his youth. *Surely she will be at her daddy's funeral. This is my opportunity to finally know what really happened. I will not let her leave again without answers. She owes me that much.* Charlie closed his eyes. *Lord, show me your will and your way. I don't want to pass up this opportunity, but something just feels off. Please lay it heavy on my heart when the time is right. Until then please give me peace.*

Charlie opened his eyes and allowed the calm to mold around his heart. "Thank you," he whispered under his breath.

<hr />

Charlie stood in the Turners' living room that evening. A tinge of embarrassment flushed his face when he realized that the extra squirt of Armani cologne might have been too much. Guilt flooded him as he inventoried the extra measures he'd taken, including ironing his French blue button-down, gingerly working paste through the unruly waves of dark hair, and assessing his look twice before walking out the front door. *Why do you still affect me like this?* Charlie wondered as he scanned the family pictures on the mantel hoping to see Abigail's face. They were all pretty self-explanatory, except for one. In the sea of pictures, one of Abigail caught his eye. She stood in front of a large, rustic wooden cross wearing shorts, a white T-shirt, and hiking boots. Her blond hair fell just below her shoulders, and her eyes were bright with joy. Charlie glanced over his shoulder, coughing into his hand to deflect the boulders pounding his ribcage. He'd not been to their house since the week she left for college. Not much had changed except for this picture. He couldn't tell where she was, but based on the vast grassland behind her, he assumed Africa.

A hand landed on his shoulder. It was Wesley, with his wife, Donna, beside him. "Hey man, thanks for coming." They embraced.

"Wouldn't have it any other way," Charlie responded, scanning the room before greeting Donna with a hug.

"Mom said you were here. I was out back with some of Daddy's old friends reminiscing about his early days doing tent revivals. You know something about that, doncha, Chaaalee Boy? I think your idea has this ole town excited."

Charlie's mind wandered to the front row of a dusty old tent nestled beside his mama as his daddy moved from behind the pew like he was gliding across hot coals. Thinking of those days made him smile.

"Honey, I'm gonna go grab a bite and give you guys a few minutes," Donna said with an easy smile, and she made her way through the throngs of people milling around the house.

Questions burned Charlie's throat until he couldn't wait another minute. But before he could speak, Wesley leaned in and whispered, "I know that look, and I don't know if she's coming. Mama said she wasn't even sure."

Charlie's heart thudded. "Have you talked to her?"

"I have, but she wouldn't say one way or the other."

More questions peppered Charlie's throat, but he stood quietly, not sure what to say, while searching the room for answers.

"Look, man," Wesley said, leaning in again. "I know that you two have unresolved stuff between you, even now, so many years later. I know you never got the answers you needed. I hate that for you, man.

I do. But when she left, she pretty much disowned my dad, and they stopped talking."

Anger rushed to the surface. "If that was the case, then why didn't she reach out to me?"

Wesley looked uncomfortable. "Look, man, this is not the time or place to do this."

"Do what?" Charlie asked. "You know something, don't you?"

Wesley shifted from side to side, crossing his arms. "Dude, you know you are my brother."

Charlie cut him off. "But she's your sister. Is that what you were about to say?"

Donna walked up and handed Wesley a blue Solo cup. "I thought you could use some tea." Assessing the looks on their faces, she asked carefully, "Did I interrupt something?"

She looked at Wesley, who was shifting from side to side, arms crossed tapping his chin.

"We're fine here." He paused. "We are fine, aren't we, Charlie?"

"Yeah, man, we're good." Suddenly he needed air. "I hate to cut out, but I'm beat. I'm gonna go say bye to your mama and take off. I am so sorry for your loss, man, I truly am," Charlie said, giving Wes a tight embrace.

Charlie made his way into the kitchen, where Mrs. Turner was talking. She turned and took Charlie's hands. "Thank you for coming," she said, lowering her head. She paused as though she couldn't find her words. Finally, she looked up at him. "Right now, Charlie, I need you to know something that has weighed heavy on my heart for years," she said, easing them away from the people she was standing with.

"Okay," Charlie said, taking a breath and easing his hands into his front pants pockets.

Ellen's eyes filled with tears, and her voice trembled. "My husband was a good man, Charlie. Everyone loved and respected the work he did with his ministry. He loved the Lord and served Him well."

Charlie nodded his head. She was right. He was well respected and had brought many souls from the darkness to the light. He would give Reverend Turner that.

"But there was also the man that I lived with, the one that was the father of my children, the man that led our household." She blotted the end of her nose with a tissue. Ellen looked around as if to make sure no one was within earshot before she spoke. Everyone seemed to pick up on the privacy needed for their exchange and left them to talk. "The way everything was handled when Abigail left…" She paused. "The way you were left to suffer with no answers"—her eyes filled with pain—"was very difficult for me and for Wesley. I know that you boys even came to blows at one point, almost costing you your friendship. And you have to know, Charlie, that I have always loved you like one of my own. You practically grew up in our home."

Emotion welled up in Charlie's throat.

"I hate that he's gone now. The years were softening his heart." She looked at Charlie squarely. "I feel like given more time, he would have made peace with this, with you."

Charlie listened intently. He didn't know how to respond.

"That's why I think it's time for you to know the truth. But it's not my truth to tell," she said, reaching into her simple, square, black leather shoulder bag and retrieving a pen and paper.

Charlie's heart leaped.

"I know that a lot of time has passed, and you've moved on with your life, so you can do with this what you will, but I feel like this is the right thing to do. I feel like this is what the reverend would want to do had he been given more time." She scribbled on the pad.

His heart thudded in his chest, but his expression was steadfast and calm.

"I'm giving you Abigail's contact information. If you want answers"—she hesitated—"it's only fair that she be the one to give them to you." She handed him the paper, holding it firmly in his palm. "I need to get back. There is much planning to do." She leaned in, brushing her warm, soft cheek against his. "Thank you, Charlie, for coming tonight and being there for Wesley. You've always been such a good friend." And with that she turned and made her way back to the group.

Not until after he'd escorted Wes and Donna to their car and seen them safely off did he dare to pull the piece of paper out of his pocket. *I cannot believe it. That number has a US area code. How long have you been back, Abby?* The key to answers he'd waited years for was finally within his reach.

The funeral came and went. No Abigail. Charlie started each day with prayer and reading extra scriptures about forgiveness and peace. He rubbed them into his spirit like a healing salve, repeating them over and over in his head as he worked on the church.

Some days he struggled with the idea of forgiving Reverend Turner and Jonathan Myers, but most days he struggled with guilt over the struggle itself. He'd come to the unwelcome conclusion that he was not nearly as spiritually evolved as he thought a man should be who leads thousands to the cross, but he was determined to overcome— that much he was sure of. Plans for the revival were in full swing and provided Charlie with a sense of purpose and hope that he couldn't put a label on, and he did not want to try.

Early signs of spring offered Charlie a sense of renewal every day. This day Charlie awoke from a vivid dream about Chandler. They were walking in a lush green meadow with flowers blanketing the ground and towering mountains in the distance. He could still feel the warmth of his son's tiny hand in his when he opened his eyes. Only this time he didn't cry. He couldn't remember the details of the conversation that they'd shared, only the joy that Chandler evoked as he spoke. To hear his son's voice was a precious gift. He knew now more than ever that his little boy was happy and okay and that a change had taken place in his heart.

He had a meeting with Pastor Dalton at ten. But he knew there was something he had to do first.

Within the hour, Charlie was on his motorcycle heading for the Heavenly Homes Memorial Garden. He pulled in and parked the bike on the gravel drive just across from a large oak tree in the distance. There was no one to be seen, only clear blue skies filled with herds of billowy clouds easing along. A gentle breeze cascaded around him as if to say "Welcome." His heart felt solid yet pliable. The long-awaited resolve that he'd longed for was finally within reach. Charlie stepped gingerly around the gravesites, careful not to walk over anyone's plot. As he approached the large oak tree, he smiled, carefully taking a seat on the concrete bench in front of two gravesites. His forearms rested on his thighs as he searched his spirit. The words flowed slowly but deliberately.

"Mama, Daddy, I know I haven't been out here as much as I should since I got home, but I have been working hard to become the man you raised me to be. I wanted to make sure that I could come here and be that man. I've known for a while now, deep in my heart, what I needed to do to be whole again…but couldn't seem to find a way past the hurt.

"I wanted to come here to lay witness in front of you both because I knew that with you it had to be from the purest part of my spirit in order to truly honor you and to honor the Lord. Mama and Daddy, thank you for raising me to be the man that I am today, and thank you for introducing me to the Word. I certainly didn't understand why planting those seeds were so important back then, that's for sure. But I wouldn't have survived this last year if it weren't for the foundation that you both laid so rooted in the gospel. And I know it's time to make this right."

A surge of emotion crashed over him, and Charlie fell to his knees and lowered his head. "Lord, I come to you with a servant's heart." Tears flowed freely as he continued. "I know that it has taken me way too long to get to this place, and for that I ask your forgiveness. I've known all along that you have been waiting patiently for me. You came after me, Lord, leaving the ninety-nine. I don't even know what I did to deserve that, but today I am here"—Charlie paused with emotion and then continued—"with my mama and daddy, who served you well, asking you to forgive me for my unforgiveness. I've wrestled pretty hard with this, harder than I could have imagined. Before the worst tragedy imaginable erased my world as I knew it, the one that I thought to be so well constructed into a pile of rubble. I'm so grateful you never gave up on me. It's taken a lot of pain to bring me here. But I am here, and for that I will be forever grateful, Lord." Charlie paused, resting his hands on his thighs, face to the sky, eyes closed. He inhaled deeply, fully engaged. He took his time allowing the words to work their way softly into his throat, resting on his tongue. Charlie savored the warmth of the sun on his face, quietly inviting the Holy Spirit into this sacred moment. Finally, he opened his eyes, gazing at his parents' headstones before speaking.

"I forgive you, Reverend Turner. I know you had your reasons for the decisions that you made, and with God's grace, I accept those decisions. Maybe one day, in His timing, I will get the answers. But today I let go of this."

Charlie inhaled deeply. "Lord, this one has been even harder, but I know today for the first time that I am finally ready. And I mean that. I forgive you, Jonathan Myers. I pray peace on your troubled spirit and release all anger and hate in my heart for you. May God's peace blanket you just as he has wrapped me in the warmth of His love, allowing me to find my way through this."

Charlie sat in silence, peaceful. No more tears fell. He took his place back on the bench, his forearms resting on his knees, with his mama and daddy.

Chapter Twenty-Four

After much planning, the day arrived for the first of the three tent revivals, and Charlie got up extra early to shower and pray. He stood at the backdoor sipping on his coffee, soaking in the beauty of the colorful annuals and the fragrant wisteria. Grateful that his typical pre-message nerves were not quite as bad, Charlie made his way down the stairs and sat on the swing, easing back and forth. Birds in the trees sang, as if to entertain him, and he swayed with his thoughts, sipping coffee and allowing the message to sink into his spirit. He'd been working on it for days, adding the final touches just before bed last night. No question, he was gradually getting back in his jet stream. Finding forgiveness had unclogged the murky gunk from his spirit and reestablished the connection that had been missing for a while, the one that provided him with inspiration and details for his messages.

Charlie felt a gratitude unlike any he'd felt before. In a mere few weeks, the church would be complete, along with the revivals, and it would be time to move on. Part of him longed to go back into ministry full-time with Wesley and the church that they started together, but another part of him, the part that hadn't fully recovered from the loss, didn't want to turn back. Charlie sat for a moment imagining his life back in the senior pastor role with the pressures and constant travel. He sighed. In the same breath, he recalled the charge he felt onstage when delivering a message that would change people's lives. *I can't turn my back on my gift, but what is my life supposed to look like now?* Charlie glanced at his watch. It was time to go.

Charlie's breath hitched when he pulled into the empty parking lot. This was the first time he'd seen the actual tent up and ready to go.

Memories flowed as he sat in his daddy's truck with his hands planted on the steering wheel watching people arrive and take chairs into the tent for setup. He couldn't help but think about Abigail and the first time they'd met. He opened the Bible on his lap and pulled out the frayed piece of paper. He knew that today was the day, and without hesitation he dialed.

Before touching the Send button, he whispered, "I trust you. I know that everything you do is for my good." *Send.*

In an instant there was a long beep followed by the words "The number you've reached has been disconnected." Charlie dialed again. Surely there was a mistake.

He dialed the number three more times but got the same message.

He placed his phone on the console in disbelief.

Then he laughed and shook his head, not sure why he was laughing. "Okay, I get it." He didn't understand the buildup to this, but he trusted, and that was what was important.

"Okay. I'm good. I got this," he said, smiling to himself. "All right, Lord, I am yours. Do with me what you will. Use me today for your purposes. Open my spirit to your word."

Charlie made his way to the tent and met Jeremiah, who was carrying two armloads of metal chairs.

"Well, good morning, Pastor," Jeremiah said with a wink.

That felt good. "Back at ya, Jeremiah. Here, let me help you," Charlie said, easing some of the chairs from his arms.

They made their way into the tent and lined the chairs up evenly along the back section, completing the setup. The podium at the front was the original from the church that they'd had in storage since replacing it some years ago. It was caramel-colored wood and had a carved cross on the front. He imagined his daddy standing behind it with his hands firmly planted on the sides, leaning into the fire of his message. He could see his mama in a lavender shift dress on the front row, left hand lifted to the heavens.

"So, you ready for today?" Jeremiah asked, brushing one of the seats with his hand, removing dust.

Charlie stood, arms crossed, warm from the inside. "I've never been more ready. Have you seen the pastor?" Charlie asked, looking around.

"Not yet, but I'm sure he isn't far behind. He's preaching before you, right?"

"Yeah, he'll take the first half, and I'll take the second. I appreciate him giving me this opportunity."

"Personally, I can't wait. Ya'll gonna set this place on fire. I just feel it in my bones."

Charlie laughed. "Well, I have to admit I did go a bit Pentecostal a few times with my sermon notes in the living room this week. It reminded me of those days watching my daddy pacing the floors buzzing with the Spirit."

"You definitely get it honestly."

"As my daddy would put it, 'Charlie, you come from a long line of conduits of the Holy Spirit.'"

"I can hear him saying that" Jeremiah responded. They paused and took in the transformation taking place around them. "I have to tell you, Charlie, I have seen the Lord hard at work on you for months now, and it shows. You remind me of the young man that took the podium just before leaving Sinclair," he said, placing his hand on Charlie's shoulder.

"It feels different now. I'm in a good place, a grateful place. I didn't know if I would ever make it back. But I'm here and only by the grace of God."

"Amen," Jeremiah said as the pastor's wife, Joanne, walked up with a worried look on her face.

"Excuse me, gentlemen, but may I have a word with you, Charlie?"

"Of course."

"I'm gonna go see what else I can do. I'll catch up with you later, my friend." Jeremiah tilted his head toward Joanne. "Ma'am."

Joanne was in her mid-sixties with shoulder-length blond hair sculpted into careful curls sprayed in place firmly. She wore navy-blue slacks with a flowered cotton blouse and matching cardigan. A simple gold cross rested just below her collar. "Charlie, I hate to be the bearer of bad news, but David has a stomach bug, a bad one. Bless his heart, he tried to come and didn't make it out of the driveway."

Charlie felt calm. "I'm so sorry to hear that, Mrs. Dalton."

"Well, you're gonna have to do the revival on your own. He was so disappointed. He said ya'll been working on the sermon together, and he was just beside himself with excitement. Heck, the whole town is."

"Now listen. You tell the pastor that everything is going to be fine. I am pretty familiar with his sermon notes, so I feel confident that I'm okay."

"Are you sure? I mean, this was supposed to be both of you, and he just feels terrible about this."

"I promise you, Mrs. Dalton, I've got this," Charlie said, relaxing into the calm serenity emanating from deep within his soul.

She sighed. "Okay. Well, I better get home and take care of him. He's just pitiful, Charlie. Pitiful." She lowered her voice to a whisper. "He's a terrible patient. Big ol' baby when he's sick. Course, he'd never admit it."

Charlie shook his head. "I understand. Most men are," he said with a smile. "Give him my best and assure him that I will be fine."

"I know you will, Charlie. I think you might put our little one-horse town on the map. I only wish I could bear witness to your sermon today." She sighed. "Okay. Well, I must go," she said, and she made her way out of the tent as the choir filed inside donning purple robes.

The choir director greeted Charlie with a handshake and made her way to the front of the tent to practice. Within minutes song echoed in and around the tent, filling it with an energy so powerful, warm, and humbling that Charlie was certain this day was going to shake a lot of foundations. Charlie took a seat in the back row and lowered his head in prayer. Enveloped in a soulful hymn, he was suddenly overwhelmed with doubt. Beads of moisture formed on his lip as he looked up at the choir director with a forced smile. Placing his head in his hands, he wondered if he would even remember the message. Charlie took two slow, deep breaths attempting to regulate the thundering in his chest. Finally, he decided to shut down the negative self-talk and power through this message. Within a few minutes, people began filing in, what Charlie referred to as the front-row early birds. He brushed his damp palms along his pants. He greeted each of them, warmly shaking their hands and making small talk. His heart rate slowed enough to eliminate the quiver in his voice as he continued greeting people.

But soon Charlie's heart raced with excitement as the tent began to spill over. More people than he could count shared stories about his daddy's ministry and how well thought of he had been. He'd never been prouder of his heritage.

Just before time to get started, his phone rang. It was Wesley.

"Hey, man, what's up?" Charlie said, moving to the outside edge of the tent for privacy. "Are you ok?"

"I just wanted to call and tell you how happy I am for you. How are you feeling?"

"It actually feels kind of surreal and wonderful all at the same time. You know it's like this is exactly where I belong right now. And turns out Pastor Dalton is sick, so I'm doing the whole thing," Charlie said, swallowing hard.

"Dude, that's crazy. God has something bigger for you. I just feel it." He paused. "On a different note, Mama told me 'bout last night."

Charlie lowered his voice. "She did. I tried Abs's number, and, well, it was disconnected."

There was a pause. "That's strange. Dude, I am really sorry. Look, I know it took a lot for you to do that. Get past this, and let's hook up and talk, just me and you."

"Okay," Charlie said. "And thanks, Wes. I'm just trusting God, and honestly, man, I'm ok." Charlie looked at his watch as nervous energy ping-ponged in his chest. "But it's that time, so I gotta run."

"All right, preacher man. Go in there and give them a good old-fashioned dose of Nettles brand ministering. Elroy and Mary Francis would be so proud of you."

Charlie's insides lit up at the mention of their names. "That's exactly what I plan to do."

"You know why?"

"Why?" Charlie asked.

At the same time, they said, "Because you come from a long line of conduits of the Holy Spirit." Then they laughed.

"Thanks for calling man. It means everything."

"You know if I could be there, I would."

"I do. I'll tell you all about it later."

They hung up just as the choir was moving into a soulful hymn. Charlie stepped into the tent and made his way to the front row. He wondered if the message would get stuck in his throat. Hands were clapping, and the energy began permeating his anxiety like a warm, heavy summer's rain. He'd forgotten what it felt like to be washed by the waters of the Most High. The words "thank you" ran on a loop in his mind until the singing stopped. It was time. Charlie stepped behind the podium and looked up. *I'm home.*

Once Charlie began to speak, words of power and grace flooded from him like a river white capping with the Holy Spirit. Charlie's body hummed and buzzed as if a hive of bees had taken up residence in his chest.

"I am in awe of God's grace. I hope that today will ignite a passion in you all to love and serve one another, to forgive and, most importantly, to trust in His plans because, my friends, He does not make any mistakes. Can I get an amen?" A resounding amen echoed throughout. "I remember those early years of ministry, the fire in my belly, the desire to fill that space of emptiness in the lost souls with the promise of hope, redemption, and forgiveness." Charlie paused. "I remember feeling like somehow I had it all figured out and so it was my calling to lead those that had gone astray because I knew the answers, and I was going to lead them down that path of righteousness," he said with emphasis. "Looking back, I felt somehow immune to the drama." He made quotes with his fingers. "I had a wife, what I thought was the ideal marriage, a nice home. Then came my son, and all the while I am building His kingdom brick by brick, church by church. People would even say to me, 'Charlie, how do you do it? You have it all.' I think my chest would puff up a little because I actually bought into the hype. My hype. I believed that I was somehow immune to the trials and tribulations, that I was not created to experience that—no, I was the shepherd, and God wanted me to tend to His flock, and that protected me from all of the drama of the actual sinners. I thought living right and doing His will equated to immunity to the suffering of those that I was ministering to." Charlie paused and looked around. "I got comfortable. I got so comfortable walking everyone else out of their weaknesses and mess that I didn't even recognize my own. You know that saying, I could not see the forest for the trees?" he asked, gaining agreement from the crowd. "Well, that was me. I was standing in the middle of a dense forest and couldn't see one single tree.

"Then one day just a year ago, my whole world fell apart in ways that I could not comprehend or even process. I lost my wife…my son…and the firm foundation that I'd stood on since I started this ministry crumbled beneath my feet. I was lost, broken, defeated," Charlie said, walking along the front row. "I'm sure many of you can relate to that feeling of, Will I ever come back from this? How can I trust a God that would allow this to happen? Why would he choose to make a mockery of my life when I was doing everything right? Can you relate, my people?" he asked emphatically, and heads nodded in agreement. "How could He turn His back on His faithful servant? I asked myself over and over.

"So, I stopped trusting Him. Instead of leaning into my faith, I became engulfed in the flames of anger and unforgiveness. And that's when the enemy stepped in. You know what I am talking about, don't you. When you are weak and angry, thirsting for something, anything to quench that need for understanding," he said, raising his voice," he steps right in, telling me that it was all my fault that my family was gone, that I was being punished for being a bad husband and father, that I should have put them before God, and since I didn't, I deserved to suffer." Emotion welled up in his chest as he spoke. "The enemy preyed on my desperate need for answers by providing me with a reality that fell in line with my grief." Charlie paused, wiping his temple.

"And I believed every word, every whisper, every lie because I was broken. Because I wasn't leaning into what I knew to be true." Charlie grew silent. "Until one day in the midst of my darkness, He reminded me that He would never leave me nor forsake me. He reminded me of the sacrifice that He made for my salvation, and He reminded me that He would always leave the ninety-nine to find me because He *is* and always has been the ultimate shepherd," Charlie said with passion. "Have you ever felt so lost and alone that you could not even pray? Have you ever wondered, God, why have you forsaken me? What did I do wrong?" Charlie said, clasping the sides of the podium as the energy rose.

"My friends, I say this to you as someone who has sat in the ashes, who has wandered through the wilderness, who has allowed the enemy a seat at my table." He paused. "As someone who thought that he was somehow *above* this kind of struggle." He held the gazes of his people. "But when I finally invited Him in, when I stopped believing the lies and remembered His promises, my eyes were opened. I began to see one tree at a time. And eventually those trees gave me life, they gave me forgiveness, they gave me redemption."

Charlie looked around. "My friends, no matter what you are here facing today, I want to testify to you that you are never alone," he said, building volume. "Lay your sorrows, lay your worries, lay your transgressions—lay it all, everything you have at the feet of the one that gave it all for you. He is waiting on you today. He wants to take your hand and walk beside you. He will lead you out of the darkness and into the light because that's what He does," Charlie said powerfully. "He shows up, He shows out, He makes beauty out of ashes, He leads you from darkness to light, he leads you to forgiveness that once felt impossible to find," Charlie said, pacing the aisle as people stood up shouting amen.

Adrenaline-filled words boomed like a transformer struck by lightning. "There is not a problem that He cannot solve, an addiction that He cannot walk you out of, a marriage He cannot save, an illness that He cannot cure. He is a miracle-making, powerfully loving and giving, show-up-and-show-out kind of Father," Charlie said, raising his hands. "Can I get an amen."

The tent erupted. Charlie's insides buzzed as he looked around, moved back to the front, and took his place at the podium. The invitation to salvation was given, and over half of the people in the tent fell to their knees. Charlie prayed over the multitudes until the very last person was saved.

"Can I get some praise today for Jesus?" Charlie said as the tent erupted, and the choir sang one final song before the closing prayer. Charlie bowed his head, moist with the sweat of salvation, and prayed from the deepest, most gifted part of his spirit.

Afterward, he stood outside the tent for over an hour, just as his daddy would've done, shaking hands and talking to people. His heart was full, but he still wondered if he could've done better.

Jeremiah walked up as the last of the worshipers were making their way to their cars. He extended his hand and pulled Charlie in for a hug, "Son, I haven't seen nothin' like that since your daddy was alive. Just as I thought—you set this town on fire."

Charlie smiled and embraced Jeremiah. "Thank you, my friend."

"I think it's safe to say that you have found your way back. That was powerful."

"Jeremiah, I am just so humbled right now." Emotion lodged in his throat.

"You made something real special happen in this little town of ours today, and everyone can't wait for next week. I haven't seen or felt the Spirit like that in a mighty long time. I'm proud of you, son, and happy that you're finding your way."

"Thanks, Jeremiah. If it weren't for your friendship, I don't know where I'd be. This season in my life continues to teach me so much. Honestly, I didn't know if I would survive it at times. I'm just trying to find my way back. And I know we serve a good God." Charlie flashed a reassuring smile at Jeremiah as beads of self-doubt blended into his sideburns.

"Amen. So how about I treat you to a piece of that pecan pie you love so much? Heck, I will even throw in a plate of fries."

They laughed.

"I think I may take you up on that. I just need to get a few things before I head out."

"Okay, well, I'll see you at the diner."

"Sounds good, my friend."

Charlie stood in the center of the tent in silence. He was in awe of what he'd experienced but concerned about the trepidation he had felt before the revival began. He yearned to ease back into the familiarity of his former life. He hoped that somewhere in the vast rubble of pain, he'd found a steppingstone to start reclaiming his life. He closed his eyes and inhaled, whispering, "Lord, help me do this."

Chapter Twenty-Five

The tent was quiet.

Charlie made his way back toward the podium to collect his Bible. Taking a moment to catch his breath, he closed his eyes and gave thanks for all the salvations today. Suddenly, he heard a voice.

"Charlie?"

His heart leaped. He turned around, and standing in the opening of the tent was Abigail. She still looked just like an angel with the sun shining through her hair. No question she was the same girl he'd said goodbye to all those years ago. Her hair was a bit shorter and darker, but otherwise she hadn't changed. She still took his breath away.

"Abs." Charlie shook his head. "Is that really you?"

"Yeah, Charlie, it's me," she replied. They slowly made their way toward each other without breaking their gaze, meeting in the center of the tent. Without hesitation they embraced. Charlie held her close, taking in her familiar fragrance blended with lilac. The intimacy of their embrace stirred up emotions, some painful. Charlie pulled away and stepped back in disbelief that she was standing right there in front of him.

Abigail suddenly looked uncomfortable as she responded to the distance Charlie had created.

"I'm sorry. Maybe I shouldn't have come," she said, turning to leave.

Charlie stepped forward. "No, please. Don't go. I just…I'm surprised to see you. What are you doing here?"

"It was just time, Charlie. I should have come sooner."

Charlie wasn't sure how to respond.

Abigail's shoulders fell back into place, and she forced a smile. "Anyway, you were pretty amazing today."

Charlie could barely breathe. "You were here this whole time? How did I not see you?"

"I kind of stayed in the back. I thought it was better that way."

She was still the most beautiful girl he'd ever seen. *How is this even possible?* Charlie tried not to stare. The questions were slowly bubbling to the surface, bringing with them an ache that he had felt so immune to only moments earlier.

"I was hoping that we could go somewhere and talk. Maybe sort through some things."

"Okay," Charlie responded, out of balance. "Did you drive here?" he asked.

"Actually, no," she said, pointing to the bicycle she had ridden growing up leaning against a tree.

"How about we just put it in the back of the truck, and you ride with me?" he asked, hopeful that she would oblige.

She nodded with a small smile. "There's no one to mind me being alone in a truck with you now."

Charlie lifted the yellow beach bike into the back. "This ole bike has some mileage on it."

"Yeah, most of it between our houses."

"That seems like a lifetime ago."

"Yes, it does," she said.

He walked to the passenger side of the truck. Their hands landed on the handle at the same time. She eased her hand away and looked at him. "Charlie?"

"Yeah?" His heart landed in his throat.

"It really is good to see you again."

He smiled back and opened the door. As he walked around the back of the truck, he stopped for a second. Seeing her in the front seat felt like a dream. *How could this be?* The corners of his mouth turned up, and he shook his head. God's plan was definitely taking an interesting and unexpected turn.

Charlie slid behind the wheel and turned the key, at a loss for words. When he looked over, she had a quiet expression on her face, the one that usually was present before they had a serious talk. He remembered it well.

"You okay?" Charlie asked. When their gaze met, he realized that time had overshadowed the memory of how blue her eyes were.

She nodded, and Charlie pulled out of the parking lot.

"So, where are you taking me?"

"The lake. I have a blanket in the back that we can sit on. It's such a pretty day. Unless, of course, you would rather go somewhere else."

"No, that's perfect."

Being near her filled him with unexpected conflict. A part of him wanted to take her in his arms as soon as the truck stopped, and another part wanted to scream at her for ever leaving.

He pulled onto the dirt road leading to *their* spot, eased the car into park, and grabbed an old blanket from the back of the truck that he'd used to cover some furniture. When he moved to her side of the truck, her head was lowered. He could tell she was on the brink of tears. Charlie opened the door, and she looked up with a slight smile.

They made their way down the path to the spot under the broad oak tree that looked just as it had the many times, they had taken shelter beneath its branches. Charlie spread the blanket out and allowed her to find her place first. He sat beside her, draping his arms around his knees. Sunshine danced and reflected off of the water, and Charlie was reminded of the comfort and pleasure they'd found in each other's arms in this very spot. He shook off the memory, afraid she might read his mind somehow. When he looked at her, they both chuckled. She was thinking the same thing.

"We had some good times here, didn't we?"

Charlie felt the heat rising under his shirt. "We sure did." Fire filled his cheeks, but he kept her gaze.

"You haven't changed at all," she said as if she was soaking him in.

"Neither have you," Charlie responded, melting into the ground beneath him.

They both turned away and looked out upon the glistening sky. Time hadn't watered down the intensity of their connection.

Charlie wanted to ask her where she'd been and why she had left, but the words felt lodged in his chest. "Can you believe how much this area has developed since we were kids?" he asked instead.

"No, it's crazy. I see Judge Alford's place hasn't changed a bit though," she said, leaning back onto her arms.

"No, it hasn't. It's actually on the market. Whoever buys that place will have their work cut out for them for sure."

Abigail looked at Charlie. Her eyes held a fear-tinged pain that took him back to the day they said goodbye. "Do you remember the last time we saw each other?" she asked.

"Of course, I do. I wish I'd known that would be it." Charlie picked up a smooth stone from the ground beside him and rubbed it between his fingers, watching the light dance playfully off the water. The pain returned.

"I need you to know that I had no idea, Charlie." She shook her head and looked up as if searching for the right words in the blue sky above them. "Gosh, this is hard," she said, folding her legs together and pulling her skirt over them. "That day something felt off. I just didn't know what…I should have never left."

Charlie tried to release the sudden rush of anger from his heart into the stone, skipping it across the water and looking directly at her. "Then why did you? Why did you leave me like that, Abs" he asked, surprised by the sticky web of grief spinning throughout his chest. "That nearly broke me. I need you to know that. I didn't think I would ever get past you."

"But you did, Charlie. And I don't blame you for that."

Charlie looked at Abigail sideways. "I'm confused here. How could you?"

She interrupted. "Wait, that came out wrong. I am sorry, Charlie. What I meant was you moved on, and I'm glad. You deserved happiness and a family." She paused, looking instantly embarrassed. "I'm so sorry. I just keep stepping all over my words." She looked down, taking a deep breath before looking back at him. Her eyes were gentle and sad. "I heard about your family, Charlie. I can't even begin to tell you how much my heart hurt for you." She placed her hand on his arm. "You've been in prayers every day since."

Charlie searched the clouds for a response. This was overwhelming. His emotions were all over the place, and the mention of his family made him feel like coming out of his skin, so he stood up and walked to the edge of the lake. Abigail joined him, and they stood together in silence for a few seconds before she spoke up.

"You know I have thought about this day for so long. I have rehearsed this moment more times than I can remember. It seemed a whole lot easier in the safety of my car, my house, my bathroom in the mornings while brushing my teeth, in the market while I sorted through the good apples and the ones that were bruised…" She trailed off into the memory before making eye contact with him. "But then I found out that you were happy. Then you were married with a baby on the way. I pretty much lost my courage by then and…" She hesitated. "And I didn't think it would be right to disrupt your life again, so I put it off, waiting for the right time, but it never came. Life just kept happening, and I let it. It was easier to drift with the current, ya know?"

Charlie was thoroughly confused by the combination of her words and obvious struggle. "No, I don't know, Abigail. I'm not following you. You could've picked up the phone at least once in the last ten years and told me. It's not like you left and I immediately got with

Marianna. Why didn't you call me? Days, weeks, years passed. Nothing. It made no sense. In my heart I knew that you wouldn't just leave me like that." He looked down, and said, barely audible, "God, I loved you." Charlie turned slowly to her, slipping his hands into his pockets. "You broke my heart."

Abigail looked away, pained. She turned back to him and held his gaze, at a loss for words.

Anger filled his eyes. "I was devastated. No one would tell me anything. Wes said you were doing mission work, and that was all I got. And the fact that it all sounded like a load of crap made no difference." Charlie paused. "And your daddy." Charlie turned to catch his breath. "I don't want to be disrespectful, but he was not kind. He didn't display the compassion of a Godly man with me. Not once."

Abigail crossed her arms, gnawing at her bottom lip. He could tell that she was searching for the best version of her story now that she was no longer rehearsing.

"Abigail, for cryin' out loud, tell me! We're here. We're grown up now, not two kids in love."

She looked up at him with tears in her eyes. "I was pregnant, Charlie."

Time stood still.

"What did you say?"

Abigail looked directly into his eyes, sobbing. "I was pregnant."

Charlie stepped back. Was she telling him the truth? There was no way that she would have kept that from him. Charlie's fingers raked through his hair, grasping it as he looked around, trying to comprehend what she was saying. Abigail stood, arms across her chest, red-cheeked and crying. She was shaking her head saying she was sorry.

Do I have a child, or did she have an abortion? "I want the truth Abby, the whole truth. Right now."

"Okay," she said swiping beneath her eyes. "That day, the last day...I left and headed to school. I started feeling sick on the drive, and it just got worse. It hit me out of nowhere. I got so sick that I went straight to the student health center. I couldn't keep anything down. That's when they did a pregnancy test. The first person I called was my mom. I was so scared. She and my daddy drove down that night, making me promise that I would not call you or anybody else until they got there. I was scared out of my mind, Charlie."

Charlie's heart was beating so hard he could barely breathe.

"When they got there, my daddy told me there was no need to unpack, that school would have to wait. I was devastated. I begged them to let me call you, but they wouldn't allow it. I was afraid, Charlie. I've never seen my daddy so mad. My mama just kept saying everything would be okay, even though her eyes told me something totally different. That night we stayed at a hotel while my daddy made a bunch of phone calls. He sent us out to get food, saying he would have this handled by the time we got back." She paused. "You have to know that I begged my mama to let me call you, but she wouldn't go against what my daddy said."

Charlie's feet were frozen in place. He could not believe what she was saying. *How could you?*

"So, when we got back that night, he told us both that I would be going on a mission. He had it all worked out. I would fly out the next morning and go live with a family that he knew through ministry work in Canada. Once the baby was born, I would go back to school, and I was never to tell a soul. I would give the baby up for adoption, and that would be it. Problem solved." Abigail became angry. "He didn't care, Charlie. I was so distraught. It's like I was spinning out of control along a cliff, and all I got from him was how ashamed he was of me."

Charlie watched her struggle remembering the effect her daddy had on her. He'd always made her feel less than. He wasn't surprised at how Reverend Turner had handled this. "I can barely wrap my mind around this, Abby. So, where's the baby, my baby?" Charlie asked, breathless.

"Let me finish. Please."

"Okay."

"So just as he said, I was shipped off to live with a family in Canada. They were good people, and we became very close."

"Stop for a second. Did they not have phones in Canada?"

Abigail sobbed. "Charlie, my daddy convinced me that you'd be better off without me and that if I really loved you, I would give you the opportunity to go to school and build a life. So, I did what I thought was right. Charlie, he shamed me. He made me feel like this was all my fault. It's all rather ironic considering the man he actually was."

Charlie listened, mouth agape in total shock. He needed more answers. "What about the baby, Abigail?"

"I fell in love with this little person growing inside of me. I knew I couldn't give her up."

Charlie's heart raced. *Her?* He looked away, trying to process her words.

"The family I was living with assured my dad that everything was worked out. The baby would be adopted, and I would go on their next long-term mission to Africa."

"So, you did go to Africa?"

"Just hold on. I gave birth to our daughter."

Charlie felt light headed. "I have a daughter?" he asked.

"Yes, Charlie. Her name is Francis."

Charlie cupped his mouth. "You named her after my mama?"

"I did. I know how much you loved her, and I needed you to be part of it somehow."

Emotion and fear welled up. "Where is she, Abby? Where is my daughter?"

"She's here, Charlie. My mom has her." Abigail stood quiet as if waiting for Charlie's response.

Charlie walked closer to the water, fingering his hair and trying to process the reality of what she was saying. He wasn't sure if he should yell at Abigail for keeping his daughter from him or take her into his arms in a joyful embrace, so he stood quietly, watching the clouds move across the sky. Finally, he turned to her and held her gaze. She looked as though she might crumble into a pile of dust at his feet and blow into the ripples of wake slapping against the bank.

"I'd like to meet her."

"Okay."

"Does she know about me?"

"Not until recently." Shame covered her face. "I told her you were dead."

Darkness encompassed Charlie's peripheral vision. *Don't pass out* ."You told her what?"

Abigail talked fast. "I know you're mad, and I don't blame you, Charlie, and I am so sorry. I am. Francis wouldn't speak a word to me for days when I told her."

"Then why, Abigail, why would you do that?" Charlie shook his head in disbelief. "I would have married you. I *wanted* to marry you."

"I was scared, Charlie, and if I could go back I would do it all different, I swear."

More anger bubbled to the surface, feeding the heat in his face as Charlie thought about the years he'd missed with his daughter. "So, she'd be what, like…"

"She's almost twelve." Abigail walked closer to Charlie, pleading. "Please, Charlie. I'm so sorry."

Charlie walked past her, grabbed the blanket, and headed toward the truck. He was fully immersed in the loss of his daughter's first years. "I can't believe you did that to me, Abby. I just…" Charlie stopped himself before he said something he couldn't take back. He opened the flat bed of the truck and removed the bike while Abigail stood crying. "Your parents' house isn't far from here. I'm gonna need you to make your way back from here. I…I just…I need a minute." He avoided her gaze.

Abigail took the handlebars. "You will never know how sorry I am Charlie."

He watched her ease onto the seat and pedal down the trail. When she was out of sight, he leaned onto his knees to catch his breath. *How could I have had a child all this time? Chandler had a sister that he never got to meet. Why would you do that to me, Abby?*

Charlie sat on the flat bed of the truck until darkness surrounded him. Depleted and confused, he finally slid behind the wheel and drove back to the house.

Chapter Twenty-Six

Charlie woke up after three hours of sleep and sat on the edge of the couch thinking of Francis. *I have a daughter.* A smile spanned his face as he pictured telling Chandler that he had a big sister. He imagined him jumping up and down, begging to meet her. The absence of that moment created an ache that Charlie leaned into, lowering his head. He prayed for peace and guidance but felt numb.

Charlie grabbed his phone and stood up. It was early, and Wes would be up by now. Charlie spent much of the night excavating conversations they'd had over the years, looking for hints of Wes's knowledge, and had come up empty. Charlie cringed at the thought of his best friend keeping this kind of information from him, but he was giving him the benefit of the doubt. He'd had Charlie's back on more occasions than he could remember, and he chose to believe that this would be no different.

The coffee started percolating as Charlie dialed the number. Wesley answered on the first ring.

"What were you doing, sitting on the phone?"

"Charlie Nettles, the man, the myth the legend," Wesley mused, putting Charlie on speaker. "I just got done with my run. How's it going, preacher man?"

"Well, that's kind of a loaded question."

Charlie hesitated before his delivery.

"You there, Charlie?"

"Abby came to see me yesterday."

Wesley switched him from speaker phone, his tone suddenly serious. "I didn't expect that."

"How long have you known that I had a daughter, Wes?"

Wesley was quiet. "Man, I'm sorry, but before we go there, you need to know that Abigail made me promise that I wouldn't say anything. She wanted to tell you herself."

"How long?"

"A year maybe."

"You've known this for a *year*?" Adrenaline rush. "A year? You sure it wasn't longer than that?"

"Look, I was pretty upset when I found out, too, man. That's my niece." Wesley sounded nervous. "Charlie, a year ago you were having struggles with Mar; the timing seemed bad. But I told Abigail she had to find you and come clean. But when you lost Mar and Chandler, she just didn't want to add to your stress. I pressed into her as much as I could. I told her that you deserved to know."

Charlie was quiet, trying to regulate his breathing.

"You there, man? I really am sorry. You have to know what a bad spot I was in. I struggled real hard with this. Charlie, say something."

"I understand, man. I get it. I just wish she hadn't waited so long to tell me. That part just tears me up. I had a daughter out there all this time."

"Not that I'm trying to defend her, but from what I can gather, my daddy came down on Abby pretty hard, Charlie, and you know they had a weird relationship anyway. I mean, listen, I think it was wrong, I do, but I have to say I was pretty happy to find out about Francis and remove some of the mystery as to why my sister left. I will never get that time back with her, Charlie, or with Francis."

Charlie's head swam in circles. "All right, man. I gotta go. I have a lot to chew on—"

"Wait, you said you saw her?" Wesley asked.

"I did," he said, looking out the kitchen window, focusing on the arbor.

"Well, you know I have to ask. How was it seeing her again?"

Charlie thought about it for a minute. "Confusing. It's like that chemistry was still there—for me, anyway—but I'm just so upset with her right now, and I feel guilty even saying it out loud. Honestly, I don't know how to unpack this."

"Charlie don't beat yourself up. What you had with Abby was intense, and that doesn't mean you never loved your wife. Ya'll have a history; that's a fact. And who knows why this is happening now. Charlie, I've seen the Lord working on you and walking with you on this. Trust His plan. Instead of leaning into your own understanding, lean into His. In a way man, this is like a miracle. You've been blessed with a second chance at life, and by that I don't necessarily mean with my sister but at being a dad."

A lump formed in Charlie's throat. Chandler's face filtered through his mind. "Yeah, I can see that."

"Look, do the best you can to sort through this with Abby. That's the first thing. God will give you what you need. He will show you the way. I believe that with my heart."

Charlie took a long pull of coffee and inhaled. "You're right. There's no question that the Lord has been right by my side working on me and with me. I think I'm just in shock."

"Hey, man, listen, you will find your way through this. I know losing Mar and Chan shook you to your core, tested your faith. But you are human, Charlie. And you will navigate this the way you navigate life, with trust and the assurance that He has good plans for you. And hey, you've got me. I mean, that should provide some level of comfort." Wesley was trying to end the conversation with his typical brand of humor, but it felt hollow.

"It does."

Charlie hung up and leaned onto the countertop, squeezing the sides of his head. He topped off his coffee and made his way to the swing in the backyard. He needed the sanctuary of the arbor to clear his head. As he eased back and forth attempting to relax in the ritual of his first cup of coffee for the day, he heard a crackling sound. He turned as Jeremiah approached with a white paper bag in his hand. "I bring biscuits and good tidings," he said with his typical upbeat demeanor.

"Good morning, Jeremiah," Charlie said, relieved.

"Since you're usually the first one on-site in the mornings, I figured you were sorting through some stuff, and what better way to help you do that than biscuits and buttermilk gravy?"

"So, you heard?" he asked.

"Word travels fast in this small town of ours. How are you doing? I know you haven't seen her in quite a while."

Charlie shook his head. "I am a little messed up about it. Honestly, I think I'm just trying to wrap my head around the fact that I have a daughter."

Jeremiah turned to Charlie. "I know, son."

"Am I literally the last person to find out?"

"No, I think I found out by accident. I just happened to pull up over at the Turner place to drop some pies off as she pulled up. That Francis is a pretty little thing." Jeremiah smiled.

"Does she look like me?"

"I think she's a good balance of you both."

"Hopefully she doesn't have my crooked toes."

They both laughed.

"So how are you doing with all of this?"

"I don't know, Jeremiah. I'm wrapping my head around the fact that I have a daughter." He was quiet before taking a sip of coffee. "But the struggle is with Abby. I'm having a hard time reconciling her not telling me. That part is testing this preacher's resolve. I spent all last night just going over it in my head and praying. Basically, on a loop, and I'm still just at a loss. We loved each other, Jeremiah. I mean, I know it was young love and all, but she was my person. I trusted her like nobody else. It's hard to get past that."

"She's human, Charlie. We all fall short at times."

"True. I wrote the handbook on that one," he said, forcing a smile.

"Let me ask you something, son. If someone came to you looking for Godly advice with this very scenario, what would you tell them?"

Charlie sat for a minute before erupting into a quick burst of laughter. "I'd tell them where to find you."

Jeremiah laughed. "I don't know about that. I could offer them a slice of my pie." The breeze danced around them as Jeremiah's tone became more serious. "Charlie, you were blessed with a gift that most don't have. I think you know what to do. Listen to your spirit, son. Continue asking for guidance."

Charlie took a pull of coffee. "Why is it that doing the righteous thing is the hardest?"

"Nobody said it would be easy, just worth it," Jeremiah said, patting Charlie's knee and standing up. "Enjoy those biscuits, son. You know where to find me if you need a slice of that pie today," he said with a wink.

"Thanks, Jeremiah. You're a good man and a good friend."

Charlie listened as Jeremiah pulled out of the driveway, resting his head on the back of the swing, closing his eyes, and inhaling the fragrant sausage gravy, considering eating them with his fingers—

"Charlie?"

Abby. Charlie opened his eyes, startled by the sound of her voice. Abigail stood in front of him in jeans and a white linen button-down tucked in. She wore leather flip-flops with a pale-pink polish on her toes. Her hair was pulled into a ponytail, with tiny pieces of sandy blonde hair framing her face. *Why do you have to be so beautiful?*

"I hope you don't mind me stopping by without calling. I was afraid you wouldn't talk to me." She stood with her fingers laced in front of her, waiting for a response.

Charlie pursed his lips and signaled for her to sit down. Her presence, the warmth of her body so close to his, threw him off balance. His forearms rested on his knees as he worked to compartmentalize the plethora of feelings. "Would you like some coffee?" he asked.

"I'm good, thanks. So, yesterday didn't exactly go as I'd planned."

Charlie inhaled deeply looking ahead.

"Charlie, I need you to know something."

Her stare warmed the side of his face. "I'm listening."

"I'm going to try to say this and not get too emotional, but it's important that you know how I felt…about you—us," she said, tucking one leg under the other. "Giving you up was the hardest thing I've ever had to do. Honestly, the only reason I made it was knowing that our daughter needed me."

The words "our daughter" echoed in his ears.

"I felt so alone. I was pregnant and thank goodness for the Thompsons. They were the family I lived with. They kept me sane. I wanted to call you so bad, Charlie, more times than I can remember. It just became this ever-present ache. But my daddy—I wish I could've stood up to him, but I felt like such a disappointment, Charlie. And he had me convinced that I would ruin your life. I don't know why I believed him, but I stayed away. Of course, over time it became clear to me that I'd made a mistake, but by then, it was too late." Her eyes filled before she blinked away the tears, looking up at the sky.

You could have come back to me or just told me I had a child.

"I did the best I could, Charlie. The years passed, and I lived in Africa working with women whose families had ostracized them after a sexual assault. I somehow related to them. They'd also been tossed aside, kind of like my daddy did to me." A tear crested her eye, and she swiped it away. "They helped me heal, Charlie. They showed me what forgiveness looked like. So, I began sending my daddy letters when Francis was just two. I never got a response. Until two days before he died. I got a call." More tears. "He asked for my forgiveness. It was the first time since I was a little girl that I felt like he loved me." Abigail sobbed. Charlie laid his hand on her shoulder. "I told him all about Francis, how she looked just like him when she pouted. He thought that was funny. We laughed." She inhaled deeply and looked into Charlie's eyes. "And finally, we said goodbye, but not before he told me that he loved me, that he'd always loved me. It was one of the most beautiful moments of my life, Charlie."

"I'm really happy for you, Abs. I know how much you needed that, how much you deserved that."

The leaves around them rustled lightly as the swing eased back and forth. After a few moments Abigail wiped the tears from her cheeks and looked into his eyes. "So how did you end up in ministry? I always knew you were special, but you really took it to a whole new level," Abigail said, breaking the silence.

Charlie thought for a moment, then he turned his face to hers. "It was you."

"Me?" She furrowed her brows. "Really?"

"I was in a real bad place when you left, and my Daddy must have known that I needed a distraction, so he started plugging me more and more into the youth ministry at the church. For a while I just kind of went through the motions until one day I was talking to this kid in the group, and he told me how much I'd helped him get through some struggles. And for the first time in my life, I knew what ministering to another person felt like, and it just ignited something in me. It's like something woke up inside me, Abby, and the next thing I know, I am filling in for Daddy one Sunday when he got sick. It sealed the deal for me. So, when I left for school, I knew that I would need to be part of some type of ministry, so I started one. Me and Wes. It just grew from there."

"Do you think if I'd stayed you would have taken that path?"

"Eventually, maybe. I don't know that I would have been able to see past those blue eyes of yours, though," he said catching her gaze. "What about you?"

"I have a little place in North Carolina, just outside of Charlotte. I'm working with an organization that helps trafficked women. Francis has adjusted well. I swear that kid is resilient. She's a lot like you." She smiled but then became serious. "I've always wanted you to be part of her life, Charlie. I know how wrong I was, and I have lived with that guilt for a long time. Keeping our daughter from you never felt right. Never. I hope that somehow you can find it in your heart to forgive me. I am so sorry."

Charlie searched the gray skies above them for a response. He took a long breath before turning to her. His heart flipped when their eyes met. The truth filtered into his spirit carrying a response. "I believe you. You could've continued to stay away, and you're here now. That's what matters. And I do forgive you. I'd already forgiven you for the other parts of this, but then you showed up, and my feelings have been pretty twisted up." Charlie looked ahead, relieved that the words didn't get hung up in his throat. "How could I not forgive you, Abs?" he muttered, barely audible. His feet swept along the ground.

"In the past year I've wondered, more times than I can count, if I would ever find even the smallest bit of joy again." He shook his head. "Losing my wife and son…"He cleared his throat and took a sip of coffee. "Well, let's just say I survived somehow. Only by the grace of God. Most days I resented the morning sun because it meant I was still here…without them. The situation with my wife was complicated, but with my son, I still have my days. I am forever changed by his loss." Charlie turned to Abigail. Her eyes were soft as she listened. "But now…but now I have a daughter, and it's like the joy that I thought was lost forever has found its way back to me again. It feels kind of like a miracle to me, Abs."

She smiled softly.

"And for that I am grateful," he said, swiping a tear away. He wanted to say so much more. "Does she want to meet me?" Charlie asked, praying for a positive response.

"Yes, very much so."

Charlie smiled and raked his fingers across his scalp. "I have a daughter."

Abigail smiled back at him. "Yes, you do."

"I feel like I should be passing out cigars or something."

She laughed. "If that makes you happy, Charlie Nettles."

Abigail's familiar tone made him want to take her in his arms even more. "So how should we do this?" he asked.

"I'll leave that up to you."

"Okay."

Abigail eased off of the swing and looked around. "You've done a good job keeping up this place. It takes me back," she said, meeting his gaze. "It's really good to see you, Charlie."

Charlie stood up, heart beating faster than normal. She was still so beautiful and familiar. Time hadn't erased their connection, and from the look in her eyes, she knew it too.

"I guess I better be going. Just let me know where to meet, and we'll be there."

"How about Jeremiah's for dinner? Let's say six? I know that's fast, but we have a lot of catching up to do."

She smiled. "That would be great, Charlie."

He could tell there was more that she wasn't saying, but this wasn't the time. Not yet.

She inhaled deeply and tucked her hands into her back pockets. "Well, okay. Six it is."

Chapter Twenty-Seven

Charlie dried off, scrubbing the towel back and forth along his head and then tossing his head around, fingering the waves of hair into place. He stood in front of the limited clothing options in his closet and settled on a pair of jeans and a pale-blue V-neck T-shirt. Nerves crested his chest, settling in his abdomen. He felt like he was going on a first date, but this was so much bigger than that. He'd stood in front of thousands of people feeling more at ease. *Okay, Charlie, get it together.*

Within minutes he was cruising toward the diner. The air worked wonders, but he prayed that his clammy palms would dry up. Questions peppered his brain. He was meeting his daughter for the first time and had no idea what he was going to say.

He pulled into a space by the front door, lifted the helmet from his head, and shook his hair loose. Charlie scanned the diner nervously, but no sign of them. Just a few couples scattered around in booths and an older couple at the counter seats. He tucked the helmet under his arm and walked inside as Jeremiah walked out of the kitchen with a fresh pecan pie.

"Perfect timing, my friend," Jeremiah said, easing it into a glass cabinet behind the counter.

"Smells good."

"You meeting someone?"

"Yeah, actually, I am."

"How many will be in your party?" he asked with a sly smile.

"Three," Charlie replied, unable to hide the warmth in his cheeks.

"I see. Well, I'd say you might want to sit in your old booth," Jeremiah said, grabbing the menus.

Charlie slid into the booth and placed his helmet on the seat beside him.

"You okay?"

"I feel like a herd of elephants are trampling over my guts right now," Charlie responded, rubbing his hands along his pant legs.

"So, today's the day? You're meeting her?"

Charlie inhaled deep into the flutter. "Yes."

"Take a breath, son. Can I get you some tea?"

"That would be great, thanks." *What do I say? Hey, nice to meet you? Or hey, so you're Francis. I am your dad? Nope.* Charlie twiddled his thumbs and looked at his watch again. He looked up as they were walking in—

He waved them over. *This is it. Oh my gosh. She's stunning .*

He didn't want to stare, but Francis took his breath away. She was the image of Abigail but with his almond-shaped eyes. He swallowed hard as they approached. She was tall for eleven and willowy with long blond hair. She wore a pink fitted skirt just above her knees with a white cotton T-shirt that carried a tiny pink ruffle of eyelet lace around the collar. She walked slowly in front of Abigail, who draped her arm around Francis's shoulder. Charlie's heart pounded as he stood up.

"Hey, sorry we're late. I got held up at the phone store," Abigail said with a nervous smile.

Francis stared up at him, her eyes full of innocence and curiosity. Before he could speak, she extended her hand to him. "Hi, I'm Francis."

Charlie swiped his hand along the side of his shirt before taking hers. "Hi, I'm Charlie. It's really nice to meet you."

"Likewise," she said with a confident smile.

You're magnificent. She reminded him of a baby gazelle with just enough age to appear graceful but still a bit awkward. Charlie greeted Abigail with a light kiss on the cheek. It felt good but strange. "Please, have a seat. I just ordered some tea." Charlie moved his helmet as Jeremiah approached and placed a large Mason jar glass of tea in front of Charlie.

Abigail eased from behind the booth, and they embraced. "Jeremiah, it's good to see you again. I didn't get a chance to give you a proper hug when you stopped by Mama's house."

"It's good to see you too, and who is this young lady?" he asked, turning his attention to Francis.

"My name is Francis," she responded.

"Well, it's a pleasure to make your acquaintance. What can I get you ladies to drink?"

"I'd love a water, no ice, and Miss Francis, what would you like?"

"Well, I know you want me to drink water, but I prefer a Coke."

"I bet you do." Abigail laughed. "Ok, I will make an exception this time, but you know we don't do soda."

"I know, Mommy."

"Eleanor will come take your order in a bit. I just wanted to stop by and say hello. It feels a bit like old times tonight," Jeremiah said, handing them each a menu. "Okay, enjoy. Pie is on me tonight."

Francis wiggled in her seat. "I like pie. A lot." They all laughed at her enthusiasm. "What flavors?" she asked.

"Pecan, key lime, or chocolate, but the pecan is what this ole diner is famous for," Jeremiah replied with a smile.

"Pecan it is," she responded, looking at Abigail with a hopeful grin, cocking her head sideways. Charlie found it difficult not to stare. Her eyes were green like pale blades of grass at the beginning of spring, and they danced when she spoke. He was already smitten.

"Okay, pecan it is. That okay, Mom?"

"Absolutely. Thanks, Jeremiah," Abigail said.

When Jeremiah walked away, Francis folded her hands in her lap and looked at Charlie. He wasn't sure what to say, but that was his cue to talk. "So, uhhh, how do you like Sinclair so far?" he asked.

"Ummm, on a scale of one to ten, ten being the highest and best, I would say an eight. But a lot depends on the pie." Her lips curled into a hint of a smile as she studied him.

He was impressed with how confident and well-spoken she was. She was not your average eleven-year-old.

"You know, when your mom and I were just about your age, we sat in this same spot and ate fries and drank milkshakes."

"With my Uncle Wes?" she said.

"Yes," Abigail said.

"I haven't met him yet."

"You'll like him. He's a good guy, and funny too," Charlie said.

Abigail's phone rang in her purse. "Sorry, guys, let me cut this off." She pulled it from her purse and read the number. "I hate to do this, but I have to take this. It's work, and they need an answer. I will be right back." She turned to Francis. "You okay, Bug?" Francis smiled.

"I got this, Mom."

Charlie was taken aback. "You say that a lot?" he asked.

"Say what?" she said keeping his gaze.

"I got this."

"As a matter of fact, I do. I like to say it."

Charlie smiled inside. "I like to say it too."

For a moment they sat quiet. Charlie wasn't sure where to take the conversation.

Eleanor approached and placed the drinks on the table. A grin covered Francis's face. "I love soda." She took a long slurp from the straw. Charlie followed suit, taking a gulp of tea.

"So, what's it like talking in front of all of those people all the time? You ever get stage fright?"

"Well, honestly, I do still get pretty nervous, and I've been doing it a long time."

Francis leaned on the table, whittling the straw in the corner of her mouth. "I had to do a play once at school, and I didn't get nervous one bit. Mommy says that I am going to be a performer."

"A performer? Really? I can see that. So, what is your talent, Francis?" he asked, relaxing a bit. "I bet you have lots."

"I like to sing. Mommy says I have a gift. Well, actually, she says I have many gifts, but this one is my favorite."

Charlie shook his head and smiled. She was so much more than he could've ever imagined.

"Can you sing, Charlie?"

Charlie chuckled. "Uhhh, no. Definitely not one of my gifts."

"Well then, what are yours?"

Charlie thought for a moment. "Well, I think reaching people for Jesus is definitely one. I also like to build things."

"Like what?" she asked, taking a sip of her drink.

"Well, see that birdhouse up on the shelf over there?" Charlie said, craning his body around and nodding in the direction of the back wall of the diner. "I built it."

Francis's eyes opened wider than normal. "Wow, that is pretty cool. Maybe you can teach me how to make one of those. We have lots of birds where we live, and they could use a home."

"I'd like that, Francis."

"So, you ride a motorcycle?" she asked, craning her neck to see his helmet, but she continued before he could respond. "I've always wanted to ride one, but Mommy would never let me."

"I do. I like to ride. It helps me relax." Charlie picked up the helmet and slipped it onto her head. "It looks good on you."

Francis wiggled her head around and held the sides. She posed as if he were taking a picture. "Will you take me for a ride, Charlie?"

Abigail walked back in the door shoving the phone into her back pocket. "I'm so sorry, guys. And what do you have on your head, Miss Priss?"

Francis held her pose, smiling. "Can I ride with Charlie, Mommy, please?" she pleaded.

Abigail slid into the booth and tapped the top of the helmet. "We'll have to see about that."

Charlie shrugged with a smile at Abigail. He shifted gears, easing the helmet from Francis's head. Static fanned from her hair, and she giggled, touching the ends. They all laughed.

For the next hour, they chatted and ate. The conversation was light and more about sharing their lives up until this moment. Charlie learned that Francis weighed seven pounds, six ounces when she was born and suffered from colic for the first three months, wearing Abigail completely out. She loved her time in Africa and wanted to go back one day to see her friends there.

The tiny scar on the outside of Francis's wrist was from a fall when learning to ride her bike. Charlie felt sad that he hadn't been there to teach her, but he kept listening, grateful for this time with her. Abigail showed him baby pictures on her phone as he sat enamored. He flipped through the pictures slowly, drinking in all that he'd missed. They laughed, and a few times he got choked up but hid it behind a cough to regain his composure.

By the time pecan pie slices were placed in front of them, Charlie's belly was full, but his heart was fuller than it had been in a long time. He leaned back and smiled as darkness landed on the parking lot.

"So, who wants another piece of pie?" Charlie joked, rubbing a circle on his belly.

"I'm as full as a tick," Francis said with an exaggerated sigh, leaning back and mimicking Charlie.

They all laughed.

"Where did you hear that, silly goose?"

"Mom, I didn't just fall off the turnip truck."

Charlie and Abigail looked at each other and burst into laughter.

"I see you are picking up on some of Grandma's southern sayings."

"Not just Grandma. I heard a lady at CVS when we were in line. She had lots of them."

Charlie watched them interacting, his heart filling like a pan of freshly poured cake batter. A slow, easy smile rested on his lips.

"Well, I hate to cut this short," Abigail said, looking down at her watch, "but I promised Grandma we would be home in time to visit some before bedtime."

"Aw, Mom, can't we stay just a little longer? I was hoping for a ride on the motorcycle."

Abigail looked at Charlie for help.

"It's late, Francis, and it gets pretty chilly. And I don't have a helmet that would fit you," Charlie said with a light shoulder shrug. "I bet your Grandma is really looking forward to seeing you. Plus, I have to get up with the chickens tomorrow to work at the church."

Francis pointed and laughed. "I'm gonna remember that one too."

"You better." Charlie wondered if they could see the glow he felt on the inside wishing this dinner would never end.

In the parking lot, they stopped at her white Jeep Wrangler, and he opened Francis's door and waited for her to climb in.

"You're something else, Francis."

"So are you, Charlie." She giggled.

Charlie eased the door shut and walked around to Abigail's side. "I can't tell you how grateful I am for tonight. Thank you for bringing her. It means everything."

"I know it should have been sooner, Charlie. And a thousand times more, for that I am truly sorry. But it sure is good to see you." Charlie held the door as Abigail slid behind the wheel, whispering. "And I am pretty sure she thinks you're amazing."

"No secrets!" Francis shook her finger playfully.

"I was just telling him how much fun we had," she said looking back at Charlie.

"That's right. It was good to meet you, Francis."

Francis smiled at him and buckled her seat belt.

"So how long are you planning to stick around?" Charlie asked.

"Not long. Francis and I need to get back home."

Fear rolled over Charlie. "Okay. Well, I would like to spend as much time as I can with you guys until then."

"I know, Charlie. We'll figure something out. I'll call you," Abigail said.

And he shut the door, but not before saying, "Ya'll drive safe."

The ache of watching her pull away returned.

Chapter Twenty-Eight

Warm sunlight spilled through the new stained-glass windows in the sanctuary as Charlie rolled the walls with fresh white paint. He was alone with thoughts of the second tent revival when he heard the rub of feet on the drop cloth behind him. He turned to see Abigail and Francis, both in jean overalls. They looked like twins with matching ponytails. He smiled.

"We thought you could use some help," Abigail said, arms draped around Francis's shoulders from behind.

"Wow, are you painting this all by yourself?" Francis asked, looking around in amazement.

Charlie laid the roller down. He pulled a rag from his back pocket and worked it over his hands as he made his way around the covered pews. "I can't think of a nicer surprise, and no, I just happen to be the only one in here right now." As he drew closer to them, it was as if he was standing in front of the past and the present.

"I hope you don't mind. Mom left for a day trip with some of her friends, and I just figured why wait for a call."

"I'm glad you didn't wait. And I'm glad you're both here."

"This place is cool," Francis said, staring at the colorful stained glass. "And this is where the choir is going to sing?" she asked, stepping up onto the stage beside the covered podium.

"Yep, and up there," Charlie said, pointing to the ceiling above her, "Is where the sound system will be. For the first time ever, this place will have its own sound system."

Abigail and Charlie exchanged a look. "This is amazing, Charlie. It's so different now. And bigger. You guys have really accomplished something here."

His heart warmed watching Abigail and Francis entranced by the change.

"So, put us to work, Mr. Nettles. We are at your service," Abigail said with an easy smile.

Charlie responded but couldn't stop watching Francis dancing around the stage humming aloud. "She is something else, Abby."

"She should be. She comes from good stock."

"Yeah, she does." Their eyes locked, and he looked away. The muscle memory in his heart was working overtime.

"Okay, so let me run and grab a few more rollers and pans."

"I'll help." Abigail turned to Francis, who was pirouetting in place. "I'm going to help Charlie. Be back in a sec, okay?"

"Okay, Mommy," she replied without missing a step.

Charlie led Abby through a corridor that emanated fresh paint, and he opened a large closet door. He leaned over and retrieved two more pans—and their faces met only inches apart. Charlie stared into her eyes, breathless. Their lips moved to meet without hesitation—until a sound from the sanctuary startled them both.

Charlie eased back and listened. He was mesmerized.

An angelic voice filled the air.

They stopped just shy of the doorway listening. Mouth agape, Charlie turned to Abigail. "She is amazing," he whispered.

"That she is."

Emotion rose in Charlie's throat as he eased around the corner, watching her. Eyes closed; her voice built to a crescendo before softly singing the last note.

Charlie's hands took on a life of their own clapping loudly, and she opened her eyes. She giggled, pulling at the hem of her skirt, suddenly shy. The more he clapped, the more color her cheeks took on.

"I didn't think you could hear me," she exclaimed, hopping off the stage and running to Abigail, wrapping around her and squeezing tightly.

"That was nothing short of spectacular, Francis," Charlie said, shaking his head. "I've never heard anything that big come from someone so petite."

They all laughed.

"I get embarrassed," she said, still clinging to Abigail.

"Well, you have a very special gift. Don't ever be embarrassed about that."

"I keep telling her that," Abigail said, caressing the top of Francis's head before kissing it.

"Mommy, can I go outside and play?"

"You don't want to help us paint?" Abigail asked as Francis skipped from one foot to the other in place, shaking her head no.

"I think it should be okay. Charlie, what do you think?"

Charlie almost stuttered, feeling the weight of her acknowledging his role as Francis's father. "Uhh, yeah, I would say just don't take your shoes off. There could be nails on the ground. And stay close."

"Gotcha," she said, giving the thumbs-up.

They both watched as she skipped out the back door.

"We mean it. Shoes stay on, Francis," Abigail called behind her.

The door slammed shut, and they were alone in the silence of the sanctuary. Charlie shook his head in wonder. "She is something else, Abby. I'm at a loss for words."

"Yes, she is." Her eyes glistened as she spoke. "I tell you, Charlie, that little girl is my world. I don't even remember my life before her." Suddenly her cheeks flushed. "Well, of course, I remember. It's just…"

They laughed in unison while Abigail cupped her face. "Okay, Charlie Nettles, enough, put me to work."

"All right," he said with an easy smile. "Follow me, ma'am," he said, and he led her to a wall with patches of spackle.

They worked together, rolling walls and keeping the conversation light. Charlie brought Chandler to life with stories of him as a baby, taking Abigail from birth to the day he died. A smile covered his face until that moment. Charlie paused and lowered his head. "Sometimes it's so hard. I miss him."

Abigail put down her roller and walked over to him. Without a word, she placed her hands on him and pulled his body to hers. Charlie reciprocated, holding her close. This felt natural. They were quiet, simply embracing Charlie's pain.

"I'm sorry I wasn't here for you, Charlie. I'm so sorry."

Charlie created enough distance to look into her eyes, still holding her. "You're here now."

She smiled. Their faces moved easily until their lips were mere inches apart. Abigail pulled away. "I'm sorry. We...I mean, I..." she said, taking a step back. "You still make me feel...so much. I don't think I can breathe," she said, eyes closed. "You have to understand, Charlie. It has just been me and Francis for so long. I've made so many mistakes."

"We've both made mistakes Abigail. This, right now is not a mistake."

Time stood still as he searched her eyes for answers. Without hesitation he pulled her body to his, placing his mouth over hers, lost in the longing he'd felt for her all of those years. She responded by wrapping her arms around his neck deepening their kiss. Years of loss, sadness and yearning swept over them as they embraced. Her familiar warmth and desire made it difficult to ease away. Their foreheads touched as they stood breathless. "I don't know what to say." Charlie muttered.

"Me either. I feel lightheaded." Abigail smiled. "I guess we should probably go check on Francis."

"Yea, you're right." Charlie said smoothing his hair inhaling deeply. Simultaneously they looked at one another and laughed. Charlie shook his head. The connection was still there.

They made their way to the back door. "That girl better still have her shoes on." Abigail said, looking back at Charlie.

They opened the door as two church members ascended the steps with rollers in hand. "Hey, Brian. Hey, Natalie," Charlie said a bit startled.

"Hey, Charlie. How's it going?" he said, extending his hand. "Looks like we're it for paint today, huh?"

"Looks that way. Hey, I want to introduce you to Abigail Turner."

They both greeted her with warmth and handshakes.

"Well, I guess we better get to it," Brian said.

"I'll be back in a minute to help. Did you, by chance, see a beautiful little girl with blond hair running around out here?"

"No, it's kind of quiet here today."

"It is," Charlie agreed. "The rollers and supplies are ready. I'll make my way back in shortly."

Charlie and Abigail began calling out Francis's name with no response.

"Maybe she's around back," Abigail said, bordering on concern.

"You go around that way, and I'll go this way," he said, picking up the pace, moving in the opposite direction.

They met back at the front steps of the church. Fear rose in his chest when he saw the growing panic on Abigail's face. "Charlie, this is not like her. She wouldn't just wander off."

Charlie took a breath, scanning the area around them looking for possible places she could hide. "You don't think she took the path to the lake, do you?"

"Surely she wouldn't go that far. That's just not like her."

"I just have a feeling. Wait one minute," Charlie said. He ascended the stairs in record time, opened the door, and asked Brian and Natalie to keep an eye out for her in case she made her way back. Worry rose in his chest as he closed the church door behind him. He braided Abigail's hand into his and held it to his lips before speaking. "We're going to find her. There is a logical explanation. She's okay, Abs. Let's take the path and see if she went that way first."

Abigail stopped him. "Charlie, Francis doesn't know how to swim. If she went to the lake…"

Charlie stopped her. "She hasn't fallen in the lake, and we are going to find her."

They walked along the trail calling out her name. As they reached the edge of the lake, Charlie yelled her name, praying for a response while surveying the area.

"Oh, God, Charlie. Where is she? This isn't like her at all," Abigail said, on the brink of tears.

The possibility of tragedy striking again washed over Charlie as he picked up the pace to a jog. With each step he prayed aloud with such fervor that the hair on his neck stood up. Abigail remained silent, squeezing his hands tightly as if he were her life raft. Suddenly he heard a tiny voice in the distance.

"Did you hear that, Charlie?" Abigail asked, raising her eyes to meet his.

They both heard it this time.

"I heard it," Charlie said. It was in the distance, but they knew it was Francis.

As they moved quickly through the tall grass, her voice grew closer. Finally, in the distance, a patch of trees appeared at the water's edge. Her voice continued to grow until they finally spotted her.

"Mommy, Mommy, help me! Charlie, help!" Francis screamed.

Charlie spotted Francis about fifty yards from the shore in a red kayak waving her arms, her face red with fear. "I lost the paddle, and I can't get back, Mommy. Help me," she screamed.

"Oh, no, Charlie. We've got to get to her!"

"Hold on, Francis. Don't move," Charlie said, scanning the bank for another kayak or small boat.

"Baby, hold on. Just be still. We are here. Charlie is coming. Don't move."

"I'm scared, Mommy," she said grasping the sides of the kayak, wobbling. Within seconds Francis began waving her arms wildly, swatting at the air and screaming. The kayak began to wobble wildly as Francis struggled to swat and maintain her balance.

Charlie kicked his shoes off. "She's in trouble," he said, diving headfirst into the water just as the kayak capsized. Francis flailed and screamed, but within seconds her head dropped below the surface. Abigail's screams filled the air as Charlie swam as hard and fast as he could. The distance between Francis and the shore was much greater than he'd anticipated. His arms were burning by the time he reached the capsized kayak. He took a deep breath and dove down. The water was a brownish yellow, and he could only see a few feet in any direction. His chest burned as he broke the surface filling his lungs to capacity. Panicked, he dove again, this time a bit deeper, working in a circle. The water felt like a vast wall pushing against his body as he waved his hands, praying to feel her body. Abigail's muffled screams pushed him farther down. *Where are you, Francis?*

Finally, only a few feet below, her body hovered with outstretched arms, motionless .*Oh God, my baby girl.* Air hunger squeezed his chest as he reached her, took her arm, and swam to the surface. Her cheeks were losing their color, and her lips were no longer the color of cotton candy. He paddled as the panic moved his tired limbs forward. *Lord, keep her safe and give me strength.*

"I have her, Abby! I have her!" he sputtered, swimming toward the bank.

"Oh, God, Charlie! Is she breathing!" Abigail screamed as they pulled themselves out of the water.

He laid her on a small patch of grass. Adrenaline rushed through his veins. Abigail's voice became status. *This cannot happen. I cannot lose another child*, he thought, placing his head on Francis's chest. *Nothing.* Panic rolled across him as his hands took on a life of their own remembering what he'd learned in CPR class. He continued compressions on her chest over and over. Nothing. The world around him moved in slow motion, and his ears rang loudly. "I won't stop. I will not lose you too." He could hear Abigail's muffled cries. *I've got this, I've got this.*

A rain shower of warmth filled him as he heard the words "No, son, I've got this." They were so clear that Charlie stopped. He was completely still as Francis's face came into focus. Within seconds water spilled out the sides of her mouth as she gagged for air. A burst of emotion rolled over Charlie as he eased her onto her side and patted her back, struggling to say, "That's it, baby. Breathe. You're going to be okay." His eyes met Abigail's, and they wept.

Charlie lifted Francis onto his shoulder, holding her head. "Thank you, Father," he whispered as Abigail held them both.

Chapter Twenty-Nine

The following days were a blur of completing the final punch list for the church and spending every available moment with Francis and Abigail. When the opportunity presented itself, Charlie pulled Abigail's body to his for a quick kiss. He'd been trying to take it slow until their encounter at the church, but his heart had other plans.

The second tent revival arrived, and Charlie felt prepared. Even so, he wondered if the message was lackluster compared to his powerhouse message of the first revival. He grappled with the knowledge that he had chosen to spend all his free time with his girls instead of fine-tuning the message multiple times, as he would have done before.

Abigail and Francis sat in the front row, just as he and his mama had when he was a boy. This alone should have brought him to a full-circle moment, but not today. Abigail gave him a knowing smile as Francis fidgeted in her seat, turning her body sideways and watching people meander in. His heart rate increased as anxiety mixed with doubt soaked into him like a paper towel slowly absorbing liquid from a smooth surface. Charlie eased to the front of the tent pretending to organize his papers and Bible on the podium while anxiety morphed into raw panic. He eased onto his seat behind the podium, lightheaded, fighting off a full-blown panic attack. He lowered his head and closed his eyes, praying with every ounce of his spirit for strength. He wiped the palms of his trembling hands along the front of his slacks and tried to appear calm as people continued making their way in. *Lord, why is this happening? Please, I beg you, show me your will for this day, for my life, for this message. Please don't let me disappoint these people and you. Forgive me for not giving this message the time it needed. Please don't let me fall short today, Lord. Please tell me what you want today. I am laying this at your feet asking for help. How will I ever make it back to ministry if I can't even handle one message?* He hoped that anyone watching him would just assume he was praying in preparation for the message. He continued to ask for help over and over in his mind for what seemed like a lifetime. The air around him bustled as the choir filtered in taking their place in front of the tent.

It was almost time to start, and he teetered on the brink of a meltdown. The volume in the tent grew as Charlie sat frozen. His hope waned, but he waited, eyes closed. As though a blanket straight from the dryer was wrapped around his shoulders, his heart began to slow, his palms dried, and clarity saturated him like the precious oils that were rubbed into his Savior's feet. His Father—not the one that raised him but the one that created the stars in the sky—gently spoke to him. Charlie listened intently before standing back up. His breath no longer labored; he would not deliver the message he'd prepared for today. Instead, another message was laid out to him in detail. *Thank you.*

Charlie folded the notes he'd prepared and tucked them inside his Bible as he stepped in front of the podium. "I want to welcome each of you today as we come together to share in a message of hope and reassurance of God's everlasting grace for each of us. Let's first go to the Lord in prayer." Charlie bowed his head and offered words of gratitude for this day of worship. His eyes opened, and a smile covered his face. He felt truly blessed. Charlie tucked his hands into his front pants pockets and looked at the many faces before him. His smile widened when he caught Francis trying to discreetly give him a thumbs-up. "I'd prepared a different message for our second revival, but as you all arrived, the Lord laid it on my heart to deliver a different message today, His message. So, forgive me if it is not polished or delivered in just the perfect way, but I am going to trust in what He has led me to present to you," he said, confident that the message would hold great meaning not just for everyone in attendance but for him as well.

"Today I would like to share a message with you about second chances." Charlie quieted momentarily to arrange his thoughts. "There was a time in my life when I took my seat at His table not fully understanding what it meant. I felt like I'd earned it with my works of service, the years of commitment to bringing people from darkness to light, of conveying his messages. I was proud of my nameplate with Charlie Nettles right there at God's table," Charlie said, holding his hands in the air to illustrate his point. "And while I had part of that correct, I was missing so much more," Charlie said, processing the epiphany he was experiencing as the words flowed from his lips. "But when tragedy struck—and it will likely strike many of you in this room if it hasn't already at some point in your life—I made the decision to take leave of His table. I didn't realize at that moment what a precious gift it was." Charlie shook his head. "I was *so* filled with anger, unforgiveness, self-doubt, and uncertainty that I determined I might be beyond repair. I didn't think I was worthy any longer to sit at the table. Can anyone in here relate to that? Have you made a decision in your life that created such trauma that you felt no longer worthy of a seat at the table, or when tragedy struck you listened to the lies of the enemy telling you that this was your life now, you were made to suffer, that somehow the bad that had happened in your life was somehow your fault, and you believed it?

"This was the narrative that tragedy created in me. No second chances for me. I doubted myself, I doubted my destiny, my ability to preach again. I doubted that I would ever love again. I doubted that anyone, even the Lord, could repair the damage in my soul," Charlie exclaimed.

"And I am going to be totally transparent right now. I was plagued with self-doubt up until the moment you all sat in your seats this beautiful day. I bet you didn't expect to hear that," he said, slowly making his way down the center aisle. "But we all have messes to clean up, amen. You see, I felt like my life ended with my son's and my wife's deaths. That tragedy, in my mind, stole any chance that I had at some version of a happy life, of a normal life. Has something ever stolen your belief in second chances? Have you been beaten and broken… and yet here you stand today as a testimony of a grace-giving God," he said with emphasis as one by one people rose to their feet lifting their hands. "How many of you have felt overwhelmed with grief, loss, devastation, disease, sadness, hopelessness? You don't need to raise your hands because you know who you are. You see, I know what it is like to live in a long season of loss and doubt. I lent my ear to the enemy and didn't even know it. 'No second chances for you' is what the enemy whispered in my ear." Charlie's volume grew as emotion bubbled into his throat. "The enemy had me convinced that my life was over and that I should live in unforgiveness, in anger, in loss, and in sadness. He whispered to me, 'Charlie you've got this, you're good, wallow in your unworthiness, rest in your new life, this is it—this is as good as it's going to get,'" Charlie said striding along the aisle.

"And you know what? I listened to that voice for a while, but then, slowly, I started listening to the voice of the one that speaks truth, the one that says you always get a second chance because you've always had a seat at His table."

The tent erupted as Charlie strode back to the podium. "Today, give yourself permission to live a life of abundance, a life of joy. You cannot change your mistakes or heartaches of yesterday, but you do have power over tomorrow. Jesus died on the cross so that you would never have to question whether or not you deserved a second chance so that no matter how far away from His table you wandered, no one could ever take your seat. There is no person, no power, no mistake, no sin that can ever steal your seat at the table. Do you hear me, my good people? Do I need to say this again?" Charlie said, raising his fist vehemently as the tent continued to erupt in praise. "When you are broken and filthy with the stench of disbelief, when you are plagued with addiction, tragedy, family drama, marital strife, He will take your hand and lead you to your seat at his table. He will never deny you a second chance. Can I get an amen."

The tent erupted in applause and praise. "This is your day for victory!" Charlie's face flushed as he signaled to the choir director. Praise and worship music lifted the energy even higher as Charlie raised his hands. "Today I want to invite you to accept your seat at the table. If you've never met Jesus, if you've never stepped into all that God has for you, I want to invite you today."

Abigail stared at Charlie intently with her arm draped around Francis's shoulders. One by one people stepped out of their seats and walked to the front, where Charlie stood, and knelt on the ground. One by one Charlie prayed with them. When the final amen resounded in the tent, bringing the day to a close, Charlie relaxed in the familiar peace of ministering and the realization that he, too, deserved a second chance.

<hr>

The next day Charlie stood in the garage working on a birdhouse.

"Hey, you." A tap landed on Charlie's shoulder. He turned, sweeping Abigail into his arms and spinning her in a circle.

"Hey, you yourself," he said, kissing her deeply.

Abigail spoke softly. "So are you always going to be this happy to see me?"

"Oh, yeah. That will definitely never change."

Abigail grinned and squeezed him tightly before sliding out of his arms. "You are the same boy I knew all those years ago, Charlie Nettles, only more handsome," she said, moving behind him to watch him work.

Charlie smiled while sanding down the sides of a three-story Victorian-style birdhouse. "I think this is my best one yet," he said, savoring the warmth of her arms wrapped around his waist.

"This reminds me of old times. The smell of gasoline and sawdust and you sanding away at one of your bird houses," she said.

Charlie swept his hands lightly over the corners. "I wish I'd had time to teach Chan more, show my boy how to pull beauty out of simple pieces of wood."

Abigail moved to the side of the workbench, facing him. "I sure wish I'd met him."

Charlie looked up as he sanded. "I do too. He was one of a kind. And he would have been so crazy about the idea of having a big sister. You would have loved him, Abs," he said with a heavy-hearted smile, swiping the roofline one last time. He refused to allow sadness to fill him at every mention of Chandler's name, so he took a breath and shifted his mood. He'd been looking forward to spending the afternoon with Abigail all week. "I'm about to wrap up. Did you pack the lunch, or do we need to stop by Jeremiah's?" he asked with a grin.

Abigail smacked his arm lightly. "Charlie Nettles, you are the one that invited me."

He interrupted her midsentence. "I got this. You don't think I would invite you on a picnic and expect you to bring the food, do you?"

They laughed as Charlie placed the sandpaper on the work table and rubbed his hands together, dust coating the concrete around his feet and the front of his cargo shorts.

"So, how's our patient?" Charlie asked as he cut the light off and lowered the garage door.

"Unhappy. She still has a little bit of fever, so Mom insisted on watching her. The doctor said it's just a bug."

"Well, at least she isn't throwing up anymore. Maybe we should just wait until she feels better."

"My mama practically pushed me out the door. I think she likes having someone to take care of. She said Francis reminds her of me at that age. Plus, with Daddy gone, I think we serve as a good distraction."

"I can see that," Charlie said, opening the screen door with a clack. "Hang on; let me grab the food," he said, disappearing into the kitchen while Abigail stood at the bottom of the concrete stairs. Within seconds, Charlie emerged carrying two brown paper bags. He leaned down and kissed her, pausing to look into her eyes.

"Your chariot awaits," Charlie said, flirting.

"So, your daddy's truck is our chariot now?" She laughed.

"Oh, no, dear Abigail. I have a special treat in store for you on this beautiful day," he said, walking into the garage. He uncovered his motorcycle, and a second helmet sat on the seat beside his.

She smiled. "Now that's a chariot."

Charlie opened the saddlebags flanking each side of the motorcycle and placed the bags evenly into them.

"You bought me a helmet," Abigail said with surprise, removing it from the seat.

"I did," Charlie said, easing it onto her head, pushing a tendril of hair from her eyes. His heart swelled.

Abigail moved it around on her head like a curious child. "Is it supposed to be so snug?"

"Yeah, silly. Be still," he said, pulling the strap under her chin and snapping it on the side. "Now, let's look at you." *God, I adore you.*

Abigail laughed. "Okay, let's do this."

"I like your enthusiasm. And you look pretty cute in that helmet, I might add," he said.

Charlie placed his helmet on before straddling the bike and backing it out of the garage. He turned the ignition on to a loud rumble. Abigail walked over. "Okay, just use that pedal to hop on," he said. Abigail put her foot in place and swung her leg over the black leather seat.

Within minutes they were on the road. Abigail's hands pressed into his sides as Charlie gained speed. The sky was a picturesque bright blue filled with clouds that replicated the ceilings of Versailles, acute with detailed edges. Abigail finally leaned onto the backrest, loosening her grip, her body relaxing against his. He hoped that she'd share his passion for the open road. The wind hummed by as the sun held them in a warm embrace. It felt perfect.

Charlie eased onto the dirt pathway leading to Lake Jenson. Flecks of sunshine twinkled on the lake's surface. Charlie slowed to a stop. Déjà vu eased over him, reminding him of their many trips to this very spot.

Abigail placed her hands on his shoulders, swung her leg over the seat, and stepped onto the ground. "That was a blast, Charlie," she said, fumbling to unstrap her helmet.

"Let me help you with that," he said, carefully sliding it apart, holding her gaze. "I'm glad you enjoyed it. It's like therapy for me."

"Motorcycles and birdhouses. You are a strange but adorable mix, Charlie Nettles."

"You know I love it when you say that" he said, pulling a folded blue plaid sheet from one of the saddlebags.

A glow covered her face. "Say what?"

"My name. Like you did when we were kids," he said with a grin.

Abigail looked at the ground and then up at Charlie, shaking her head. "You know this is just all so crazy. You. Me. Here."

Charlie shook out the sheet, and it floated onto the grass. "I will take this kind of crazy any day," he said.

Abigail turned and faced the lake, lost in thought. "This old lake just never loses its allure," she said as Charlie wrapped his arms around her from behind. "I love this place. But it does feel kind of strange being here after what happened with Francis."

"That's why I brought us here. We have to reclaim it in our way."

Abigail looked into his eyes. "Me and you."

Their lips met, and Charlie's heart fluttered. Time stood still. Charlie stepped back and leaned over. "Madame, a fancy sheet for two and a menu filled with culinary delights," he said, attempting a French accent and extending his hand to her. "May I?"

"Yes, you may," she said, cocking her head to the side playfully.

"But first may I interest the lady in a dance?" he asked, pressing her hand to his lips and lingering.

Without a word, Abigail eased her arm around his neck as he secured the other over his heart. Their bodies blended together as he hummed no song in particular. He no longer felt guilty for loving her still. He'd shared a part of his heart that held no regret, and Abigail had lived in the deepest part from the very moment he met her outside a dusty old tent when they were just kids. They continued swaying to the soft humming of Charlie's voice and a chorus of rustling leaves. He'd never felt more at home than in this moment. *I want to hold you like this forever.*

Abigail looked up at Charlie. "This really feels good, Charlie." He pressed his lips softly on her forehead, languishing in her familiar smell. "And to think you still have the moves…with dancing, that is," she said, color filling her cheeks.

Charlie smiled and eased her into a spin with a dip. The sound of their laughter echoed through the air and across the water.

"Is my lady hungry?"

"Indeed, she is."

Charlie placed the bags on the sheet and patted the ground beside him.

She sat cross-legged, watching intently as he retrieved the food.

"So, we have a little pecan pie," he said, reaching back into the bag. "Burgers, fries, and two relatively melted chocolate shakes," he said, licking ice cream from his knuckle.

"This is great, Charlie." She leaned over and kissed him softly. Her lips were warm.

"I never thought I'd be sitting here like this with you again," he said.

"And yet, here we are," she said, arms outstretched behind her, eyes closed. A wall of shiny blond hair moved behind her in small wakes. "This is nice." She whispered.

Charlie moved his hand along her cheek, savoring her porcelain skin beneath his fingertips. She opened her eyes and looked at him. No words were exchanged. None were necessary. Finally, Charlie took her face fully into his hands and kissed her. His body yearned for more as she responded to his touch, but he wanted to take a different path this time with her, so he pulled away.

"I think we better eat," he said with a breathy smile.

"Yeah, let's eat," she said, equally off balance. "So, Francis declared to me and Mama that she wants you to teach her to swim."

Charlie looked at her sideways. "Talk about grabbing the bull by the horns."

"Yeah, she called it a defining moment. I just cannot believe some of the things that come out of her mouth. That kid is an old soul."

"I'd say," Charlie replied, and he took a sip of milkshake. "Pretty courageous move if you ask me. I would love to teach her. I don't want this place, our place, to have a bad connotation, ya know? It holds such good memories for us, and I would love to share that with our daughter."

Abigail's eyes filled with tears.

"Hey, what did I say? What's going on?"

Abigail closed her eyes, placing her hand over Charlie's.

"Abs, talk to me."

She looked at him, eyes glistening. "I just never thought I would hear those words—*our daughter*. It just feels so good. I'm sorry. It's just been so long that I've wanted this."

Charlie moved closer, looking into her eyes. "You will never have to want for this ever again. I promise you, Abs. I will always be there for you and Francis. Always."

"I know. This all just seems so surreal." Abigail paused. "Charlie, there is something else that I need to tell you."

Charlie's heart skipped a beat. Her expression was serious. "Okay."

"It's taken me a long time to reconcile so many things. I think a part of me wished it wasn't true, so I just hid it away."

"What are you talking about?"

"My daddy, Charlie."

Charlie looked at her sideways, not sure where this was going.

"He wasn't the man everyone thought he was," she said, squinting at the sky above. "Not even Wes knows what I am about to tell you."

Charlie listened intently.

"One day when I was probably eight or nine, Mama dropped me off at the church. She'd gotten called to one of her ladies' groups, and she said Daddy was there doing some paperwork and he'd look after me. It was a Saturday, so no one was supposed to be there. She said she'd be back in about an hour to get me." Abigail took a breath. "So, I go in the back door. It was unlocked. I called out for my Daddy but got no answer, so I made my way to his office. The door was shut, and I heard muffled sounds coming from inside. Without a thought I opened the door. There he was on the couch in his office, half naked with the church secretary. I thought he was going to have a heart attack. The look on his face was like someone had poured cold water down his back. I slammed the door and ran out of the church as fast as I could. I was standing outside when he made his way down the back stairs where I sat shaking and crying."

Charlie listened, in shock.

"He proceeded to tell me that I misunderstood what I saw and that I couldn't tell Mama. He said if I did, she would take me and Wes and move away. I was too young to understand, but I knew that I didn't want to leave our house and my friends. So, I agreed, but it ate me up inside. The worst part is that he continued carrying on with her for years after that. I confronted him just before I left. I told him that Mama deserved better and that it was time to tell her the truth. I threatened him."

"Oh, Abs, that's unbelievable."

"So, when I ended up pregnant, he sent me away. I could've told Mama the truth, but I just couldn't break her heart twice," she said, tears filling her eyes. "I couldn't disappoint her again. It would've killed her. She loved my daddy. So, for her sake I carried this with me, all these years. You're the only person that I have ever told."

"I'm at a loss, Abs. You shouldn't have had to carry this, ever," Charlie said, running his hand along the back of his neck. "So basically, he sent you away for his sins, not ours. This wasn't really about us."

"Oh, it was still about us, but that just gave him the incentive to follow through. If it had gotten out that I was pregnant, it would have scarred his perfect reputation, and he was not having that. So instead of sacrificing himself, he sacrificed his own daughter."

They both stared out at the lake in silence. Charlie inhaled deeply and turned to her, placing his hand on the side of her face. "I love you…so much, and you should've never had to carry any of this by yourself. I'm so sorry he did that to you, to us. I know sharing this with me was hard, but I appreciate it more than you know. What he did was wrong. You need to remember that." Abigail leaned into his hand. "I promise you this. You will never have to walk alone and carry a burden like that ever again." He kissed her lightly on the lips, and they embraced.

"I've made my peace with Daddy. I'm okay now," Abigail said, wiping her cheeks with the back of her hand. "Can we go back to dancing now that I've messed up the mood?"

"You can never mess up the mood," he said with a smile. "Are you sure you're okay?"

"Yeah, I am. I promise," she said, smiling back at him.

Charlie pulled her close. "While on the serious subjects, we haven't really talked about what's next. I'm guessing it's about time for you to go back to work," Charlie said.

Abigail took a sip of milkshake. "I was going to talk to you about that. I'd hoped to be here for the last tent revival and the ribbon cutting of the church, but I think we may have to go back."

Disappointment swept over Charlie. "That's okay. I totally get it."

"I'm sorry, Charlie. I really wanted to be here for you." She paused. "So, what's your plan after the revival? You going back to Georgia?" she asked.

"I don't know, but we'll figure something out. I want to be wherever you and Francis are."

"So, me, you…this really is really happening?" she said as if she were taking a bite of ice-cold watermelon on a hot summer's day.

"I love you. Plain and simple. This old heart can't take losing you again. And Francis. I just want to be her dad and take care of you guys. Mind you, I am currently and gainfully unemployed right now, so I have a few kinks to work out."

They laughed, fingers entwined, lying back. A warm breeze carried the faint fragrance of their diner food. They were quiet for a while, simply enjoying this time together. They stared at the old oak branches spanning over them as the sun peeked through, finally turning to dusk. Hours passed as they rested in each other's arms. Charlie closed his eyes, inhaling Abigail as she folded perfectly into his side. He knew with certainty that she was the missing puzzle piece. At that moment he knew exactly what his final message would be, and he'd never been more grateful.

Chapter Thirty

The distant echo of car doors slamming caused Charlie to pause before stepping out onto the back stoop of his daddy's house. Today was the day. Abigail and Francis were leaving to go back to Charlotte, and the revival was tomorrow, with the ribbon cutting at the church the following day. Emotions swirled around in his chest like a potter's wheel forming a beautiful creation. He smiled as they walked toward him. His bare feet landed on the grass, and he inhaled the fragrant magnolias that overshadowed the garage. Francis smiled brightly as she ran and leaped into his arms. He closed his eyes and held her. Lilac and baby powder filled his senses. They'd grown close quickly, and gratitude flooded through him like a mountain stream, refreshing him with every thought of her. He felt love again, the kind he carried in his heart for Chandler. She was a miracle, one that he'd never imagined when he lost his son.

"Good morning, beautiful girl," Charlie said before easing her onto the grass.

"Good morning," Francis replied. "And good morning to you my other beautiful girl," he said, leaning over, brushing Abigail's forehead with a kiss. She pulled him into her, resting her head on his chest as Francis skipped toward the arbor swing.

"How am I gonna do this, Charlie? The thought of driving away from you today…"

Charlie turned and faced her. "This is it, Abs. Me, you, and that angel right over there," he said with a reassuring smile. "You absolutely sure you can't stay for the weekend?"

"As much as I want to, I just can't. My director said she really needs me to come in tomorrow to get a jumpstart for the week on a new project. What could I say?" she said with a forced smile, resting her forehead on his chest. "She's been so understanding."

"It won't be long, Abs. We are going to figure out how to be a family." Charlie's heart skipped before the words finished crossing his lips.

"I hear you. My head knows that, but my heart still remembers our last goodbye near this very spot. And tomorrow is so important. I just hate to miss it," she said, looking up at him softly.

Charlie wrapped his arms around her. He wanted her to feel safe. "I know you would be there if you could. It's really okay, and I promise you, Abs, we will never be apart again. Not like that."

"Mommy, Charlie, see how high I can swing," Francis said, pushing off the grass, head back, looking at the white clouds billowing above.

"All right now, not too high," Abigail said as they made their way over to her. "Scooch over, sis," she said, nudging Francis and caressing the top of her head.

They all eased onto the swing, with Francis in the middle. Charlie's arm encompassed them both, with his hand resting on Abigail's shoulder. If time stood still at this very moment, he would be content.

"So, are you excited about the tent thingy tomorrow?" Francis asked, needling the fabric of her pink T-shirt between her fingers.

Charlie smiled. "I am. It's a pretty special weekend," he said, wishing silently they could attend.

"I know. I wish we could stay, but Mommy says she's gotta work," she said, playfully taunting Abigail.

Abigail patted her leg. "You know I would love to stay, but we have been away from home for a while now, and it's time to go back."

"But that's not fair. We could go back Monday. It's only a few days, Mommy."

"I know, Lovebug, but I have no choice. My director needs me to come in tomorrow. We already talked about this."

Francis curled her lips, pretending like she was crying. Abigail pulled her near and planted a kiss on the top of her head. "Don't even try the puppy dog face."

Charlie wanted to make the same face and beg her to stay a few more days, but this was hard enough. He imagined the following days absent of them, and a spool of pain unraveled. Instead, he pasted a smile on his face. "In the blink of an eye, we'll all be together again. And we can FaceTime every day. It will be like we aren't even apart." The words hollowed out before he could finish the sentence. No amount of FaceTime would adequately quench the thirst he had for their actual presence.

Francis studied his face. "You promise?"

"I promise," he said, followed by a kiss on the top of her head.

They eased back and forth in silence for a few minutes. A comforting stillness surrounded them until Francis spoke up. Her voice was smaller than normal, lacking her typical animation. "Can I ask you a question, Charlie?" she said, eyes fixed on her lap.

"Of course. Anything," he said.

She hesitated, picking at a string hanging off the cuff of her jean shorts.

Abigail took her hand and squeezed it. "It's okay. Just ask," she said.

Charlie placed his hand on her shoulder. "What's on your mind, Francis?"

Francis looked up at Abigail, who nodded before looking back down at her lap. "Well, ummm. So, I have been thinking. And since we are going to be a family one day..." She hesitated. "Would it be okay if I called you Daddy?" The words shot out of her mouth, and she buried her face in Abigail's shoulder.

Emotion rained over Charlie. He had to look away and catch his breath. "Hey," Charlie said, rubbing the top of her head. "Would you look at me, please?" Francis slowly turned to face him; cheeks flushed. "I can't think of anything that would make me happier."

A smile covered her face as she leaned into his side, and he pulled her to him. Abigail swiped a tear away and leaned in.

"I've never had a daddy before. This is gonna be awesome." She giggled.

"Yes, it is," Charlie said, swallowing hard into the joy that was pulsing over him. "And I have never had a daughter, and I am honored to be your daddy, Miss Francis," he said, pulling her into the crest of his arm. *Thank you, God.*

Within minutes, Francis lifted off the swing and pirouetted across the yard. Abigail's body melted into his as they watched their daughter. What felt like minutes passed as the sun began to hang lower in the sky. Abigail sighed looking down at her watch. Resting her head against Charlie's arm, Abigail inhaled and looked up at Charlie, biting her lip. "I really want to stay."

"I really want you to stay."

"But I have to go."

"I know that too," Charlie replied.

She stood up and stretched her arms high above her head as if to shake off the moments to come. Charlie stood up and wrapped his arms around her waist, his head on her shoulder as they watched Francis dance in circles singing. Abigail pressed her arm over his, intertwining their fingers.

"You know this is all gonna be just fine, right?" Charlie whispered.

"I do," she responded, tightening her fingers around his. "Okay, we better get on the road." Abigail turned to face him; her eyes heavy.

"We've got this."

Abigail forced a smile. "We've got this."

Charlie pulled her into him and closed his eyes, breathing her in. "I love you, Abs, so much."

"I love you too."

At that moment Francis ran over to them and wrapped her arms around them both.

"We're making a Mommy sandwich."

They all laughed.

"It's time to go," Abigail said, looking down at Francis and easing a stray piece of hair away from her eye.

Francis inhaled deeply with a playful sigh.

They walked slowly toward Abigail's car. Charlie bent down, eye to eye with Francis. Love filled every pore of his body. "I will be counting the days until I see you again," he said as big tears filled her eyes. Charlie immediately pulled her into him. "And I couldn't be happier to be your daddy." He held her close and prayed the time would pass quickly. "Okay, let's get you buckled in," he said, opening the back-seat door. She eased in and forced a smile as a tear rolled down her cheek. He had to look away and take a breath.

"Wait one second," he said. He jogged toward the house and bounded upstairs. He took Chandler's teddy bear from the top of the chest of drawers, clutched it to his chest, and made his way back outside to the car. Abigail stood beside the car watching. Charlie bent down beside Francis. "I want you to take care of this little guy for me until we are all together again," he said, placing the bear gingerly into her arms. She hugged him tightly, eyes closed. "I love him already," she said with a smile. "Where did you get him?"

Charlie tried not to tear up. "He belonged to your brother, Chandler. He would have been so happy that you are taking care of it for him. So, when you feel sad, I want you to hold him real tight and know that it won't be long before we are all together, okay?"

Francis nodded her head in agreement. Relieved that she no longer looked sad, he kissed the top of her head and shut the car door. Abigail wrapped her arms around him and rested her head on his chest. Charlie felt her pain and knew she, too, was trying to keep the façade going for Francis's sake. They held each other in silence. Charlie kissed the top of her head and whispered, "I just don't want to let you go."

She sighed. "Me neither, but I know this. You are going to do an amazing job this weekend with the revival and the ribbon cutting. And I am always with you, Charlie. I always have been. And God will reveal your next steps to you."

"You're right. It's been a rough year but also an amazing one. And I found you again and Francis," he said, watching her stroke the bear's head with a satisfied smile on her face.

Charlie took Abigail's face into his hands and pulled their faces together, eyes closed. "I love you, Abby. With every ounce of my being, I love you."

"And I love you, Charlie Nettles, forever and a day for added measure."

Charlie pressed his lips to hers and held them in place, inhaling her. When he looked into her eyes, there were no words left. He opened her door, and she slid behind the wheel.

"Call me when you get home," he said, easing the door shut.

Francis waved at him from the back seat. Abigail blew him a kiss before backing up. He watched them as they disappeared into the distance until they were a mere speck.

He stood at the end of the driveway for a few minutes dazed, missing them before the headlights disappeared into the distance.

As he turned and made his way toward the house, his neighbor stepped onto her stoop to water two large ferns with long cascading leaves. "Good morning, Charlie," she said with a warm smile.

"Good morning Mrs. Landry."

"This is a big weekend for our little town. I can't wait to get back into the new church. We're planning to attend the revival tomorrow too."

"It's going to be quite a weekend," Charlie said, hoping he wouldn't have an anxiety attack like he didn't before the last one.

Chapter Thirty-One

Charlie awoke from a peaceful slumber to the sound of his cell phone ringing. He'd worked on his notes for the revival until ten o'clock last night and had fallen fast asleep. He rolled over, took the phone in one hand, and propped his arm under his head. A smile covered his face.

"Good morning, Daddy." Francis smiled as if the words were a prize that she'd just won at a fair.

"Good morning," Charlie said warmly.

"This is your official wake-up call. Mommy said you might have butterflies since today is the revival." Abigail leaned in behind Francis. "Hey there. Are you ready, Pastor Nettles?" she said with a knowing smile.

"I am," he said, trying to push down the trepidation he'd been feeling. Francis moved on and began chatting about a song she'd just learned as Abigail stood behind her injecting comments. Charlie watched them in awe, wondering how he could take a screenshot of them without disconnecting FaceTime. The newness of his little family would never wear off. He sank into his pillow laughing while listening to Francis shift from subject to subject. She reminded him of the preteen version of her mother.

Finally, Abigail asked Francis to give her a few minutes alone to talk to Charlie. Francis blew Charlie a kiss and skipped away. Abigail took the phone and leaned back against a dark-green armchair. "So, can I tell you how incredibly handsome you are when you wake up in the morning?"

Charlie hmmphed. "I don't know about that. This hair is a little on the crazy side," he said, combing his fingers through a handful of wavy hair, smoothing it out. "But thanks," he said, watching her eyes follow him in a way that made his insides flutter. He shook his head. "I don't know what I did to deserve you, Abs. God, I love you."

"I love you too, Charlie. So, are you really ready for this weekend?" she asked.

"I am," he said with hesitation.

"That wasn't very convincing."

"I know. Before the last revival, I literally thought I was going to melt into a puddle before it started. I've never had nerves like that before, and it just makes me wonder if ministry is still my calling."

"Charlie, you have been through a whole lot. I think you need to show yourself a little grace. No matter what you'll make the right decision. That I know for sure."

Charlie thought for a moment, trying to reconcile what his future would look like without ministry in it. "I know you're right, Abs. I just never thought that I would be so conflicted even after both revivals turned out good in the end. Or at least I think they did," he joked.

"They absolutely did. Don't start second-guessing yourself now. And if that is not in your future, you'll know. You'll feel it in your heart when the answer is ready for you." She paused. "You've been through so much, Charlie. And look at you. Your mama and daddy would be very proud of you."

"I just wish they were here. They'd love Francis. And Daddy would definitely have some words of wisdom for us, and I can only imagine what he'd say."

They both laughed.

"Yeah, me too."

They talked for another forty-five minutes until Charlie reluctantly looked over at the clock. "As much as I hate to do this, I need to run. I promised Jeremiah I would stop in the diner this morning."

"Call me later, okay? I can't wait to hear all about the revival. You're going to be amazing today, Charlie. I believe in you. I only wish we could be there."

"Thanks, Abs."

A comfortable silence filled the space between them. "I hate to hang up, but I guess I'll let you go for now. You've got this."

An epiphany rolled over him like a warm ocean tide. "I love you, Abs. Tell our girl her daddy loves her."

She blew a kiss and said, "Love you" before the screen went dark.

Charlie held the phone to his chest and marinated on her words and what they'd meant to him his whole life. Finally, he sat up, shook his head, and said aloud, "I've never had this." With excitement, he hopped into the shower and then headed to Jeremiah's Diner.

——⊙——

The smell of hot bacon sizzling on the griddle met Charlie as he opened the door to the diner. It bustled with activity as Jeremiah came out of the back and greeted him with enthusiasm. "Well, good morning to you, young man. You ready to get this little town fired up?" he said over his shoulder, waving for Charlie to follow him. The corner booth had a small white tent reading Reserved.

Charlie laughed. "Since when do you reserve tables?"

"Well, I think this occasion deserves to be properly acknowledged, so today we make an exception."

Charlie sat down, and Jeremiah slid into the booth across from him.

Jeremiah folded his hands on the table in front of him. "This is a big weekend, son. You ready?"

"Hopefully."

"You knocked the other two out of the park. I think you'll be just fine."

Charlie hoped that he was right. "A good message can get lost if the preacher is breathing in a paper bag," Charlie joked.

A short, plump waitress with dark curly hair approached the table with coffee cups in one hand and a pot of steaming coffee in the other.

"I took the liberty of ordering us some coffee to start. Thank you," he said to her with a smile and then brought his focus back to Charlie.

Charlie wondered what was on Jeremiah's mind as he poured creamer into his cup out of a white ceramic dispenser.

"Would you like to order?" Jeremiah asked.

"I think I will just have coffee for now, but thanks."

"Okay, I think we're good for now."

"Enjoy," she said, and she disappeared behind the counter and into the kitchen.

Jeremiah studied Charlie with a knowing look as if waiting for Charlie to say something. "It's been around a year since you showed back up. You really have made strides, Charlie. I am proud of you, son," he said, holding Charlie's gaze.

The warmth of Jeremiah's words covered him like a summer rain. "Thank you, Jeremiah. Coming from you, that means everything. It's been the hardest year of my life," Charlie said, allowing emotion to settle gently into his words. "I continue to question myself, God's plans for me. I'm still not sure, but I finally realized that I'm not in control. I let go of the anger and pain. I had to forgive. Myself, Mar. It's been a journey. But here I sit. I have been given another chance at love, at parenting. It's overwhelming, actually," he replied, carefully sipping the steaming coffee. "For that I am grateful."

"There's no question in my mind that you will make the best decision for your future. Of course, with a little help from above. So… this is a big weekend for you on many levels, and I wanted to give you something that held meaning. Something to commemorate this new journey you are taking." He paused. "I think I found the perfect gift for you." He slid out of the booth. "I will be right back," he said, disappearing into the kitchen.

Within seconds Jeremiah reappeared carrying a tall box wrapped in birthday paper.

Jeremiah pointed at the paper, amused. "The sign of a bachelor."

They both laughed as he placed the box on the table in front of him. "Man, this is a big ole box. What have you gone and done?"

"Well, just a little something for you to take with you on this next leg of your journey. Kind of a reminder of where you've been and where you may be going. That part's up to you," Jeremiah said in a fatherly tone.

Charlie tore the paper away with the excitement of a child. He folded open the top of the box and peered inside. A smile covered his face as he reached inside and eased the contents out gently. "Man, this takes me back. I had completely forgotten about this one," Charlie said, placing a large white birdhouse with a steeple and cross on top. He looked at Jeremiah, who watched with satisfaction.

"I added a fresh coat of paint. But this beauty has a strong foundation because that's all it needed after all this time. I've had that birdhouse just outside my sunroom on the back of my house for years. Every morning when I drink my coffee, I watch to see who is visiting my little church. A sparrow made it her home for a time, had some babies, and then they moved on. It's brought me a lot of joy over the years. But it's always reminded me of the birdhouse preacher who not only built a birdhouse church but built a ministry. One that has touched the hearts of so many folks."

Charlie turned it carefully, inspecting and remembering every stroke of sandpaper that created it. "This birdhouse. It's something special, my friend. You have made this weekend even more memorable than I could've imagined."

"Well, I'm glad you like it."

"And Jeremiah, thank you for taking an interest in that kid who was trying to figure it all out. I hope you know what a difference you made."

Jeremiah leaned back. "You gonna make an old man misty now," he replied, touched.

Charlie continued to admire the gift. "I love this, Jeremiah. This is very special to me. I will never forget it."

Eleanor refilled their coffee as they talked about the revival and ribbon cutting. It was the perfect segue into this final revival. The pieces of his final messages were falling into place.

Chapter Thirty-Two

Charlie awoke to the sound of birds chirping outside his bedroom window. Today he hoped to lean into whatever purpose and future that God had in store for him. The journey had been long, and it was time to celebrate the spiritual surgery that had been performed on his heart. His stomach jumped just enough to humble him.

Charlie slid from beneath the covers and landed soundly on his knees beside the twin bed. For a moment, uncertainty wafted over him like a feather. He lowered his head and closed his eyes. *What if the message falls flat? What if no one meets Jesus today?* What-ifs landed on his skin like a hornet making its way across Charlie's spirit, so he prayed. "Please, Lord, soothe my spirit. Fill me with your goodness and use me this weekend. Use me to wake up those who are sleeping, to reignite the fires that have been smothered out in people's spirits. Show me, Lord. I invite you into this message. Use me to cause a brush fire of revival in this town, use me to introduce you to those that don't know you yet. Use me," he exclaimed. "And Lord, I trust that you will reveal my next steps."

Calm settled in his chest as he showered and prepared for the day. He smoothed his hair with one hand and carried his Bible in the other, taking in the details of the house that he grew up in as he slipped his leather loafers on beside the couch. He could see the younger version of himself sitting at the little kitchen table while his mama cooked, and his daddy talked about his plans. Every corner triggered a memory, some good some bad.

He finally made his way to the front door and turned around. It was as if his mama and daddy were standing there smiling. "Thank you for teaching me the word. And thank you for always believing in my purpose. I am so grateful that God chose you for me. I love you both so much. And this weekend I'm gonna make you both proud. And Daddy, I am praying that your brand of preaching will seep through my pores as I stand in front of that crowd today setting the room on fire with the Holy Spirit." Charlie imagined them both, hands in the air, saying, "Amen, son. Amen." Charlie smiled to himself and closed the door behind him. His journey was starting to make sense.

⸺◦◦⸺

The time for people to arrive was near. Charlie pulled his phone from the back pocket of his brown slacks. He'd not heard from Abigail and Francis this morning, leaving him wondering why they'd not reached out. Her phone continued to go to voice mail, and he slid his into his back pocket. He wanted to hear their voices before the revival.

Charlie stood at the entrance of the tent welcoming everyone as they came in. To his relief, he was filled with a calm that could only come from God as he shook hands and made small talk with the townspeople. Before long, the seats were full, and the walls were lined with people of all ages. His senses were heightened by the excitement saturating every corner of the tent. He was reminded of those days long ago as a boy when his daddy would look at him and say, "You feel that, boy? That's the spirit of the Most High. He's here and raring to go." Charlie never understood that feeling as a boy.

He slowly made his way to the front and stood beside the choir. Members of choirs from the churches in surrounding counties had come together for this day, intending to raise the roof with a combination of gospel and mainstream praise music. The room quieted, and Charlie approached the podium. He swallowed into the emotion welling up in his throat as he looked out at the sea of faces, some familiar, others not.

"I want to thank each and every one of you for joining me today. I'd like to start by sharing with you a story of God's redemptive grace. Some of you may know me; others may not. My name is Charlie Nettles, and I moved here in middle school when my daddy, the late Elroy Nettles, took an assistant pastor job at the church."

Movement caught his eye at the back of the tent. Charlie's breath hitched. Abigail and Francis eased in. Smiles covered their faces, and joy filled Charlie's chest.

"My mama and daddy would be so proud right now to see me here, in this tent with all of you fine people." Charlie looked straight at Abigail. "I am forever grateful for their decision to move here all those years ago." He paused and smiled. "Ya know, my daddy always told me that I came from a long line of conduits of the Holy Spirit, and today, my friends…" he said with emphasis. "And today we are going to *praise* the Most High with so much joy just like all those preachers that came before me with the power and promise that only generations of ministering can bring. Can someone give me an amen."

The tent erupted in praise.

He continued, raising his hands in the air. "With so much power that the heavens will roar right along with us," he exclaimed, shaking his head, enveloped in the Spirit.

Charlie made eye contact with Francis, who was bouncing up and down with excitement. Amens reverberated in the air as the choir began to sing a powerful and lively praise song that surged through Charlie like an electric shock wave. At that moment, he knew what his daddy was feeling, with saturated sideburns, so lost in the Spirit that the words no longer belong to you. As the choir quieted to a humming background melody, Charlie began to speak while energy bounced around the room like a beach ball as people clapped and praised. Charlie delivered the most powerful and spirited-filled message of his career in ministry. No nerves, no anxiety. The choir carried the emotion to levels that left a steady chill running up Charlie's spine. Everyone sprang to their feet, singing and praying, some crying, others shouting amen. Every time he looked at Francis and Abigail, his heart nearly exploded with gratitude. The hours felt like seconds as he wrapped up, vibrating from the inside. He led everyone in a powerful closing prayer while the choir hummed and swayed to a melody in the background. Transformation flooded the tent, and Charlie knew that his mama and daddy were right there with him, standing proudly. He ruminated on the history and culmination of generations of preacher men and women who'd stepped into their destinies leading Charlie to this very moment.

When finished, Charlie folded into the people, shaking hands, trying to reach everyone in the tent. It was important that they knew how much he valued their presence today. Shaking the last hand, he made his way to Abigail and Francis, who were standing at the back of the tent, and scooped them both into his arms.

"That was amazing, Charlie. I'm so proud of you," Abigail whispered in his ear.

"Thank you, Abs," he said, holding them close. "I couldn't believe it when I looked back to see you guys. It was the icing on the cake."

"Yeah, Mommy told her boss that work would have to wait just a little longer." Francis giggled.

"So not sure how the job front looks for me," Abigail said, shrugging. "I guess we can live on love, huh?"

They laughed.

"Absolutely," Charlie responded as Jeremiah's hand landed on his shoulder.

"Son, that was something else. Our little town needed that kind of revival. The hairs on my arm are still standing up," he said with a hearty laugh.

"Thanks, Jeremiah. Man, it's been a journey, but today was something else."

"God showed up and showed out," Francis said with excitement.

"Yes, He did," Charlie responded.

"I am heading to the diner. Why don't you folks come on over and have some hot pie fresh out of the oven?"

They all shared a look and shook their heads yes.

———◦◦◦———

Daylight transitioned into nightfall as Charlie and Abigail watched Francis sing and dance barefoot in the grass by the swing that was now her stage. They eased back and forth, enjoying the show until she fell across their laps exhausted.

Charlie embraced the soft buzz of her breathing. "Our girl is worn out," Charlie said.

Abigail leaned into the crook of Charlie's arm.

"I can't tell you how perfect you both made this day," he said, stroking her hair lightly.

Abigail looked up at him, holding his gaze, "I just realized that we are a family now, and nothing is more important Charlie. Nothing."

He kissed the top of her head, inhaling her. "When I was standing up there at that podium and I looked back there and saw you, it took my breath away. And the only thing I could say in my mind was 'Thank you.' You and Francis are living proof of God's grace, Abigail. I never dreamed that he'd take all of my brokenness and put it perfectly back together, but he did."

"Yes, he did, Charlie." She paused. "What's next, Charlie? For you, for us?"

Charlie rested against the smooth wood of the swing, content. "This. If this is all I had, it would be enough. I've been blessed, and I fully intend to find ways to give God the glory in whatever I do."

She smiled. "And we are finally going to be a family."

"Yes, we are."

"I just love saying that."

"So, are you ready for tomorrow?"

"Yeah, I am. Tomorrow is truly like a homecoming. I just wish Mama and Daddy were here to see this."

"They are, Charlie," she said with certainty and a long yawn. "Well, I guess we better get going," she said, curling her lips into a slight frown. "I promised Mama a slice of that pie, and I am sure you need to prepare for tomorrow." Abigail rubbed Francis's head. "Time to go, lovebug."

Francis stretched her arms across them with a sleepy grin, reminding Charlie of Chandler for a split second. "Wake up, pretty girl," he said.

They eased off of the swing and made their way to the car. After goodbye hugs, Charlie watched them pull away. He sighed with satisfaction.

He walked back into the house and stood at the kitchen table staring at the steeple on top of the church birdhouse. This day had been rich in inspiration and gratitude. He marveled at the grace that was given to him in his darkest hour as he lowered his head in prayer.

Chapter Thirty-Three

Warm, golden sunlight crested the horizon as Charlie stood at the kitchen window. *God's paintbrush*, he thought. Coffee filled his sinuses as he took a long pull of the steaming liquid. He'd slept peacefully and had awoken without an alarm clock, fully rested even though he'd not fallen asleep until after midnight. He'd realized that his message for the ribbon cutting had been marinating in his spirit since his childhood. Elroy and Francis Nettles had soaked him in his purpose from as far back as Charlie could remember.

Charlie showered and slipped on a lightweight, navy-blue V-neck sweater paired with a white T-shirt and a pair of pressed beige slacks. The uncertainty of his path ahead no longer held a shadow of doubt over him. He trusted with every ounce of his being that God was going to guide his path with each step that he took in faith.

Opening the back door, he inhaled deeply, savoring the fresh morning air, and letting his mind drift to Chandler. If only he were here to share the joy Charlie felt. He sighed, resting his head against the smooth wood. "Daddy loves you so much, Chan. So very much. I hope you don't ever forget that" he said in a whisper as he saw movement from the corner of his eye. Perched motionless on top of the arbor swing was a red bird. Charlie smiled. Love blanketed him like melted butter as peace settled in his heart.

⟞⚬⟝

White clouds billowed overhead against a backdrop of iridescent blue sky as Charlie approached the church steps. He was early, but he needed a few hours of quiet to go over his message and prepare himself mentally.

The hours of hard work had paid off, and the church exuded the warmth of a Thomas Kinkade painting. Charlie unlocked the door to the sanctuary and stepped inside carrying the church birdhouse. He was met with the smell of fresh paint and wood. Studying the detail of the beautiful stained glass in the windows depicting angels and images of Jesus reminded him of sitting in the front pew as a boy. Today was a homecoming that Charlie could not put into words or even thoughts. It was a complex menagerie of all that he'd aspired to become and do throughout his life. This was the day that he would truly start over even though he had no idea what that would look like long-term.

Charlie moved toward the podium at the front of the sanctuary taking in all the work that the people of Sinclair had made possible with their generous donations. He eased onto the front pew and placed the birdhouse on the navy cushion beside him. Resting his elbows on his knees, he lowered his head to pray. "Lord, I just want to thank you for never leaving or forsaking me, always bathing me in your love and grace, leading me back to my purpose. This year has been so many things. There were times when I couldn't find my way to you because of pain, anger, and unforgiveness. I lost my wife, my son. I lost the life that I'd worked so hard for. But this last year, you've shown me what I needed to do to find my way again. I had to learn to lean into my faith like a child depending on their father for support and direction. You showed me that you are a loving redeemer and provider. Bringing

Abigail back to me was such an unexpected blessing, and I will spend the rest of my days honoring this new life you've given me, never forgetting what is important. Please bless me this day that I will bring light to the darkness for those in need and that I will properly honor the importance of this day in Sinclair for you and the people that entrusted me to welcome this new chapter. I also pray for your guidance, asking you to show me my next steps, make my path clear, and show me how to move forward in this new life in a way that is a blessing to you and those seeking your kingdom. I trust you, Lord. And I finally realize that you've got this. You've always had this."

Charlie sat quietly for a few moments, hands folded against his forehead, eyes closed, breathing in the closeness that he felt to God. He looked at his watch.

The church administrator walked in, flustered. "Somehow the ribbon came down. I'm putting it back up so we can get started," she said, disappearing into the supply closet before hurrying back past him.

"Let me help."

"No, I will have it up in a jiff. We should get started once I do that."

Charlie nodded his head in agreement, then stood in the quiet sanctuary for a few minutes listening to voices filling the air outside the doors. He lowered his head one final time asking for guidance and then stepped outside.

He was stunned at the number of people that had shown up. Wesley, Cheryl, Abigail, and Francis stood with Mrs. Turner near the bottom of the stairs. Jeremiah was beside them beaming with the pride of a parent watching their child take his first steps.

The crowd quieted as Charlie began to speak. "I want to thank each and every one of you for coming out today. Your support, both financially and emotionally, has made this all possible. As many of you know, Pastor Dalton is still not well, but he said to tell you all how much he appreciates each of you and how grateful he is for this community." Charlie looked into the crowd, taking in the faces around him…some familiar, others not. He asked that they bow their heads as he offered up a prayer of blessing for the day and this beautiful church that would serve so many in the community. As he cut the long, white ribbon, cheers and amens filled the air.

People began to file past him as he stood greeting some with hand-shakes and others with hugs. When the sanctuary was full and the doors were closed, Charlie took his place behind the podium. He'd placed the birdhouse beside him on a table. He took it into his hands with a wide grin, and looking at Jeremiah, said, "You know a long time ago a young man built this birdhouse. It was crafted from the flame of ministry that'd been laid on his heart. He knew that one day this birdhouse would represent so much more. And now it does." He paused. "Because that boy was me. As I run my fingers along the edges that I sanded and smoothed for hours, I am reminded of that feeling of redemption as my soul was being transformed and rooted in a long history of preaching, as that fire was growing in my belly to finally embrace and follow my destiny into ministry. But when I look at it closer, I think about what this looked like when I simply held the untouched birch between my fingers, allowing the vision to unfold and become a church. When I stood at that workbench, be-fore the vision unfolded, I began to work on the base or foundation. You see, my vision had yet to unfold for this birdhouse, but I knew that it must start with this first, crucial step. This particular part of the birdhouse had to be the most durable and strong, so as to hold the rest of the structure upright in the winds and rains. It would need to be sturdy enough to house families of birds and their babies. So, I knew this first step was an important one."

He placed the birdhouse back onto the table and stood in front of the podium, locking eyes with Francis and Abigail, who were in the front row. "As this vision came to life, as I trusted God to work through me, guiding my hands, it became this beautiful church with a steeple, similar to this very building that we are so blessed to be sit-ting in today. Years passed, the roof weathered a bit, the rope holding it frayed some, and the little stoop loosened just slightly. But do you know what held the structure together?" Charlie paused and looked around. "The foundation. So, all it took was a few minor repairs and a fresh coat of paint to bring it back to life," Charlie said smiling in Jeremiah's direction.

"You see, we are much like this birdhouse. When we let Jesus into our hearts, we allow him in all of his grace to establish a foundation. One that will not crumble with sorrows or troubles and one that will sustain us even when the winds of life's struggles and disasters rip the roof off. Even then, the foundation remains intact. This beautiful church right here," he said, looking around, "it too was built with a strong foundation, headers and footers made of steel, and poured concrete for strength and endurance." He paused, embracing the warmth from the stained glass, meeting the gazes of those around him. "We are much like this building and even this birdhouse, except our foundation is built on forgiveness, love, grace, and trust in God's plans. It's built on the knowledge that when we are weak, He is strong because He is that foundation." A lump formed in Charlie's throat as he reflected on his struggles. Charlie looked at Abigail as tears filled her eyes.

He took a breath. "You see, if we let Him, He will help us rebuild when those storms of life tear us down. He will pour out a redeeming love to us all unlike anything we've ever experienced. He is the master architect, and there is no wind strong enough to destroy the foundation that He will build inside you if you simply allow Him. Trust Him. Let Him in when you are scared."

Charlie walked along the center aisle. "I am guessing that there are those of you today battling the storms of life. It may be addiction, infidelity in your marriage, a child that has gone astray. It may be a diagnosis that feels hopeless. You may be suffering a loss that has left you hollow inside." Charlie watched transformation taking place in the tear-filled eyes of those who were obviously struggling. "But let me assure you of this one truth today. If you are sitting here, in this room, you are meant to hear this message. You are building that foundation by being here if you don't already have one, and there is nothing— and I mean nothing," Charlie asserted with power and emotion, "that God's redeeming grace cannot heal in you, that cannot give you the strength to rise up and believe again. There is no wind, no rain, no storm that can ever touch that foundation. Because it is strong," Charlie said making a fist, "and unshakeable. You see, God doesn't build your eternity on sand, my friends. He builds your foundations in Him and the precious blood of Jesus. Can I get an amen today," Charlie said as the fires of Pentecost worked their way up his neck.

"You are never alone; you are never forsaken. Can I get another amen?" he said as Abigail and Francis stood. "You are a child of God, my friends, and your spiritual house is built on elements that no man, no woman, no entity can destroy." Sweat beaded up on his brow. "No matter where you are, He is there. No matter how many times you get lost, He will find you. And no matter how many times you turn away from Him, He will always welcome you home, my brothers and sisters." The air popped with an electricity that only the Holy Spirit can provide as Charlie continued to a crescendo. "When you have a foundation that has been laid by the Most High God, you will always be redeemed. Do you hear me?"

Charlie took a breath and turned to the choir behind him as they sang and clapped. He raised his hands, eyes closed, lost in the lyrics.

As the music slowed, Charlie began to speak. "I want to ask you all today one simple question, and don't respond aloud, because this is for you and only you. This is your moment." Charlie stood quietly. "Can you stand strong on your foundation?" he asked, surveying the room. "For those of you that have a foundation cracking and crumbling beneath your feet, I want you to know that today you are here to repair the damage that has been done." His voice rose to an adrenaline-filled pitch. "I am here today because you are worthy of a house built on a solid foundation, you are worthy of strength and stability, you are worthy of a shelter that can withstand life's hurricanes, you are worthy of a foundation of grace and endurance. You are worthy of a foundation anointed by the blood of Jesus, allowing you and me to live in a home that will withstand every single storm."

He eased the back of his hand along the dampness of his brow. "Today as you stand on His foundation, in His house I want to invite you to build your own." Charlie stood in front of the podium. "Won't you let him give you everything you need to get started." The room was quiet. "All you have to do is step forward."

People of all ages eased down the center aisle and landed on bended knee at the front of the church as deacons prayed with them and around. It was no surprise that well over half of the people in that room either dedicated or rededicated their lives to Christ. Others around him stood praying with hands on each other's shoulders, whispering into their purpose.

Charlie watched in wonder as Abigail made her way to him holding Francis's hand. "I'd like you to pray over our family, Charlie. Will you do that?"

Charlie placed his hands on Abigail's and Francis's shoulders, forming a circle as he began to pray. Tears rolled down his cheeks as he embraced this moment that he knew was truly the final piece of his puzzle.

At the end of the prayer, they embraced as many around him did as people made their way back to their seats.

"Before we wrap up today, I just want to say what an amazing community this is. You good folks sitting here today are the foundation of this church. The wind, rain, and a big ole oak tree may have destroyed the roof and the walls, but what a foundation these walls sit on. And what a foundation you all form for one another, this town, and this church. But most important is the foundation that has been established with many of you today, in your hearts, in Christ. I can't promise you that there won't be storms. I can't promise you that you won't be scared as the winds of change or heartache blow around you, but I can promise you this. No matter what happens, your foundation will always be right there to rebuild on. And finally, that same foundation will strengthen with every prayer you say, with every moment of gratitude, with every song of praise that you sing lifting His name."

Charlie looked around the room and smiled. "Now let us pray."

Charlie locked the sanctuary doors, but not before taking in the beauty around him one more time. Jeremiah, Wesley, Cheryl, Abigail, Mrs. Turner, and Francis stood outside chatting as he made his way down the steps.

Wesley pulled him in for a hug and shoulder pat. "Man, I am just speechless. That was on fire."

"Thanks, Wes. I couldn't ask for more."

Jeremiah placed his hand on Charlie's shoulder. "Son, that was truly amazing. You blessed us with some down-home, evangelical preachin' today, I'm not gonna lie. I thought for a minute it was Elroy standing up there."

They all laughed.

"It felt good. I can't even describe it, Jeremiah."

Francis walked up and said, "You raised the roof," making quotations with her fingers, giggling.

"Yes, we did," he said, rubbing the tendrils of hair away from her eyes.

"Well, what do you say we all go to the diner? Pie is on me," Jeremiah said.

They all agreed and began making their way to their cars, Charlie walking hand in hand with his girls.

"So, what's next, Mr. Nettles?" Abigail asked.

They stopped and looked into the other's eyes as Francis ran ahead to catch up with her grandmother.

"Well, first off, I gotta make you an honest woman."

She laughed. "I like that answer."

"But it will be a surprise. You won't even see it coming," he said, teasing her. "And I was thinking about maybe making an offer on Judge Alford's place. What do you think?"

"Well, I do know a guy that is very good at building things. I'm sure he could have that ole place good as new. Maybe I should give him a call."

"Maybe you should," Charlie said, placing his hands on her cheeks, drinking her in, his chest pliable and warm with all their memories. "I love you. I will always love you, Abs."

"And I love you too," she said, holding his gaze. "Forever and a day for good measure."

Charlie pulled her body to his and held her, eyes closed. He finally understood what true redemption felt like as he said thank you over and over in his head, holding the woman he loved.

ACKNOWLEDGMENTS

Over the years, I have been incredibly fortunate to be surrounded by so many helpful people who have made this journey possible. First and foremost, thank you, God, for planting this seed in my heart and in my imagination all of those years ago. My characters evolved through many nights of waking up at 3 a.m. and writing down ideas that would not allow me to sleep.

Writing is a time-consuming passion, and I'm so grateful to my husband, Robb, for his continuous support and love. I'm also incredibly thankful that he conspired with Denna, the best friend a girl could ever have, in the most loving way to nudge me towards the finish line. Their unrelenting encouragement removed all of my fears.

The love I have for my beautiful family inspires me daily. Laken, Luke, Ryan, and Jake, every experience while raising you guys is reflected in my writing. I count my blessings every single day for our party of six. The day each of my grandbabies was born forever changed me. Israel, Jonah, and Levi, I will always love you from the deepest part of my heart. It goes without saying, Joshua, I'm forever grateful to you for the way you love my daughter, those babies, and our family. I truly admire you.

I grew up with a single mom, Rosie, for many years. Every night, I saw her retire for the evening with a book. Her love for reading was evident by the paperbacks resting underneath her bedside table. That stuck with me. Her love for me was so unconditional. She was always front and center, cheering me on. Oh, how I miss her beautiful smile and contagious laughter. I was also blessed with my daddy, Doug, whose stable presence in my life has been a gift. I have always been able to count on you. My stepdad Ray left this world way too soon. I will forever treasure our adventures together. To my brother Steve, I'm so thankful for becoming your friend in life and not just your little sister. To my big sister Rene', your resilience in life amazes me, as does your love of books. When my niece and nephew were born, I got a glimpse of what loving a child would feel like. Candace and Cameron, your Auntie will forever be your biggest fans. I want to remember my Grandmother and Grandfather Ford as the ultimate examples of family commitment for me growing up. To my Grandmother Gaskins, who had the uncanny ability to see things exactly as they were and express them in ways that only she could. Bob and Ruth, thanks for raising my soul mate to become the man who makes my heart sing and inspires my stories.

When I was learning about the church and how it operates, I was so blessed to have Dr. Tim Phillips share his plethora of knowledge. I would also like to thank Aaron Chovan for taking time out of his busy schedule to help me feed this dream and share his ministry knowledge.

Becoming a writer definitely requires thick skin and an overt willingness to welcome constructive criticism. I could not have made it without Nicola Wheir's brilliant guidance as she carved away the fluff and helped me develop this story. Sandra Johnson, a fellow author, was my first writing teacher. I credit her for fanning the flames of my desire to become the best writer possible. She also painted a realistic picture of choosing the life of a writer. It's not always easy, but man, it is worth it. I aspire to grow with each new writing adventure.

Since childhood, I have been so fortunate to be surrounded by a beautiful, diverse group of friends. It started in kindergarten with Crickett. Forty-nine years later, you are still my confidante and biggest supporter. Growing up, Denna and Denise were absolute constants in my life. We were a puzzle of three with a friendship that has now spanned decades. God knew we would need each other for so many reasons as we navigated this life. Many friends from childhood impacted my life in an immensely positive way. Jenny, Catherine, Monica, and Shany, thank you for being part of so many stories that shaped me as a person and writer. Gammie, knowing you are no longer a phone call away will never be okay with me. I will always treasure our friendship. Misty, my mystical supplement and health guru confidante. Our laughter is magic. Fast forward to my friends who impacted my world as I ventured into adulthood. Katherine, my soul sister, only you and I get our jokes, and I love that about us. Your faith is beautiful. Jeannie, you were one of the very few who read my work from beginning to end and encouraged me to keep going. I thank you from the bottom of my heart for that. And a big thanks to your husband and my friend Jon for always sharing his creative ideas and his willingness to write music for my future projects. Bev, your strength in adversity is awe-inspiring. Your smile never fades. Thanks for letting me be part of that. Patty, no matter what has happened in my life, you've had my back. You've always been part of my story. To my loving prayer warrior, Pamela, thanks for always being a phone call away with your hands raised high. Nova, I'm forever grateful for the day you left NY and became my friend. Susan, you exemplify strength in loss. I admire you so much. Windy, my dear friend who honored me with my Godson Myles, you both mean so much to me. Rachel, distance and time never overshadow our connection. Amy, your steady presence in my life since we met as aspiring actresses has been a gift. You, Kimberly, and I share a chapter that fueled my creativity and led me to my love for creating characters. Nicole, the years have only deepened our friendship. Your loving spirit is a treasure. Mande, thanks for your adventurous spirit and loving heart, which always encourages me to step outside my box. David, my dear friend, I treasure the rich history that we share, always.

Over the years, I have cultivated many other deep connections that have influenced my writing. These are the individuals that I don't see or speak to as often as I'd like, but when we get together, no time has elapsed. You know who you are. I treasure you. To everyone along the way who has shared an encouraging word, you have no idea how much I needed it.

A big thank you to my work family at Exit REC for cheering me on in everything I do.

When I started a book club 6 years ago, I had no idea that I would learn so much from this fabulous group of women. CHP book club, listening to your insights as we've traversed various genres over the years has opened my mind. Thanks for believing in me.

To Roy and Alexandra from Palmetto Publishing, the publishing process was a bit overwhelming at first, but you walked me through it with ease. I'm grateful for that.

My hope is that this book, born out of a lifetime of experience, love, and faith, will inspire readers. May God's redemptive love shine through the pages.